A Space Apart

Meredith Sue Willis

A Space Apart

Meredith Sue Willis

Irene Weinberger Books
An Imprint of Hamilton Stone Editions
Maplewood, New Jersey

Irene Weinberger Books Edition ISBN 978-0-9903767-2-9
Irene Weinberger Books is an imprint of
Hamilton Stone Editions
P.O. Box 43, Maplewood, NJ 07040

Library of Congress Cataloging-in-Publication Data
Names: Willis, Meredith Sue, author.
Title: A space apart / by Meredith Sue Willis.
Description: Maplewood, New Jersey : Irene Weinberger Books, [2016]
Identifiers: LCCN 2016027015 | ISBN 9780990376729
(acid-free paper)
Subjects: LCSH: Families--West Virginia--Fiction. | Conflict of
generations--Fiction. | Domestic fiction.
Classification: LCC PS3573.I45655 S6 2016 | DDC 813/.54--dc23
LC record available at https://lccn.loc.gov/2016027015

The first edition of this book was published by
Charles Scribners Sons, 1979 ISBN 0-684-16071-4 .

The second edition was published by
Authors Guild Backinprint.com, 2005 ISBN 0-595-34398-8

The E-book version is published by
ForeverlandPress.com

Chapter 4 Appeared in a slightly different version in *Phoebe* Magazine.

See more about Meredith Sue Willis at www.meredithsuewillis.com

To Andy

Other Books by Meredith Sue Willis

Fiction

Higher Ground
Only Great Changes
Trespassers
Quilt Pieces (with Jane Wilson Joyce)
In the Mountains of America
Oradell at Sea
Dwight's House and Other Stories
The City Built of Starships
Out of the Mountains
Re-Visions
Love Palace

For Children & Young Adults

The Secret Super Powers of Marco
Marco's Monster
Billie of Fish House Lane
Meli's Way

About Writing

Personal Fiction Writing
Deep Revision
Blazing Pencils
Ten Strategies to Write Your Novel

A Space Apart

Chapter 1
Mary Katherine

The parsonage was filthy when Mary Katherine and her father moved in. The closets were piled with rusty hangers and brittle magazines and bed sheets that rent when you touched them. The place had been empty since the sudden death of the last pastor, so she wasn't expecting Better Homes and Gardens, but it did seem that Galatia First Baptist could have afforded to hire someone to do the rough work. All the sinks had elliptical orange stains from the sulfur hard water, and the living room furniture released clouds of dust when you sat down. It was an affront to turn the house over to them in this condition.

The new minister was her brother John Scarlin, not their father. John was seminary-trained, the equivalent of a master's degree, and he had been the minister of a church up in Pennsylvania for two years. Their father was a preacher too, homemade and self-ordained. In the last few years he had narrowed his doctrine to the point where no one came to his church anymore except Mary Katherine, and he was ready to excommunicate her when he got sick. She had quit work to nurse him in the old combination general store and church five miles outside of town and then John called and said he had the church at Galatia. Pack your bags, Mary Katherine, John told her. We're moving to town and we're going to be a family again.

The old Preacher used to take them into town to buy clothes or to see the doctor, and he would always point out the big yellow First Baptist Church with its bell tower and chimes and say, That is a Judas church where they claim to be Baptists, but you can smell the incense like Catholics. When she and John were old enough to be bused into town for junior high and high school, John would point at the church too and tell her, One of these days I'm going to be the preacher at that church and I'll make them get back to the Bible.

And he had done it, he was coming back and they were going to live in town on Church Street with the elm trees and above the elm trees the red and green roofs of the best homes piled up the sides of the hills and above them broad fields and a few cows, and higher still on ground so steep it had never been farmed were woods, and above the prickly rim of the hills, just sky. Not a glimpse of the tipples and strip mines and slag heaps of Black Run where they grew up. Looking at Galatia you would never know it was the coal mines feeding everyone. Mary Katherine and John were finally going to live together there in a graceful place, a house on the same lot, sharing the same semiglazed bricks and forsythia bushes as the First Baptist Church. Except that the inside of the parsonage was filthy.

The main question in her mind as she started to clean it—with no vacuum cleaner—was whether the insult was to John, or to her, or to both of them and what they came from. It's because of who we are, she thought first, it's an insult to both of us, on her hands and knees inside the bathtub scrubbing with Ajax and SOS pads and ammonia. If we hadn't been raised in that crazy way by that crazy old man downstairs they would have had more respect. If we had grown up regular Baptists instead of Second Milers. If they hadn't known us when we were wild little country children, just barely housebroken. That was going a little too far, the Preacher did his best by them, and she felt guilty, so she ran downstairs to pull him up in his wheelchair. The second day after they moved in here he had another one of his slight strokes, and ever since he hadn't been talking, although she couldn't say if it was because he couldn't or because he didn't want to.

Maybe after all it was just that they were young. The church was certainly getting John for less than they would have had to pay an older established man. And they knew they were getting a bargain too. They had heard him preach. Mary Katherine had herself gone up with the Search Committee to hear him preach, and he hardly ever raised his voice, but not a person in that poor little church of strangers in Pennsylvania didn't lean forward in their seats to get every word. After the service a lot of girls had crowded around her when they found out she was his sister. Tell us what Reverend Scarlin used to be like, they said. Tell us what he was like when he was a little boy. She had answered them without paying much attention because it was the people from Galatia who mattered, and whether or not they were going to have eyes to see what John was worth, how fine he was.

Of course they had seen. Even Emzie Wright had seen. That's why they offered the church to him, and it was the church they were offering, the church as beautiful as ever, needing no apologies. And that left the insult directed straightaway at Mary Katherine, and she knew it wasn't from the church as a whole either, it was from Emzie Wright alone, and the knowledge made the back of her jaws tight with anger, but glad to have come to the conclusion. She could imagine with perfect clear satisfaction the nasal sound of Emzie Wright's voice saying to the rest of them on the committee, Oh leave the cleanup to Mary Katherine, she's a hand to do that kind of thing. She won't have anything else to do, she isn't working. How could I work, thought Mary Katherine, how could I work at the drugstore or anywhere else with the Preacher in the

12

shape he's in and John needing me too? How could I work anywhere or get married either? Emzie hated her for not marrying her son Earl, but she had hated her long before that. You're one of the reasons I refused him, thought Mary Katherine. Not that I'd let you stand in my way if that was all it was. It wasn't a final refusal anyhow, she had just told Earl she wanted time to think. All right, said Earl in his solid way. And went off to Korea. Only after he was gone did she start to pay attention to the radio and the newspaper and to think that where he was going they fired real guns, not cowboy movie blanks.

Even so, thought Mary Katherine. I have my duty too. And she decided she would work all night every night till John came and the house was spic and span and he would never know about the insult, and she would never let them know in the church either, not a one of them, and she would never ask for help either.

The phone rang, and she turned down the Preacher's radio show. "It's Johnny, Preacher!" she said, and the Preacher closed one eye, and she said to the phone, "Oh, he's okay, he could talk if he wanted to. He's just sitting here listening to Gangbusters."

She loved talking to John on the telephone. His whole voice right in her ear. He said, "I hear you're polishing the parsonage room by room."

"Who told you that? You just think I never do anything but clean—"

"No, I really did hear it. Emzie Wright told me. I don't want you overextending yourself, Mary Kay."

"You talked to her? Long distance?"

"Yes, I had to talk to her, and the Shinns and everyone on the Committee and the Board of Deacons. I have some big news."

She had heard more bad than good big news. Still, he sounded happy, so she put on a smile to listen.

"I got married," he said. "I had to inform the committee and the Board of Deacons right off. I had to make sure everything was okay. I was afraid they would take back the call."

"They wouldn't take back the call!"

"It was pretty sudden by anyone's standards. I had to do some fancy explaining."

She waited for hers, and when it didn't come, said, "What about me and the Preacher. Do you want us to move out?"

"Mary Katherine!" In his deepest voice that he usually saved for grief and mourning. "Mary Katherine, what do you think? I told the committee first because I had to be sure they wouldn't withdraw the call. I'm coming the same day, as I said, nothing is different. She says she's depending on you because she can't imagine what it's like to be a preacher's wife. We're both depending on you."

Mary Katherine said, "There's no stove. The old one didn't work and the new one may not be here in time."

"In time for what?" Things around the house made him impatient, he never wanted to be bothered.

"In time to cook a decent meal for you on Friday night."

"It doesn't matter! Lord Have Mercy it doesn't matter. We'll all go out to eat. Or tell Emzie and Thelma and some of the women, and they'll bring covered dishes—don't worry about it!"

Emzie and Thelma, she thought, and then, Why didn't he tell me first, even if they had taken back the call, I should have known about it first. Off the phone, sitting on the steps with her forehead pressed against the bannister, she started thinking, And John, what would have happened if I'd been the one to call you up and say Oh by the way I decided to marry Earl after all and he's coming to live in the parsonage with us too.

But then the problem of the beds popped up in front of her. She had to find another bed, and she only had twenty dollars in the bank. "Preacher," she said, "I'm going to bring down the little bed for you in the den and take your bed upstairs because Johnny got married. What do you think about that? I'll have to buy a cot or something for me. Not that you care what you sleep in, or me either, but who am I going to get to carry the beds? Now I have to have curtains too, there's nothing to do but make curtains. What do you think of Johnny getting married, Preacher?" He might have shrugged the slightest bit, but he kept his eyes closed. She could feel mean things coming up in her throat and she said, "It runs in the family, doesn't it, getting married in a hurry?" She headed for the kitchen before she could say anything else and tried to scrub the old wax off the linoleum. Later she gave the Preacher his bath, and after she had put him to bed she finished scrubbing and slept on the couch and when the morning light woke her through the curtainless windows went and washed down the kitchen floor again.

She had not forgiven John by the night they came, but she did manage to get the house ready. The stove had come in time after all, and she had asked the deliveryman to help her switch the beds. She had a meat loaf in the oven and scalloped potatoes, and early in the afternoon she had shaved the Preacher and dressed him up in his red flannel shirt and green tie. Her greatest triumph was that she had managed after all to make curtains. She had spent all of the money after groceries on some cotton with pink leaves and blossoms and little red strawberries, and she had run up enough gathered curtains for all the downstairs windows and the big bedroom upstairs. There had been a little piece left over too, not enough to curtain her room, but enough for an apron, and she wore that now, over her navy wool dress with the Peter Pan collar. The house still had breaths of Clorox cleaner here and there, but the cooking smells were beginning to displace them, and the curtains were doing a little dance at the drafty windows. The only way she had failed to be ready was that she still didn't know John's wife's name. She kept thinking, Well, I don't have to worry because he'll say And this is Jane, or Susan or Betty. She ran to the window every time a car passed and made sure the Preacher was sitting up straight, and once, while she was plumping his pillows, almost sooner than she expected although she knew John was always on time, she heard the car that pulled over and two slams. She had one fraction of a second of stillness before they came in, two of them, John and the one whose name she didn't know, the two of them so elegantly dressed with a tailored quality she hadn't expected: John in a topcoat and hat that hid part of his face, and his wife in glen plaid gray and green like spring rain with lots of flyaway hair and a tam.

"And this is Mary Katherine," said John.

The girl came running and gave her a soapy clean kiss; she bounced off Mary Katherine at the Preacher, knelt by his wheelchair and hugged him, gave him a kiss. Apparently no one had told her that the Preacher didn't kiss, although this one didn't seem to bother him. He closed an eye. John just stood there in his topcoat smiling as the girl hugged and kissed everything in sight.

"This is Dad of course," she said to the Preacher. "I've been looking forward to meeting you, Dad, I've been telling my idea to John, that I intend to spend a lot of time with you making friends so Mary Katherine can go out if she wants to—"

"Dad?" said Mary Katherine to John. "You call him 'Dad' now?"

High pink spots on John's cheeks, an unusual sign in the sallow-skinned Scarlins, and the more familiar vertical tension line between his eyebrows. He waved his hands, smiling under the frown. "Why not? He's our father. He never denied that."

Mary Katherine said to the girl, "We never did call him anything but Preacher."

The girl hopped to her feet and John slipped her coat off of her. She hardly seemed to notice. But the suit underneath was the same gray and green glen plaid as the coat; it was an ensemble. Mary Katherine had never seen anyone wearing a real ensemble before. For just a second she stepped forward and looked at Mary Katherine, trying to figure something out. "Really? You always called him Preacher?" Do you think

I lied? thought Mary Katherine. The girl took the Preacher's bad hand and shook it in both of hers. "How do you do, Preacher. Nice to meet you again."

"That's his bad hand, nothing you do can get it warm." She stopped, having no idea of what she wanted to say to the girl except the one thing What is your name? and that was impossible to ask. She waited for John, but he was as still as the Preacher, a lot like the Preacher right now in fact, the inset brown eyes, and both of them looking at the girl who kept patting the Preacher's hand and looking brightly around waiting for someone to speak.

You don't know the Scarlins, thought Mary Katherine, if you think one of us is going to talk first.

Finally the girl laughed. "Why would you want to change his name, John?"

When is he going to say her name?

John shrugged and called her honey. "It never seemed right when I thought about it, to call your father Preacher. Besides, I guess I was thinking I'm the Preacher now."

Mary Katherine couldn't stand it anymore. "You're John," she said. "He's the Preacher. I have to go put ketchup on the meat loaf."

From the kitchen she thought she heard them whispering under cover of the Preacher's radio program. She stretched out her arms, braced them on the stove and lowered her head, trying to get her breathing regular. Questions went flying off through her mind: How long did he know her? Where did she come from? Above all, what is her name? She heard a little tap tapping and saw the girl's spectator pumps, brown and white, open-toed, everything about her so perfectly pretty.

"May I set the table? Oh, you already did it. But listen, I know this cute way to fold napkins. I'm good at things like that. Little things. I'm always fiddling with little things." Mary Katherine squeezed her eyes shut. The heels tapped closer. "Listen, Mary Katherine, I'm sorry I didn't know what to call him. I shouldn't have come barging in here fooling with your napkins either. Look, I'll unfold them—I'll put everything back just the way you had it."

Mary Katherine said, "John never even told me your name."

"It's Vera, but I thought you knew because we were introduced once, you know."

Chagrined, Mary Katherine couldn't remember anything. "Up in Pennsylvania?"

"Yes, I guess I must have blended in with the crowd. You were at his church and there were a lot of us girls—we all had a crush on

John—I was one of the Good News Thrushes, we sang? Do you remember? We had little red weskits."

Mary Katherine remembered crowds of people, and she did notice a lot of girls going off like sparklers on all sides of her. "I get stupid in crowds."

"Oh me too. People don't realize because I look like I'm talking and laughing and having a good time but I'm panicky and silly."

"Don't unfold the napkins. It's just that John didn't tell me. He didn't tell me anything till the last minute." She hadn't meant to say anything against John, but the girl nodded so sympathetically.

"John's afraid of you," she said. "He says you're his conscience. He got me scared half to death of you too. I talked nonstop all the way down here I was so nervous. I wanted to buy you flowers and I made him drive all through three different towns looking for a florist but nobody was open.

Mary Katherine found herself talking too, and again it was what she had meant not to talk about. "I cleaned all week, and when I found out about you, I made the curtains."

"You made them! You have a sewing machine? Oh Mary Katherine we're going to have fun while John is out doing whatever preachers do. We'll sew things and bake cookies. How about college—have you started yet? John says there's a state college in driving distance. Why don't we go to college together and study in the evenings? I had a semester already—"

"I never even started," said Mary Katherine. "I was working in the drugstore and then the preacher got sick."

"We might have to take turns—you'd go one day and I'd stay with the Preacher and then vice versa—I didn't mean to leave out the Preacher. That's the main thing I love about your family, Mary Katherine. I love it that you're back together again. John told me how you and he promised when you were children to live together and here you are, all three of you."

Mary Katherine stirred with fear of disappointing her. "We haven't been together very much. Johnny and the Preacher didn't get along—"

"But you're together now, don't you see? You did what you said you would. You're dependable people, just the opposite of me. I made so many promises when I was little! I was going to live in one town with my best friend forever, I was going to take harp lessons and ballet. But I always had to move. I was living with my aunt and uncle and the company was always making us move. The only promise I ever stuck to was that I was going to finish high school where I was, so I got a job as a live-in companion for an old lady and stayed when they moved. I started college there too, and then I met John."

"We had a pretty strange bringing up—"

"I know all about the Second Miler Baptists and how you had church in the little store. I know about your mother running away from the Preacher. But listen, Mary Katherine, my mother did a lot worse than that." Her eyes were very widely spaced, almost too wide to see them both at once. "I probably shouldn't tell you this, but I want you to know the worst all at once. My mother wasn't right. She took her own life."

Each of Vera's irises had a tiny black rim and Mary Katherine thought for an instant they were turning around. She didn't know what to say; no one had ever told her such a thing before, not about themselves. People told the bad things about each other, either maliciously or with love, but not about themselves right out like that. She said, "Did you—were you there?"

"Oh no. I hardly knew her. She was in an institution at the time. But listen, please don't tell John I told you. He thinks I'm a blabbermouth already."

Mary Katherine had a spell of dizziness as if Vera were some kind of carnival ride. Was it possible to live with such a person every day? Vera laughed and talked them through dinner and even the Preacher seemed to be paying attention. Mary Katherine found her eyes meeting John's from time to time and she thought she was going to get over her anger and they would all tell the plots of funny movies and be happy.

When she got up to make the coffee, John said, "Why don't we wait? Some of the church people may be dropping over and we could serve it to them."

"Oh John!" said Mary Katherine. "The Preacher spilled his dinner on his shirt. Why do they have to come tonight?"

"I'll help the Preacher wash up," said Vera.

John cleared the table and Mary Katherine started the dishes so there'd be enough when the people came. "Who's coming?"

"The Committee. Someone from the deacons."

"Why do they have to start checking up so soon?"

"Don't take the worst view, Mary Kay. They want to welcome us. They won't stay. They'll drink a cup of coffee and leave. A parsonage isn't like living in the back of the store on Black Run."

"They want a look at Vera."

"That's true." He picked up the dish towel to dry. "What do you think?"

He was looking so up-to-date. The way he combed his hair and the pleats in his pants. He had always been handsome, slender, dark hair, eyes set deep. It looked romantic in him, she thought; in a girl, in herself, it was too somber. Handsome as he was, though, as smooth as he had become, she knew him for her brother because he had come back to Galatia. He could have gone anywhere, she thought, but he had come home because this was where things took on meaning. The only place worth having your triumph was Galatia, West Virginia.

She said, "I think Vera's wonderful. Better than you."

He didn't laugh although it was a sort of tease. He said, "I don't have any excuse except confusion. I have a feeling you think you got the short end of the stick. I depended on you liking her—"

"Better than I like you right now."

He did smile a little. "Well, I'm glad. You can be pretty hard-shell—"

"I'm not hard-shell."

"I remember a time when you accused me for all practical purposes of getting you a job in a house of prostitution. I call that hard-shell."

"I was fourteen years old, Johnny, I was ignorant!"

In the corners of their mouths they both smiled a little and concentrated on the dishes. Working with John was a pleasure, not that he thought much of housework, but he could do anything, she thought, the most quick and efficient of anybody. They could hear Vera in the other room talking to the Preacher, her voice making a little singsong. John said, "But you'll help her learn how to get along with the ones coming tonight, won't you? The Shinns, Emzie and Everett Wright—"

"Emzie! Ha!"

"Sometimes Vera says things to surprise people. She has an unusual way of saying things that scares people."

"Good. I hope she scares Emzie. I hope she gives Emzie the biggest surprise of her life." Since he mentioned the Wrights, she hoped he would say something, tease her a little about Earl, but it never seemed to occur to him.

Mary Katherine and Vera were together all the time. For Mary Katherine it was a revelation, the pleasure of doing everything with somebody. They made breakfast together and did the ironing together. They planned a vacation church school that people talked about for months after, and even Methodists and one Catholic family sent their children. They made flour paste and newspaper puppets and Vera wrote plays for the children to perform. All on Bible subjects of course, but not boring at all. John thought they might be spending too much time on puppets—but that was after he had knocked over a pan of flour paste. He was proud of them, everyone was proud of them. Vera bought Mary Katherine an eyelash curler and a wardrobe of lipsticks in all different colors. Every day was a pleasure to Mary Katherine, who hadn't realized she could do so many things. They organized a singing group and made the skirts and played the piano. All summer she would get up at six o'clock to do the ironing, especially John's shirts, which Vera was bad at, and since she was up anyhow, she would put a cake or some brownies in the oven. Later she would go over to the church and type and mimeograph the weekly bulletin, sometimes with little humorous sayings and stories that Vera made up. They helped John with the shut-in visits. At first she and Vera did the kindergarten Sunday school class together, then they took turns so one of them could go to morning worship, and then the Preacher got worse and Vera had morning sickness, so Mary Katherine did more and more by herself while Vera stayed with the Preacher. Vera seemed content and Mary Katherine was enjoying herself enormously. She felt like a juggler with oranges and little white balls and champagne bottles all up in the air at once, always just a fraction of a second ahead of herself and in perfect control.

"Don't you ever run down?" said Vera. "Let's pretend like the Preacher is sick today and both of us stay home and play."

By the end of October Vera was staying in most days. Being pregnant seemed to weary her, although she was perfectly cheerful and took very good care of the Preacher. When Mary Katherine got home, Vera talked about the fascinating things that were happening to her body. I could listen to my body all day long, Vera said.

One Wednesday night at the end of the month she said she really was feeling terrible and begged Mary Katherine to stay home from prayer meeting to keep her company. John dashed across the windy alley to the church alone, and Vera immediately began to sing and wheeled the Preacher into the living room and put on the radio. Mary Katherine could hear her singing with it, much louder than the radio. She shouted, "Vera, you don't sound very sick to me!"

"You'll see," called Vera, and a few minutes later Mary Katherine had the prickly sensation in the back of her neck of not being alone.

She gasped; it was like an angel of darkness, a thing with great bat wings and a distorted face with a webby little o of a mouth.

"This is the night of retribution," it said.

Vera rolled back the stocking from her face, but it still pulled her eyebrows tight and gave her a naked, singed look. "Of course you know it's just me, but if you didn't, you would have been terrified, wouldn't you? You were pretty scared as it was."

"I thought you were supposed to be sick."

"I lied. I've been lying a lot lately because I've been working on these costumes, one for me and one for you. I've been planning this for weeks. Nobody knows about it but me and the Preacher. I borrowed the choir robes from church and sneaked up to your room and used the sewing machine—I had to pick up every little black thread so you wouldn't suspect anything. But tonight," she said, "we're going trick-or-treating."

Mary Katherine had so many objections she didn't know where to begin. "It's the wrong night. Tomorrow's Halloween, not tonight. And you're pregnant."

Vera shook out the other robe like a bullfighter's cape in front of Mary Katherine. "Try on yours. I've got the whole thing figured out, Mary Katherine. We couldn't do it tomorrow because John would be home. Tonight was prayer meeting so he'd be out, but also you told me yourself Emzie Wright never goes to it because she's too tired."

"What has it got to do with Emzie?"

"Why, she's the one who gets the retribution. Everyone else in Galatia is very nice. We're going to go to her house to put a curse on her because you hate her."

"I do not!"

"Oh yes you do. You would never admit to hating someone, but you do, you're a good hater. I wish I could hate as well as you do, but I've never been in one place long enough to hate. Well, the idea is, we go to her house and do the witches' scene from Macbeth, as best I can remember it because I don't have the book, and we're going to give her a warning to mend her ways. I've got your lines written down, and everything you say is in unison with me so you don't have to memorize—"

"We can't."

"Why not?"

Mary Katherine looked her straight in the eye, the big wide eyes, the cheerful smile and pleasantly surprised eyebrows. Why ever not? "I never should have told you about how Emzie made it hard for me about the parsonage. I never should have told you she didn't want Earl to like me."

"But Mary Kay, every time you say her name your face falls about two feet and you look like Doom. You can't hide your face. We're doing this to get her off your back."

"They'll know who it is."

"How could they ever guess? No one will know, not John, not anybody. We're just going to be witches and give Emzie Wright a scare."

"I never read any Shakespeare except Julius Caesar when I was a sophomore."

"Good, you won't know how much I forgot. The main thing you

say is Boil and Bubble Toil and Trouble. We pretend to be stirring up a cauldron."

It was the idea of being able to stare Emzie in the face that made her waver. She had been sidling around Emzie with her eyes lowered all these years. She said, "I may be wrong about Emzie. She never said anything right out to me. Mostly it's just that this person or that person told me she said this or that."

Vera draped the robe over Mary Katherine's shoulders. "What's the difference? It's not as if we were going to hurt her."

"We're grown women."

"I'm not."

"You're a mother!"

"Not yet. You don't become a mother till you've had the baby. Once I'm a mother I'll be very serious, the minute I meet the baby. But let's be wild just this once. For half an hour, that's all. I know what you're going to say next, that we can't leave the Preacher, but I say he'll be fine for that little bit of time."

She hadn't even given the Preacher a thought. What a hypocrite I am. I guess I might as well.

Vera saw she had won and threw a stocking cap at her and started to cackle. "Come on, Mary Katherine, practice! Boil and Bubble Toil and Trouble! Foul, foul, foul!"

It was a night with damp black gusts of wind that made their choir robes rise and fall and unexpectedly slap their ankles. They stood crouched over with their heads together for a few seconds in the alley between the parsonage and the church, listening to someone inside talking, some long drawn out speaker, Hebert Shinn most likely. Prayer meetings were sleepy and quiet, sparsely attended with only the front lights on, and when Hebert started praying the church would seem to get dimmer and dimmer as you tried to keep from falling asleep. I'd rather be here than there, thought Mary Katherine. They went through the parking lot and out on Waterbridge alley for their rear assault on the Wrights'. A dog barked through a fence and Vera swooped her sleeves at it, and then squatted down and called until it let her pet it.

"Vera," Mary Katherine said anxiously, "let's go." A garbage can blew over somewhere.

They had to stoop to pass under an apple tree, then step over the furrows of Everett Wright's garden. Mary Katherine got along fine with Everett and thought he was a good man. She realized now that she didn't want him mad at her. What for that matter would Earl think on the other side of the world if he knew she was harassing his parents in a witch's costume? She could usually tell what would make Earl laugh and what would cause his disapproval, and she had a bad feeling about this.

They went along the side of the house, close enough to touch the white boards. Mary Katherine thought there would be an instant on the porch when she could change her mind if she wanted to, but Vera knocked too soon. The inner door opened and Everett looked at them through the glass wearing a white long John undershirt and suspenders. From deep inside the house came Emzie's voice. "Who is it, Everett?"

"Looks like trickertreaters, Emzie. You folks supposed to come tomorrow night."

Vera dashed her flashlight beam over Everett's face and then her own. "We want the woman," she said. "We have a message for the woman."

Everett said, "We ain't bought the candy yet. You fellas look too big for trickertreat anyways."

She hadn't seen Everett since Earl left, and seeing him made her homesick. Made her hear Earl say, Oh the Army'll be all right. I'll meet some guys. It won't be so bad. All he wanted was to get engaged. I wouldn't have even had to tell anyone, she thought.

"Who is it, Everett?" First Emzie was a big blobby shadow behind him, but she squeezed him to one side and cracked the door open. "Teen-agers," she said. "The Mayor declared tomorrow night for trickertreat and we don't have anything yet, so you can just move along."

Vera fixed her with the flashlight. Wide and solid with auburn bangs hiding her forehead and eyebrows, she squinted at the light, but didn't flinch. Vera said, "Are you the Right woman? Are you the Wright?"

"I don't know who you are," said Emzie, "but you know very well who I am so go on and have your joke."

Vera let out a shriek of laughter and swooped the sleeves of her robe and started the Boil and Bubble, but Mary Katherine just stayed shrunken against the porch pillar, praying it wouldn't get worse, hearing child prayers she hadn't used since she was little run through her mind. Oh please God if you don't let this happen I'll do anything I'll never again if only please God.

"The message!" cried Vera. "I have a message about cruelty!" She had a piece of paper in her pocket that she hadn't told Mary Katherine about, and she waved it around. "Listen and take heed! *If you don't straighten up and stop being mean You shall be chased by a monster lean Each time you lay down your head to dream The sound that wakes you will be your own scream!*"

She thrust the paper at Emzie, who wouldn't unfold her arms, so she dropped it on the porch. Emzie said, "Well, Everett, I've had about enough of these teen-agers. If they don't get going now, I think you better go get your old shotgun."

"Sure thing, Emzie," said Everett, not moving a muscle.

Vera screeched and leaped off the porch, not using the steps, and took off running down the street, howling and laughing. Mary Katherine ran after her, right out on the street even though they'd agreed to stick to the alleyways, and Vera was stopping now under a street lamp and whirling and cackling.

"Stop it," said Mary Katherine, finally catching up. "Stop it Vera, what if you fell? Get on the sidewalk, what if a car came?" She pushed her onto the sidewalk. "Settle down now, Vera!"

"I don't want to go home," said Vera. "I want to stay out here for good. You didn't know I'd written a poem, did you? Did I exorcize her? Are you free?"

"I don't know. I started missing Earl."

"That's a good sign, I guess,"

"The only good sign will be if we get home and no one catches us." Vera didn't seem to realize what was fitting. Mary Katherine had never had anyone tell her either, but she had figured it out somehow. A few people in Galatia had helped her out, Gladys and Doc Rogers when she worked at the drugstore, John of course, but she had also made a study of things. When she first stayed in town on school days to work, she used to stand at the drugstore counter and wipe it over and over and watch the street like a big sunny river, everything flowing, everyone in Galatia and all the little surrounding mining camps eventually passing by or drifting in for a Coca-Cola or a prescription or a newspaper. The ones who only passed by would get talked about by the ones inside, Gladys and Doc Rogers. There goes old Mrs. Bodkin, Gladys would say. See how straight she carries her back? They say she has her own teeth too and rubs them with salt, never did use toothpaste, you hear that Doc? Never used a bit of toothpaste. I saw your friend Roe Pickett this morning, Mary Katherine. That girl has a lot of gumption, you know that? Doing so well in high school with that family she comes from. Isn't that right Doc? And Doc saying, Only Pickett in the whole bunch worth a nickel.

They were pulling off the witch robes as they went in the back door, and Mary Katherine was feeling the relief; no insidious voice saying, There's that Mary Katherine Scarlin, she's half-cracked, you know what she did at Halloween?

The Preacher was sitting by the table with a bowl on his lap, eating pieces of dry bread. The refrigerator door was open and the milk bottle spilled. He had tried to pour it in his bowl because a lot of the milk had run down his pants leg. He stared at them and nibbled on the bread even as they rushed over to clean up. Mary Katherine slammed the refrigerator door, slapped the dishrag on the floor for the milk.

"Poor thing," said Vera. "You didn't get any milk in the bowl at all."

"Take that bowl away from him till I can clean up. I was going to make your milk toast, Preacher, if you just would of waited. I told you I would. But you always have to do what you want to when you want to and now we don't have any milk at all."

"I'll mix up some powdered," said Vera, sitting down with the big pile of black costumes in her arms. She hadn't taken off her stocking cap. She seemed suddenly weary and didn't move as Mary Katherine worked on the cleanup, and then John came in.

He said, "Do we give the Preacher his bath in the kitchen now?"

Mary Katherine froze. The costumes hadn't been put away. Vera's hair was flying every which way out from under the stocking cap. Vera said, "It's a good thing he didn't decide to make his milk toast on the stove because he would have burned the house down."

John's face began to register Vera's outfit. "What are you wearing?"

"I guess we're caught." Vera yawned. "We made Halloween costumes and went out trick-or-treating."

"You went trick-or-treating? While prayer meeting was on? Mary Katherine, you did too?"

"Now don't start on Mary Katherine. I was going to do it whether she went or not and she only came along to make sure I didn't hurt myself—"

John stared at Mary Katherine. "Trick-or-treating? I can't believe it."

Vera winked at Mary Katherine. "We didn't bother any Baptists, just a couple of Catholics."

John's face reminded Mary Katherine of a time, of a sound of crockery breaking. "I don't care who you went to—don't you see how it looks? Don't you—" He started to build up pressure, but stopped with his mouth open, then screwed it shut and turned on his heel.

Oh no, thought Mary Katherine.

Vera said, "Uh-oh," and gathered up the costumes and followed him upstairs. Mary Katherine could hear their voices for a long time, first just Vera teasing and wheedling, then John answering in a monotone and gradually more fluently as Vera won him over.

And she was left with the Preacher, making up some powdered milk, soaking toast in it, and warming it both sprinkled with sugar and pepper. She watched him eat and had nothing left to do till he was finished, and as if the witchspeak had finally come over her, she began to talk to him. "Well, don't ever think I'm grateful to you, Preacher. Other people helped me, but not you. I'm not even grateful to you for teaching me to keep store and play the piano. Every important thing I had to learn for myself, do you hear, Preacher?"

After Christmas the Preacher began to catch colds. The doctor kept coming to give him penicillin shots, and he would mention that they might have to rent a tank of oxygen before they were through. The doctor checked Vera too, but she seemed extraordinarily healthy. They all spent a lot of time sitting with the Preacher. Mary Katherine hated it, especially she hated how mean her thoughts were towards him. She would sew or try to read, but there was a limit to what you could do in there with him lying in bed wheezing. One night she was trying to read a book by Pearl S. Buck, who was born in West Virginia, but there was a sort of bricked-up door inside her that seemed to keep the ideas in the book away from her. She blamed the bricks on the Preacher. It was a terrible thing, but she found herself blaming everything on the Preacher as if it were his fault she couldn't concentrate on reading and John never asked about Earl and that Vera sometimes did unfitting things. It wasn't right to sit here with bitterness when he was so sick. She had been saying mean things in her head since Halloween. Your fault I never had a mother, she thought. No one ever told me I would need deodorant. The simple everyday things she came down out of Black Run not knowing. She might as well have been raised by wolves. He worried about their souls, though, he said, because their mother was a Catholic and he suspected she had sneaked off and had them sprinkled when they were little babies. I should have moved out when John did, she thought. Then I would be more forbearing now.

John had come in one summer evening at dusk just as Mary Katherine was laying out the tureen of creamed corn and a plate of white bread. The kitchen was hot and all the doors were open to catch the breeze. John stepped in silently from the back instead of coming in through the store. He was wearing a beautiful light tan suit and a tie with green and brown overlapping leaves in the print. "I got a new job," he said.

Mary Katherine said, "It looks like you got a new haircut too."

He called out in a deep voice, "Hey, Preacher, come here and see something."

The Preacher came from the store, taller than John then, dark-skinned and straight, with thick gray hair and a little plug of tobacco in the back of his jaw. He looked over the suit, then went to the door to spit. John hung the jacket on the back of his chair.

"How about your tie?" said Mary Katherine. "Aren't you afraid of spilling something?"

"I have to get used to wearing it. I don't want to look like a hawksnester at my new job."

The Preacher said, "Are you praying or gabbing, Mary Katherine?"

She said a quick "Bless-this-food-to-the-good-of-our-bodies" so she could hear about the new job, but the Preacher picked up after her Amen and prayed for a good five minutes more.

When they finally all looked up again, John started making an apple butter sandwich and the Preacher said, "You might of said a prayer too, for the wherewithal to pay for that white suit."

Mary Katherine said, "It isn't white, it's tan."

"I got a job at the Toggery, Preacher, and I had to have a suit because I'll be selling clothes. They're giving it to me at no markup and they're taking what I owe for it out of my salary."

Mary Katherine said what she thought the Preacher would have wanted her to. "Well, Johnny, I don't know about Credit. Credit keeps you always using goods that belong to somebody else."

John made a face at her, but the Preacher said, "He don't need that suit for work, he needs it for that church he goes to now."

John served himself creamed corn and kept serving until his plate was swimming in it. "I work evenings on Friday," he said, "and on Wednesday too most weeks."

Mary Katherine gasped. "But Johnny, what about the prayer meeting?"

"I guess I'll have to miss it."

The Preacher chewed and looked at the wall.

"But Johnny, Second Miler Baptists—"

"He ain't no Second Miler," said the Preacher, quite softly, but you could hear the intake of air, the pressure building up for a real shout. "There are only two Second Miler Baptists in this room, and he ain't one of them. That church in Galatia, John, that purple synagogue that calls itself a Baptist church, I hear the preacher there wears a collar like a Catholic fa-ather. I hear they jump up and down on their knees and drink wine for communion."

"You know Johnny wouldn't go to a church where they drink wine."

"Let him talk, Mary Kay. Let him say everything he has to say."

"I hear they baptize in a bathtub in that church. With hot running water even though the Book says that in Those Days Jesus was baptized and came straightaway up out of the river Jordan. Up Out Of, John, means Immersion and not sprinkling—"

"They immerse all right, Preacher."

"The River Jordan means a river, not a bathtub." John's thumbs began to curl under his hands.

"They didn't have churches yet when Jesus was baptized, and it's warm all year round in Palestine."

"They used a river because God told them to use a river."

"The mines didn't dump in the River Jordan."

"There is a fate worse than death for those who mock His commandments."

John smacked his hands on the table and pushed away from it and started walking in a circle around the kitchen. "You think you're Moses the Lawgiver. I can't believe it sometimes. Did you ever think you might not have been the one man in the world chosen to interpret the scriptures right? Did that ever cross your mind?"

"I can read. What is right is written and what is written is right. You make your own decision to be saved or damned. It's as simple as that." The Preacher spoke out of stillness, but John rubbed his hands together and paced and shook his head.

"It is not simple," said John. "Nothing is simple. Do you see, Mary Katherine? There's nothing you or I can ever say that he'll hear. He doesn't hear us, not a word we say. I'm taking the job because you don't have clothes for fall and he doesn't make enough to keep body and soul together. I'm doing the most ordinary thing in the world, I'm taking a decent job and going to a convenient Baptist church. And I won't be damned by him for it."

"You think Eternal Damnation isn't an ordinary thing?"

"People have been damned for misleading children in their care, too, Preacher."

The Preacher stood up and stretched out one arm. "I don't want to see you in my church again. You cannot serve Two Masters."

"Well I won't serve you, that's for sure. I wouldn't serve you even if—" He seemed unable to find any words, and instead of giving himself time to find some, he threw his fist at the table and swept the tureen onto the floor where it broke evenly in two pieces and the creamed corn flowed out slowly. He leaped over it and ran through the store. The Preacher kept his arm out as if he were casting a curse on John, and Mary Katherine grabbed the beautiful suit jacket and ran after him, her voice echoing in the dark empty store where they did business and had church, where the two of them had always played. "Johnny! Johnny! Where are you going to sleep?" She caught him out on the road and he told her to come with him, she'd go crazy too if she insisted on living with the Preacher. But she was only fourteen years old and terribly afraid of going to Hell as the preacher described it. Later, when she was working in town herself and going to high school, she might have left him, but by then the Preacher had his first stroke and she had to spend time at home feeding him fried mush and milk toast while he babbled about how he was damned and going to hell. One of his confessions was that he had been a Catholic himself for a while long ago, when he was working in the city and had no one he knew. That was when he married their Italian mother it turned out, and he was the one who had them baptized Catholics, not her. Mary Katherine was ready to walk out on the Preacher for good then, but John said he had known for a long time. Why didn't you tell me? Why do I have to stay with him? You don't have to do anything, said John, but just search your conscience awhile before you decide. So of course she went back to Black Run and John got the scholarship to college and seminary, and the Preacher in the end stopped talking and Mary Katherine talked instead. You let me grow up thinking my mother was a bad woman. Well, Preacher, don't think I will let you off easy for that.

Vera came in wearing John's cardigan sweater that just barely buttoned over her nightgown now. "Changing of the guard," she said.

"I don't mind staying with him, you look tired."

"Just tired of waiting. I might as well wait in here where I'm useful."

Mary Katherine didn't even stay in the sick room to talk to Vera but fled the terrible warmth, the closeness to his breathing. Thank heaven for Vera, she thought, walking around the living room, picking up some shoes, straightening a pile of Life magazines, folding the afghan. She gathered momentum as she worked, beginning to itch in the fingers and wrists for more activity. John was writing a sermon on the kitchen table, and she asked if it would disturb him if she made a cake. He grunted No, hardly lifting his face from his notebooks and Bible.

She became cheerful as she sifted and creamed, thinking about Vera's baby, and about Earl Wright, what Vera and Earl would think of one another. Out of the corner of her eye she watched John ruffle his hair, then rest his long hands flat on the Bible as he read a passage. Everyone doing something quiet and useful. The baby growing dreamily inside Vera. Herself with the solid slap and scrape of wooden spoon in batter. She wished someone could gently lift the roof off the house and see them at this moment. God could, of course, but she had in mind something more like the deacons or trustees of the church. See what a good family John and I have put together out of nothing?

She was pouring the batter into the cake pans when Vera came in. "The Preacher," she said.

"Does he need oxygen?"

"No, he doesn't seem any different except he's trying to talk."

John closed his fountain pen. "He wants to see us?"

"He says he wants to straighten something out. He says it's a last request."

Mary Katherine couldn't help herself from letting the oven door slam. "I know you think it's hard of me, Vera, but he's been threatening to die for years. Why did he wait till now to straighten things out?"

Vera leaned her back against the wall as if she were taking a picture of the two of them and trying to get everything in. "He says he wants to confess his sins."

"He's already done that. Before he stopped talking, he told more things than I ever want to hear. I've heard all the sins already. So has John."

"He doesn't want to tell you or John or me either. He says he wants to confess to a Catholic priest."

They both stared at her, and Mary Katherine noticed with annoyance that Vera's feet were bare. All they needed was Vera getting pneumonia too.

John said, "What did he say exactly?"

"Oh, Johnny, it doesn't matter, it's just one more trick to torment us."

Vera made her jaw go slack like the Preacher's. "I-have-to-talk-to-a-priest. Get-me-a-Catholic-fa-ther."

"You don't have to imitate him. It's bad enough knowing he's crazy without hearing you do an imitation. Isn't that just like him, Mary Katherine? To decide on a deathbed conversion? Or reconversion. To see the light one more time."

"The only light he sees is hell fire."

"I guess the truth is he's always been crazy. I remember him preaching at the mines at shift change. He took us with him. My job was to watch you because you were just learning to walk, and he would stand up on one of those old wooden dynamite boxes and preach to the miners as they came off the cars. All they wanted was to get the grit off their faces and out of their throats and here was this crazy man calling thunder and lightning down on the Catholic church. Not even anything so interesting as telling them not to drink beer—they didn't so much as give a catcall. They would just laugh once or twice and be on their way."

"And all he ever wanted was for people to notice how different he was from them."

"Hey," said Vera. "Who's going down to Saint Anthony's?"

John's face lengthened and tightened. "You're kidding. We aren't having a priest in this house. It isn't going to go around town that the

Baptist minister's father is a Catholic."

"Besides, Vera, it isn't really his deathbed. You don't know him. He used to keep me awake night after night saying that the devil was putting hot coals in his armpits. He has a bad conscience."

"I know all about his conscience." Vera looked from one to the other of them, her gray eyes growing wider and wilder. "I don't think either one of you feel sorry for him. I think you're worried about your reputation."

Red bruises appeared on John's cheekbones, and the little vertical incision between his eyebrows. Mary Katherine wanted to say, Oh don't get him mad, Vera, the last time he got terribly mad he walked out on us. But John maintained calm. He picked up the Bible and put it under his arm. "We feel very sorry for him, Vera. We understand him and feel sorry for him. Let's go and have prayer with him."

The Preacher was waiting for them, sitting erect, his sharp old knees raising the blanket. The room seemed still, and Mary Katherine realized suddenly that for the first time in weeks she didn't hear his breathing. He was like a bright-eyed ghost.

John stopped near the foot of the bed and gravely turned the pages of the Bible. Mary Katherine stayed in the doorway, feeling hypocritical to be here at all. Vera whispered, "Hey, Preacher, do you want to hear some Bible?"

John found what he wanted and pressed the spine of the Bible between his palms, then looked at the old man for the first time. "If you're in trouble, Preacher, if your conscience isn't easy, that's between you and God, but if we can, we want to help you ease the burden." He glanced at the book, then up again, as if he weren't quite sure how to proceed. "Mary Katherine and I and Vera want to be with you at this time and share the comfort of the psalm: 'Oh God thou art my God, early will I seek thee; my soul thirsteth for thee.' "

The Preacher growled down in his throat. "Don't want to hear you."

Mary Katherine whispered, "He is talking."

"I said he was," said Vera.

"It's good to hear your voice again, Preacher. Is there some favorite scripture you want me to read?"

John went back to the psalm. " Thy lovingkindness is better than life."

The Preacher's good knee began to twitch. "I want to talk to a priest."

The red stains came back to John's face. "My lips shall praise thee."

"I had enough Bible," said the Preacher, and his knee began to move in time to what he was saying. "I want to see a priest, a Catholic priest. I want to see a priest."

Half a second before he did it, Mary Katherine saw what was coming and cried, "Johnny, look out!" but the covers had already slid off and the shiny, sharp-shinned leg flashed through the air and kicked the Bible out of John's hands.

John leaped backwards and bounced it once in the air but kept it from falling. The force of the kick knocked the Preacher off his pillows, and he lay on his side staring as John slammed the Bible shut and ran out with Vera following him. To her surprise, now that he was talking again, Mary Katherine's anger was less than it had been for a long time. She lifted him by the shoulders back onto his pillows and jabbed the covers back under him. "What do you think you're doing, kicking a Bible?"

"I'm changin' over. I want to be forgiven."

"Well Lord knows you need that." She got his water glass, and when he tried to refuse it, she held him by the prickly back of the neck till he drank. He coughed and spit in the glass.

"You want me to roast."

"Why don't you say your prayers instead of thinking up devilment?"

"I never could pray by myself."

"That's why you had to be a preacher, I guess."

"That's why I have to have a priest. But you don't have to do it. That boy said he'd get me a priest."

"John's not getting you anything after you kicked the Bible."

"Not him, the little boy. That little boy is good to me."

"Who, Vera? She's a woman. She's John's wife."

He fixed his eyes and snorted, as if he had proof now that she was trying to trick him.

"It's true. You'd know what was going on around here if you weren't so wrapped up in yourself. Go ahead and close your eyes, it doesn't bother me."

They were in the kitchen, John standing at the window watching the rain fall, clasping and unclasping his hands. Vera leaning her elbows on the table as she talked, and for the moment her loose nightgown hid her pregnancy. "Listen to me, John, it's only fair to get him what he wants, if it will make him feel better."

Mary Katherine said, "Oh Vera, let him rest. Wait and see if he doesn't forget the whole thing."

Vera rotated her big gray eyes at Mary Katherine. "You don't give him any respect. When you found out the bad things about him, you pretended he was dead. Well, it doesn't matter, I guess you can't help it. He's the one who did something terrible, and he's suffering."

John turned suddenly. "Who gave you the right to sit back and give opinions on the Preacher? Who gave you the right to tell Mary Katherine how to act and me I'm only worried about my reputation? You don't know anything about us."

Oh no, thought Mary Katherine. They're going to fight. "The Preacher's senile," she said. "We should all have some coffee and cake and not get excited."

John came to the table and faced Vera. "It doesn't matter whether he's crazy or not. No one is going for a priest."

"Don't fight!"

"Not me," said Vera. "I'm not much of a fighter. Especially not against you two." And she left them alone in the kitchen.

John made a fist and struck the side of his leg. "I don't need opposition from my own family."

Mary Katherine tested the cakes. It was such a mess. Vera shouldn't start things when she was pregnant.

Vera came back barefoot but wearing John's raincoat. "I can't find my shoes."

John said, "I don't believe you think you are going to bring a Catholic priest into this house."

Well, thought Mary Katherine, here it all goes. "I put them in his bedroom when I was straightening up." In her mind she began to form a letter. Listen, I have to get away from here because they are starting to fight. She didn't look at John because he thought she was helping Vera.

They followed Vera and watched her lace up her old saddle oxfords without anklets. "Well, I'm going." John straight-armed the door closed when she tried to go out, and Vera said, "Are you going to slam me too?"

"Oh, Vera, he wouldn't hit you—Johnny, you know she's right, if he wants a priest, let him have one, what do we care, I'll go for a priest—" John turned to Mary Katherine, and in that instant Vera slipped out the door, leaving it open.

John slammed it as hard as he could, and Mary Katherine could feel it in the floor. He said, "All I want is to do right. All I want is to be able to conduct a good ministry without being hindered, without giving people anything to use against me. Don't you know what they're going to say if this gets out? Don't you know what it would do to my chances?"

Mary Katherine felt sick; John's face in front of her was melting and running like candlewax. "The Preacher's crazy," she said. "It's his last wish."

John seemed to be coming out from some hypnosis. "Don't dramatize. I'll tell you one thing, though. I won't be in this house with a Catholic priest."

She ran onto the porch after him. "Your coat!"

The rain was already making gray marks on John's shoulders. "She has my coat," he said.

He paced for a few minutes under the streetlight and then went off in the opposite direction from the Catholic church. Mary Katherine watched him out of sight, then went to the kitchen table where his papers and pens were still lying around and she began to write version after version of a letter, even after Vera came in with the stranger. She kept writing and tearing up until she found just the person she wanted to be, just the person to fall in love with Earl Wright.

Dear Earl, I guess you must be surprised to hear from me after all this time, but here I am. I hope you are safe and well. How are things over there in Korea? I'm fine, and so is John, but the Preacher has been awfully sick. He's doing a little better now, though. John is married, and I like her very much. They have a baby coming soon and we are all looking forward to that! I feel too young to be an aunt! I hope the army isn't too hard. And the Communists. Well, Earl, that's about all for now except I guess you should know I've been thinking about you a lot and wishing you were home safe so we could talk over what we talked about before you left. Best wishes and keep smiling from

Your
Mary Katherine

And the next Sunday John preached his sermon on prejudice against those different from ourselves, and a couple of weeks later Vera had her baby Lee, and then the Preacher really did die, and Earl came home safely from Korea.

Chapter 2
Vera

The amazing thing was that she could feel her success as palpably as a bead between her thumb and forefinger. She had wanted the audience to forget for a moment to whisper, That's my grandson! She wanted them to forget that Easter is the holiday when the children put on the pageant, and instead to feel present at Jesus' actual suffering on the cross. She had stood in the choir box with the old spotlight and borrowed gels, and felt the people in the darkness stirring, leaning forward. She heard them catch their breath and hold it. The children moved them, and the children moved at her direction. They were all touched: Emzie Wright and Hebert Shinn and Bill Rogers, just as surely as by one of John's best sermons. Her great idea had been for the audience to provide music and text by singing familiar hymns—"I Come to the Garden Alone," and "Up from the Grave He Arose." Then there had been the colors, the blue for the Last Supper, red when Peter, played by her older daughter Lee, whacked off the Roman soldier's ear. And finally there had been the shock that she actually strapped a child up on a cross. Her own child, again, her younger, Tonie. Poor Tonie objecting to the yellow beard. Her feet had slipped off the little platform and the leather straps cut into her bare arms. Vera had heard a voice in the audience whisper Oh No! But yes, thought Vera. Oh yes, it is real, not a pretty picture, not something old and comfortable but real passion and real suffering.

"Now what?" said John. "What are you grinning about?"

Easter morning between Sunday school and church, and her Passion pageant was over. She was half sitting in the window of his office in the new building, and he was in his swivel chair. The desk had not arrived yet, but the chair was ready for it, centered on the wall-to-wall plum carpet.

He turned himself from side to side. "You weren't listening. You didn't hear anything, did you?"

She had been wafting in the warm current of her success. "I'm sorry, I'm still wrapped up in last night." There was a ghostly butterfly of what she had achieved and it was drifting away in silence. "It was nothing," she said. "It's gone. I'm listening."

It had been precisely at the moment when she raised her hand to signal the organist to chord for the opening procession that John marched down the center aisle and interrupted it. He couldn't stay out of it, he couldn't let her begin the way she had planned, he had to say Welcome mothers and fathers, and grandmothers and grandfathers to another children's Easter pageant. But I did it anyway, she thought. He tried to make it be an ordinary service, and I made it be something extraordinary.

"What I want to tell you about," he said, "is the letter I got yesterday from the Parkersburg church. I didn't mention it sooner because I knew how involved you were in the pageant. They're asking me to preach again next Sunday. I think they're going to make the offer this time."

"Will you accept?"

"I assumed we would discuss it."

"Now? Between Sunday school and church on Easter morning?"

"Well, I haven't wanted to disturb your fun the last few weeks. You've hardly been home anyhow."

My fun, she thought, and the words took on a neon flash inside her head. "Oh, John, you just like the excitement of toying with an offer from a new church in the middle of the biggest Sunday of the year at your old church."

His mouth and eyes seemed to seal, his skin to contract against his skull. She was trying so hard not to let him know what he had done to her; she couldn't bear to have him angry. She began to pull sentences out of the air, watching his face for the ones that would make the tenseness relax. She said, "We've been in Galatia a long time. Nine years I guess. Do you know that means I've lived in Galatia longer than anywhere else in my whole life? I have always felt this was the right place. You came back, Mary Katherine and Earl got together. When Lee was born, it was like I was beginning a new life too. I feel like I've had my whole lifetime here."

He had decided not to get mad. "We've accomplished a lot since we've been here. It's not as if I'd feel like we were cheating them if we left now."

"Cheating them! You practically built this educational building for them single-handed."

"They say the schools in the district where this church is are excellent. But I don't know. It's still a city. It's a big decision, but I don't want to get stale. I want to know it's the right moment and seize it. Don't mention it yet to Mary Katherine ."

"You're not quite as old as Jesus when he seized his moment."

"What has Jesus got to do with it? Why did you say that?"

Sometimes there was a strange, antic dwarf in her head that made her attack John when she wasn't expecting it herself. "Why John, I thought Jesus always had something to do with it when a minister started making decisions."

He stiffened. His tightening face seemed to draw everything toward him, to suck up carpet, window, herself. It was Easter morning and she seemed to be able to do nothing but set off one of John's rages.

She tried to apologize again, but she was saved by a scrambling at the inner door that led to the old part of the church, and in burst Tonie, long hair in pigtails, wearing an orange dress greatly expanded by several crinolines. The crinolines had been a bribe: You may wear as many as you want with your Easter dress if you'll act Jesus. I know he wasn't a girl, but I can't get any boys to do it. Lee had begged to play Jesus; she loved to act, would act any part, any time. But it had been the little kids' pageant, and it had been stretching a point even to let Lee play Peter. There were too many crinolines, and the dress curled up in the back. Vera tugged it down, and Tonie jerked away pouting.

"Who am I supposed to sit with?" she said.

"Knock," said John. "Don't come barging into my office like that without knocking."

Tonie stared at Vera from under her eyebrows. "You're sitting in the choir and Lee is sitting with her friends and she doesn't want me to sit with them."

"Well, sit with your friends. Sit with Ruthie Rogers."

"She's sitting with her family because they came today."

"More Easter Christians," said John.

"Do you want to sit in the choir with me?"

"Vera! For heaven's sake. Lee will sit with her. The friends will sit with their families and Tonie and Lee will sit with Mary Katherine and Earl and the boys."

"That's right. Daddy's idea is better, honey." She pulled Tonie's skirt down again. "I have to go to anthem practice," she said, "but I was wondering, John, why you made that speech last night just when we were about to start the pageant?"

"What speech? The welcome? I always welcome people to family nights."

"But last night was supposed to be different. I told you how it was supposed to be. They were supposed to forget it was a children's pageant."

"But it was the children's pageant!"

She knew she wouldn't have been saying any of this if she hadn't had Tonie there, an orange and blue plaid ribbon to tie. "I was just wondering," she said. "It worked out okay."

"Why are you bringing this up now? What has it got to do with—what we were talking about?"

"We better go find Lee," she said, taking firm hold of Tonie's hand. His mouth was trembling, and for an instant she felt like a great swollen maestro of human emotions. The amazing thing, though, would be that he would recover in no time, be completely serene by the time church started. He only lost his temper at home.

He said, "Why are you starting in on me now?"

"I'm not starting anything. Everything is just going on." He didn't try to stop her as she dragged Tonie out.

"Lee doesn't want me," said Tonie.

"Yes she does. Did I tell you how good you were in the pageant last night?" But Tonie seemed to have no interest in last night. A shame, she thought, because last night had been a much better place to be than today.

On Monday morning after Easter John's alarm woke Vera, but she kept her left eye closed and watched him with her right protected from notice by her pillow. He rested his head in his hands a few seconds, rubbing sleep away. Usually, when he went for his shower, she fell asleep again, but this morning she lay without moving, with a monstrous vision of the day before her. She imagined each action ahead: waking the girls, boiling water for coffee, putting out the cereal boxes, doing Tonie's braids, and meanwhile staring at the basket of white shirts to be ironed. She squeezed her eyes shut again, trying to float down, but only succeeded in beginning at the beginning, when John would wake her, go out, she would wake the girls, boil the water, and get the cardboard cereal boxes. And beyond that, the house, hopelessly untidy with toys and clothes strewn in every room, waiting like a giant baby, squalling silently, demanding its massive change and swabbing down.

She didn't look when John came back, only smelled the damp warmth from the shower. When he was dressed, he said, "Wake up, honey," and sat beside her on the bed, running a hand over her breast, down her side and between her legs. She rolled away from him.

"I'm up," she said, and added crudely, "Are you?"

Instantly, neatly, he removed his hands and stepped away. He was always offended by anything like dirty talk from her. "I won't be home for lunch. Hospital calls."

"All day?"

"Do you care?"

She felt a solid satisfaction at having offended him, at least as long as he wasn't going to be around the house to make her pay for it. She didn't move until she had heard him down the stairs and out the door, and then she hopped out of bed and burst into the girls' room, stripped the covers off of them.

Lee whined and rewrapped herself. Tonie sat up and rubbed her face, just like John, clearing away cobwebby dreams.

"Let's move."

"What's the matter?" said Lee. "Why are you starting the day so mean?"

"I'm looking for malingerers. That's people who pretend to be sick when they don't want to work or go to school. Or pretend to be asleep when they're awake."

"I was asleep. We can't both go to the bathroom at the same time anyhow."

"Just get up. Just get up and shut up and get downstairs."

A strange impulse, a halo of energy. Mostly to avoid the cartoon characters on the back of the cereal boxes, she began mixing pancakes. Lee came down first, grumbling about Tonie not giving her any privacy in the bathroom, always endlessly accusing Tonie of trying to occupy her space. But even Lee became silent in awe of the pancakes being dropped on her plate. Vera kept dropping pancakes, one for Lee, one for Tonie.

"How come we're having pancakes?" asked Lee.

"Don't look a gift horse in the mouth."

"Let us have some coffee," said Lee.

She made them each a cup of instant without much milk. Tonie made a face over hers, but Lee drank it. They were both highly wary. Vera approved of their suspiciousness and felt a secret camaraderie.

"You didn't make our lunches," said Lee, pointing at the counter where the paper bags were usually waiting.

"Pancakes aren't enough. You children always want more."

"You always make our lunches."

"Show me the contract."

"All right, I can make my sandwich. I'll make nothing but peanut butter and jelly. I'll make Tonie's too."

Tonie had been watching, and suddenly she said, "You have to braid my hair."

"Let it hang loose today."

"You have to braid it!"

"You always beg to wear it loose, so wear it loose today."

When Tonie balled up her features and started to cry, Vera sent her for the brush and comb and rubber bands, but she only braided halfway down, leaving a lot of fine hair loose in a big brush at the bottom. Meanwhile Lee wrapped the peanut butter sandwiches, ostentatiously using twice as much wax paper as needed, then, making sure Vera was watching, dropped several handfuls of chocolate chip cookies into each bag.

Vera said, "Things change. You can't assume everything will always be the same. I'm preparing you for sudden changes."

"I want them braided all the way," said Tonie.

Lee said, "I can make sandwiches as well as you can. I know how to pack a lunch. There's a picture in the scout handbook."

"Braid them all the way!"

She smiled at Tonie. "No, I refuse. Now you say 'yes' and I'll say 'no' for as long as you want to go back and forth."

"Come on Tonie," said Lee. "Let's go."

Vera was jealous of their closeness; she wasn't sure she had ever seen Lee so solicitous of Tonie. Her contrariness had made them join forces. She thought, I never had a sister to join up with when my mother was unbearable.

She stood shivering on the porch in her nylon nightie and watched them fade into the fog. Her euphoria faded with them, and she was ashamed of herself. Malicious mischief, she thought. I'm infected with malicious mischief. She imagined that these few minutes of uncontrolled spitefulness had caused irreparable damage. Now they would always look at her with nuggets of mistrust dark in their eyes. It was as if a child-Vera had suddenly appeared sticking its tongue out at rivals, determined to make them feel as orphaned as she had.

How sad, thought Vera, dropping on the couch and letting tears fall and sink into the tweed. How sad to be seven and always suspecting that when you come home your mother will be changing the rooms, or sending you to your aunt's, and your aunt is at work all day and talks about moving to Australia or Alaska and your mother is always about to get married. Later her mother did get married to a store manager for Consolidated Coal, and he moved more often than her mother had alone!

Tonie and Lee should have been sons. Mothers are what their daughters will be. It would have been better to have John be the important one because he was solid. Vera floated. Down, slowly. She floated down into her depression and on through the bottom of it toward sleep. She used to tell people that her mother had received a letter from her love saying that he could not see her again because he was married and had two children and her mother wrecked the car in a rainstorm and killed herself in despair. She used to kill off her mother in her stories to make sense of things. She used to make up a lot of stories. She saw herself on a wooden boardwalk in front of the company store on a coal mountain, and the tipple boss's daughter was whining,

"My mother says I can't play with you anymore because you story all the time. You story to beat the band." There had been other children, and the audience gave her a power she would never have had alone with the little girl. "Tell me/' she said, walking deliberately forward and making the store manager's girl back up, "do you think I'm storying when I tell you I have learned how to put curses on people? I make curses out of hot chicken blood." Vera didn't really care whether anyone believed that or not. It was enough that the manager's girl stumbled on a loose board and fell on her rump and everyone laughed and laughed and liked Vera.

The phone woke her. It was eleven-thirty, she saw, but remembered gleefully that John and the girls weren't coming for lunch. On the phone was Thelma Shinn, who wanted to get together to plan the devotions for the Women's Mission Circle. Come over, said Vera, come over in an hour and a half. She felt like talking to an adult, and she liked Thelma's jokes about her husband Hebert and the mortician business.

But as soon as she was committed to the certain hour of Thelma's arrival, a plague of nasty little objects began to parade around her ankles: from the floor newspapers to pick up, and Sorry and Monopoly games. A trail of shoes and socks. An island of construction paper and crayons. From the kitchen sticky plates and the electric coffeepot to get out of the closet and fill. And she would have to bake something quickly to serve Thelma. Brownies. The measuring cup, the egg. She got that far, then sat down at the table with the egg in front of her. As clear as revealed truth a child's voice came to her saying, "Make me. Try and make me."

At one o'clock she heard the quick little steps on the porch, the knock. She tiptoed to the door, laid her cheek against it, and listened to the faint scrape of Thelma's shoe. A clearing throat, another knock. Vera felt intimate with this coughing scraping person. It was not the Thelma she knew of course. This was a neutral being with an unpretentious knock, a gentle voice. But then there was a metallic click, the squeak of a handle turning in one direction and then the other. Oh Thelma, thought Vera. Oh Thelma Shinn! Would you really stoop so low? Would you walk in on me? Suppose I was inside with a man? Or suppose I had just run out for a coffee cake and caught you breaking and entering? Thelma gave the door an angry rattle. No, you wouldn't mind being caught. You think the parsonage is as public as the church.

Without waiting longer, Thelma gave up and clicked off the porch. Vera had an impulse to call after her, to take back what she had done, but the house pressed behind her, impossibly, restlessly untidy. It's too late now, she thought. I'll say I had the flu. I'll say I fell into one of those feverish sleeps and didn't wake up till Thelma had gone.

People would believe it. They would prefer that story to one about the preacher's wife listening through the keyhole to Thelma Shinn's breathing. The girls would be angry. Children have no sympathy for adult weakness, she thought. Illness is a pleasure they reserve for themselves. She used to love being sick. She loved the attention to the whims of her stomach, the yearnings for a vanilla milk shake or a slice of buttered toast divided precisely into four squares. But even more she loved the feverish daytime dreams she swam in, dreams without the quietness of sleep, hallucinatory dreams that she nurtured and expanded. The tale of the dagger-hand gypsies came to her during the flu when she was about Lee's age. She had amused herself with that one for years.

John believed in her flu. "You should have cancelled the arrangement with Thelma, though."

"I was just so groggy. It was stupid."

He was a good nurse. He sat beside her on the couch and held her hand, and then he fried hamburgers and defrosted green beans and organized the girls to set the table. After dinner Vera felt as if she might actually have a fever. She napped, then slept. She dreamed she was dying of leukemia and distantly she heard them all walking softly and whispering but nobody sobbed. John sent the girls to bed and leaned over her to whisper her awake, but she murmured that she was so comfortable on the couch she just wanted to stay a little longer.

She became fully awake when the upstairs was quiet. Then she unwrapped herself from her cocoon of covers and stalked from room to room humming hymns; she felt vividly in the midst of some great experience. The tweed and blond furniture, the dim night lamps, were powerful and vivid too. She began to tell herself the old dagger-hand gypsy story and how they steal the little girl, and they all have instead of a left hand an implanted dagger, because they amputated the hand in a coming-of-age ceremony. The girl is in constant danger of being initiated into their tribe. Sometimes they threaten; sometimes they save her from stupid conventional townspeople who want to make her be a lady. After a while she made a peanut butter and banana sandwich and ate a can of pineapple chunks.

During the next few days John spent extra time at the house, and the housekeeping went very well. He didn't put any fresh lining paper in any drawers, but he ironed all his shirts and braided Tonie's hair. She was especially pleased about the shirts. She liked to nap with them all working around her, the girls vacuuming, John boiling spaghetti. John

42

wanted to call a doctor as they approached Saturday and their scheduled visit to Parkersburg. Don't worry about me, she said. You go—I trust your judgment. You should see it, though, he said. It's a beautiful church—very modernistic, but not cold. An A-frame, with fieldstone ends. They want to see you too. Like this? She was wrapped in a stadium blanket and her hair had flattened to her head. What a terrible time to be sick, he said. She said, We never know what our bodies are going to do to us.

On Saturday morning as soon as he had left for Parkersburg, she closed the door to the girls' room so they would sleep. She showered and washed her hair and put on fresh dungarees, feeling pretty sure she wasn't going to start telling herself the epic of the dagger-hand gypsies today. But when she got to the kitchen, she noticed that he had washed his own breakfast dishes. They were in the drainer, droplets still clinging to the juice glass. She reached for the dish towel to finish drying them and saw that the electric coffeepot was perking just for her. Bowls set out for the girls, a banana in front of each place, an individual box of cereal: cornflakes for Lee, frosted flakes for Tonie. She dropped the dish towel and sat down. She was ready to redeem herself through work, but he had done everything for her. She never would have guessed he would remember that Tonie only ate frosted flakes.

She heard a floorboard creak overhead as they began to get up. If it was only Lee, she would read in bed a while. If both of them were awake, though, they would quarrel. The creak was followed by silence, so she was safe a little longer, but even so felt disturbed. She was listening for sounds from the upstairs so assiduously that she jumped when the intrusion came from the back porch. Mary Katherine, fresh from the outer world in a beauty parlor bubble.

"Why didn't you call me when you first got sick, Vera? You know I would have come."

"It's nine A.M. and you've already been to have your hair done. You're a wonder of the world."

"Why didn't you call me?" Mary Katherine poured a cup of coffee and set it in front of Vera.

"Don't wait on me, I'm not sick. It's a hoax. Have some coffee."

"I think I will have some. I've been drinking too much coffee lately, though. We've been staying up till all hours on the tax work. If we make a success this year, we're going to open an office, and then we won't be dependent on the mines anymore."

Vera knew she was supposed to be interested, part of her was, admiring Mary Katherine's master plan to make something out of Earl and Earl liking to brag about how Mary Katherine was turning him into a businessman. Something in her was blocking the appropriate responses. Mary Katherine appeared small, perfect in all the details of dress and expression, but reduced and distant. Vera didn't mind. It made it easier for her not to ask how the business was coming along.

"You don't have to stay, Mary Katherine. I don't know why John called you today. He's a better housekeeper than I ever was. Every evening he makes three lists of what to do. Dishes, run the sweeper, homework; he even includes his sermons. Tonie runs around the house carrying her little list, printed, mind you, so she can read it."

She didn't know if she was boasting or speaking ironically; she waited for Mary Katherine's reaction in order to know. Mary Katherine said, "It was the pageant, wasn't it? It just wore you out."

"Everyone is so sympathetic. John has been terribly sympathetic. People always are as long as they believe you. John would never nurse a hypochondriac the way you do your mother-in-law."

"'Oh, Emzie's sick enough. Her legs swell up—"

"Ha. She'll outlive the rest of us." Vera had always enjoyed hating Emzie for Mary Katherine. "She's nothing but a big tub of—guts."

Mary Katherine giggled.

"She's a big tub of guts that everyone has to drive around and play cards with. The only constructive thing she ever did was to have Earl, and as soon as she had him she started making him run errands for her. Poor Everett is just a dried up old drone. Once the wedding flight was over, the Queen Bee dropped him." She let it go, feeling something wasn't quite right. Mary Katherine didn't approve of calling Everett a drone after all his years in the mines. "Emzie and Thelma Shinn, the whole bunch of them, all they have ever done is sneak around this parsonage looking for dirty underwear under the beds."

Mary Katherine started washing out her coffee cup. "Well, yes, but they think they're doing right."

"Doing right shouldn't give you so much pleasure snooping and gossiping. Besides, everyone thinks they do right. Except me. I don't know why, but I always know I'm doing wrong."

Mary Katherine gave her a look, but ignored what she'd said. She did that a lot.

"I mean it," said Vera. "I always do wrong. But you used to hate better, Mary Katherine. You've mellowed in your old age."

"I'm going to make you a meat loaf and it'll be in the refrigerator ready for you to put in the oven."

"No! No thanks! I refuse to let you, I'm not sick. You aren't listening to me. I made this whole sickness up. Oh, on second thought go ahead and make the meat loaf. At least that way you'll stay awhile." She watched Mary Katherine assemble her ingredients. Efficient, her and John both. I'm one of her duties now, thought Vera. Excuse me—got to run—it's time for Vera's feeding. Just like the poor old Preacher. She said, "Did John tell you where he was off to this morning? It's supposed to be a secret so you have to pretend you don't know, but he thinks he may be getting a call from Parkersburg."

Mary Katherine's back was to her, kneading meat and crumbs with egg. She leaned on her arms and held still and Vera followed the effect with interest.

"You and Earl and Johnny and Jimmy should move with us. You would get away from Emzie, we'd all live in a great big farmhouse together with dozens of rooms and animals. I've always wanted to have my own cow."

The trouble was that she had stopped Mary Katherine from talking altogether.

"Are you upset? John should have told you what he was thinking. It reminds me of all the times they used to move when I was little and they wouldn't tell me we were moving until they picked me up at school. They did it because I threw such fits. Once when we were living in Johnstown, Pennsylvania, I got sick and came home early from school and got there just after they had driven off to pick me up and there was not a stick of furniture left in the house. I sat down on the porch and didn't even cry because I thought it was all over, I thought they had moved without telling me where. I just sat there thinking I was going to fade out, disappear—"

Mary Katherine turned around finally. "That's just awful," she said. "That is so sad—"

"I always vowed if I had children, I'd never make them move. I'd never put them through what my mother and stepfather put me through."

"I thought you lived with your aunt and uncle."

Something chilled Vera, a vast flock of blackbirds passing between her and the light. Mary Katherine receding again. "I used to live with my aunt sometimes until my mother got married again. My aunt was an old maid."

"But right before you met John?"

"That was my mother and stepfather. I divorced them, that's what I always say."

"Your mother's alive?"

She could not remember what she had told Mary Katherine. She hated it when she forgot some crazy thing she did long ago in a panic. "Oh sure. She lives out in Ohio somewhere. We send cards back and forth, that's about all."

"You told me once she killed herself."

"Oh Lord. Did I say that?"

"The first night I met you."

"I don't know why I said that—I was just making it up as I went along."

"You said she was in an institution and killed herself."

"She's alive in her nasty way out in Akron, Ohio. I never could get along with any of her family. She was never meant to be a mother. Listen, Mary Katherine, maybe now you'll believe me. I do wrong things. I lie. I might as well tell you what I did on Monday. I'm not sick now and I wasn't sick on Monday when all this started. Thelma Shinn came over so we could plan the devotions for the Mission Circle. The house was a mess of course, after Easter and the pageant. Thelma came and knocked and I hid myself behind the door and listened to her breathe and laughed until she went away. Don't say anything— I know it was crazy. John thinks I was asleep when she came. He's the one who called her and told her I had come down with the flu. Thelma isn't mad. People in this town will do anything for you if they think your body is sick—I got flowers and meals, everything. But they could never understand how I could be nauseated at the thought of Thelma sniffing around my kitchen again."

"You were run-down—"

"I was nauseated." She was a little nauseated now. She had lost Mary Katherine's face and was very tired of trying to explain everything. She thought that one day she would stop talking the way the old Preacher had. They thought they were rid of him, but I'm just as bad. Just as mean and rotten.

"Why," said Mary Katherine's familiar voice, a stout rope in darkness, "why don't you visit your mother?"

Glad to be given a question, glad Mary Katherine was still speaking to her, she said, "Because I'm a strange and hateful person, don't you know that yet, Mary Katherine?"

John was enthusiastic about the Parkersburg church. He had never liked modern architecture, he said, he had always gravitated toward the traditional, but this one's style combined the purity of New England Congregational lines with the warmth of fieldstone and even a touch of splendor in the seven-foot bronze cross suspended in back of the pulpit.

He was still talking about it at lunch on Monday as she spread mustard on his roast beef sandwich, poured his coffee. It became very

46

vivid to her as he described it over and over from various points of view. A pick-up-stick jumble of heavy exposed beams and that bronze cross pulling down the whole pile. She walked him out onto the porch as he was about to leave for the hospital visits. "The congregation is young," he said. "They're open to things—for example, they have a college boy on their search committee. I wish you had come."

She watched him down Church Street. Just in front of the church he met Emzie Wright with a bouquet of jonquils, coming to decorate for the Mission Circle meeting. Vera dodged behind a porch pillar and the screen of newly flowered forsythia, thinking, I wonder if I can say I'm still too sick for the Mission Circle. John gave Emzie his special half-humorous bow that he saved for large matrons of the church. Emzie loved to tell how she had put her imprint on his character when he used to board with her as an adolescent. In spite of the familiarity, though, she had a deference for office and treated him with respect. Emzie was trying to talk, aiming a finger skyward to make a point, but John eased by her skillfully, quick and cheerful. Emzie took the church steps one at a time, resting often, helping to pull herself up by the railings.

When the entertainment of Emzie Wright going up steps was over, Vera plucked a forsythia blossom with her lips and ate it. She was going to have to put their lives in boxes, the horse books and the collection of dress-up clothes and costumes they kept in a suitcase under the bed. Tonie's doll babies. All the dishes and pots and pans. She had no idea how she would ever fit all the pots and pans into boxes. Vaguely she was angry with Mary Katherine for not coming with them. When she came from Pennsylvania, Mary Katherine had been here to make all the decisions, telling her what to put where. Everything had been easier then because Mary Katherine knew how to do everything. Lee had been almost more Mary Katherine's baby than Vera's. The good old days. She had a vision of packing boxes lining a deserted dusty road as far as the eye could see.

After a while a car came down Church Street and parked opposite the church. Three people in suits got out, a woman in royal blue between a young man and an old one. Shoulder to shoulder they went directly to the main door of the church, read the little sign saying "Office" and followed its arrow around to the educational building along the passage between the church and the parsonage. Vera stayed behind the forsythia and watched them. The woman had red hair and a full but neat figure, not too different from Mary Katherine's. The older man was silvery and heavy with a deep fruity voice that carried from far down the passageway. The young man was thin and nervous, like a door-to-door Bible salesman. Just as they went into the educational building, they pointed at the parsonage.

It was the delegation from the Parkersburg church, of course. They would look for John first, politely, and they would check on the facility he had built for the Galatia church. But they were here to view the wife. There was no doubt in her mind. They had come to look at her. She had only minutes before they would knock, but she knew exactly what to do. She plugged in the electric coffeepot and dumped fresh coffee on top of the old grounds and new water in with the cold coffee. There was still a cake that Mary Katherine had made. The kitchen a mess, of course, with dirty laundry piled by the cellar door and clean shirts in their blue plastic basket waiting for her to iron them. Always more shirts. Don't let the woman say, Oh I'll help. Keep her out of the kitchen. She ran for the living room, gathered newspapers, gathered the girls' Sears Roebuck cutouts, ran everything into the den and closed the door. She could already hear the fruity voice coming back along the path. Just in time she remembered the little bathroom under the stair and whisked her stockings out of it, wiped the hairs out of the sink with a tissue.

In the mirror she caught sight of the safety pin holding her housedress together over her bosom. They were on the porch, but she could cover the old dress with an apron if she wanted to. They knocked, and their knot of voices fell silent as they waited. Deliberately she repinned her dress from the inside so that only a little of the metal would glint out at them.

She opened to them, expressing complete surprise, taking a deep breath of the woman's rosy powder. They introduced themselves, and their names fell in her ears like the wheat sown on hard ground; she remembered nothing. They complimented the church, the educational wing, her living room. She said, "And my husband tells me such wonderful things about your church. He says the architectural style isn't at all cold." She said she would just put the coffee on. She indicated the little downstairs bathroom. And surely they would stay to dinner?

"No, no, we're just passing through," said the young man, who looked awkward and on the run.

"Just passing through," said Vera, smiling at them all. "Oh yes. And you thought you'd stop in."

The woman said, "We were so sorry you couldn't make it this weekend." She hadn't taken off her white cotton gloves and she was wearing a ring too, a large pale topaz stone over the gloves.

Vera thought, Even I know better than to wear a big flashy ring in the middle of the day over my gloves. She wanted to give the stone a

48

quick rap with her fingernail, just to indicate that she noticed. And I see your dyed hair too. She wondered if this were a test of some kind.

"And will your little daughters be home from school soon?" asked the rich, thick man's voice.

"Oh my darling girls!" said Vera. Cleverly, subtly, answering the woman's overdressing and dyed hair with a theatrical toss of her head. "They'll come tumbling in at any moment. They're wonderful girls, but of course it's hard being a minister's child, the uncertainty, the continual uprootings. You never feel that you really belong in a place." As she spoke, she smiled and nodded, encouraging him to nod along with her. He sings in the choir, she thought when she had him really bobbing away.

But the red and blue woman wasn't so easy. "We understood that Reverend Scarlin had been in Galatia for nine years."

Vera saw the situation at once. The woman was the one who mattered, the intelligent challenge. "I was a minister's daughter myself," said Vera. Sympathy from the silver man. The young boy attempting to appear alert when she looked at him. "Not from around here—in California."

They don't deserve my antique cups and saucers, she thought, but she got on the kitchen stool to get them out of the highest cabinet anyway. Even the coffee server with fluting and roses. She took a pride in knowing what she was supposed to do. She broke off a bit of icing from one of their slices of cake, sucked her finger, and broke a bit off each of the other slices. I hope they catch something from me.

Of course it wasn't nice to fall upon her unsuspecting like this, but it was the accepted rule of the game. Everyone had a license to examine the preacher's wife. Wasn't she used to it, and used to Thelma Shinn and Emzie Wright having coffee together and clucking over her housekeeping and poor John having to live like that? Still, there was recourse with them. Gossiping was a foible too, and everyone agreed that Emzie and Thelma were house proud. People said, Oh, you know Emzie and Thelma, in their houses you can't put your bottom on a chair without brushing yourself off first.

With this committee, she felt how they had all the power over her, and she had none over them. They could grin stupidly and wear rings on the outside of their gloves. She could only make mistakes. Costly for John. Nowhere to go but down. Everything riding for John on this imperfect minister's wife. She saw John at the hospital doing card tricks for the little Rogers girl with the broken leg, and all the time he was thinking blissfully of his new church in Parkersburg, and at the same time, at this very moment, he was in danger and entirely ignorant of it.

The young man was looking at the bookshelf. Here—get away from my dust! "Sit down," she told him, nudging at him with the tray. "Won't you have some coffee? Won't you have some cake?"

You sit down too, they say, complimenting Vera on Mary Katherine's cake. They begin to sip and swallow, giving her the floor. They want me to explain myself, she thought. They have given me the rope. What did they want to hear? "The girls will be here soon," she said, yearning for the relative ease of that moment. Tonie would say something cute. Lee would say something intelligent. Everyone would chuckle together. She felt like describing the loveliness of her girls, how they had a picture poster of all the presidents and Lee had memorized the names and Tonie kissed all thirty-four of them good night, giving Abraham Lincoln two pecks. But the girls would be here to save her at any moment, and she didn't want to raise the committee's expectations too high. She said, "Being a parent is so much more difficult than people think. It's like being in a dream where you're on a stage performing and you have no idea what your lines are, or what cue will be thrown at you."

The young man took his glasses off and wiped them. Vera thought: Am I beginning to do something strange and he doesn't want to see it?

"The thing I'm best at is directing plays. I do all of the children's pageants. We just finished crucifying Tonie, that's our youngest, for Easter."

The young man dropped his glasses in his pocket. The silver-haired man took another slice of cake and chewed quietly, staring placidly into space. Only the woman was watching closely, watching everything. I like you, thought Vera, but this really isn't fair.

"It was too much, you know, to ask a little girl to play Jesus. She did her best, but it wasn't right to tie her up on that cross. But you would want to hear my faults too, wouldn't you?"

The woman said, "Up on a cross?"

"Well, not with nails of course. It was just a big wood and cardboard one my brother-in-law made."

The older man came to life. "The Protestant cross is not a crucifix. Our cross is empty to signify the resurrection."

She felt slapped, but didn't give up at once. "Oh of course, I know that of course—"

The woman said, "It was a pageant of the Easter story?"

"Yes, yes, and after all, they did nail him up there, didn't they? Protestants or no Protestants!" The woman had offered that hair's breadth of support, but Vera thought, That's nothing, there is no hope. She set down her coffee cup. "I suppose you all noticed the safety pin

holding my dress together. I didn't have any warning you were coming."
They made noises, a little distant chirping. "Just help yourselves to more
cake and coffee and I'll go put on something more presentable. Clothes
make the minister's wife, I always say."

She went up the stairs running, directly to the girls' room, and pulled
out from under Lee's bed the cardboard suitcase full of discarded
dress-up clothes. Her mouth began to grin, to peel back over her teeth.
She ransacked the suitcase, scattered clothes behind her like a dog
digging a hole. The open-toed red heels she had been married in, a pink
nylon hostess gown, a gift she never wore because the neck was cut so
low. She plumped her breasts half out of her bra and slipped into the
pink wrapper. In the bottom of the suitcase a lipstick was rattling, also
some lemon gloves, and then she saw an enormous green plastic ring,
a Cracker Jack prize.

They all three leaped to their feet as she came flowing down the
stairs. "Sit, sit," she said. "I just thought I'd slip into something more
comfortable." A warmth rising from her body, causing some invisible
odor to waft out and turn the men's faces red. They stayed on their
feet, but she sat, crossing her leg to show off the red shoes. "Well, back
in the hot seat. These are my wedding shoes. John questioned the
propriety of open toes, and the color of course. John has always had a
good sense of what would offend people like yourselves."

The woman was looking at her green plastic ring. She understood
the meaning perfectly. Oh dear, thought Vera. We would have been
friends, this woman might have taught me all sorts of things. Something
terrible occurred to her, that the gloves might be because of a disfiguring
rash, a skin disease. She didn't think she could bear the thought.
Somehow she had expected them to disappear when she came down
like this. Not to remain, so full and fleshly. She felt the defiant lipstick
grin fading from her mouth, her ordinary appealing smile attempting a
comeback.

"Why are you doing this?" said the woman.

Vera said, "Don't ask me that. Ask me a question I can answer."

The woman turned to her companions, but they stared past her as
well as past Vera, as if there were some contamination by gender.
Quietly, even privately to Vera, the woman said, "Listen, whatever
you're doing, you're making a mistake."

Oh yes, thought Vera, you're so right. I knew you would understand.

The silver-voiced man suddenly cleared his throat and seemed to
pump himself into life. "Yes, I believe there has been some mistake,
and I think we had better leave before there are any more." He turned
to the door, but his move was spoiled by the entrance of Lee and Tonie.

They hadn't made any noise on the porch, and they stood there now, two dark blond faces, Lee's higher than Tonie's, looking more alike than they ever had. She had the feeling that reflections or replicas of them were stationed all around the room, watching her.

The man made a wide detour around them, and the young man followed. The woman paused to say, "They are lovely girls."

Lee turned to Vera. "It isn't for a play?"

Wait, thought Vera to the woman's royal blue back. Did you hear what Lee said? What do I say to her now?

Lee made a soft howl and dropped her books and stomped upstairs.

"Tonie," said Vera, "You stand by me—" she kicked off her high heels and clutched Tonie's hand, dragged her out on the street with her. "I have to explain something to those people."

She caught up with them just as they were getting into their car, and at that same moment Emzie Wright came out of the church. Emzie planted her vast legs and gaped. She shouted loud enough to notify any neighbors at home, "Vera Scarlin, what are you doing in your nightgown?"

"Madam," said the silver-haired man to Emzie, "if you are a member of this church, I think you would do well to inform your pastor that his wife is a secret drinker."

Vera pressed close to the blue suit and rosy powder smell. She wanted to hold hands with the woman and Tonie. Without gloves, catch the skin disease. "Let me explain." And the woman actually waited with her door open, willing to listen, and Vera was so frightened now that she had the chance that she could only say, "The child—it's the little girl—"

They started the car and the woman had to close her door, but she rolled down her window to say, "What do you have against our church? You never even saw it."

"Stop squeezing my hand!" said Tonie. Tonie was trying to get away, the car was pulling away.

"I hardly got started here!" she shouted after the car.

Emzie Wright said, "Well I never thought I'd see the day. Who were those people?"

"Oh leave me alone," said Vera, sitting down on the church steps and hugging her stomach. She wondered if John would divorce her.

Lee appeared on the porch carrying a suitcase, and for an instant Vera thought she was running away, but it was the dress-up suitcase, and she shook it until the clasp sprang and clothes spilled down the steps. An old lace slip settled on a bush. Lee kicked the dresses and threw the red shoes into the forsythia. "Take your old clothes! I don't want to wear your old clothes! Stay out of my room!"

Emzie Wright stepped onto the square of lawn between the church and the parsonage. "Young lady, don't you speak to your mother in that tone of voice. You pick up those things before someone gives you what's coming to your backside!"

Up and down Church Street people had come out on their porches. They stood half-hidden behind their elm and maple trees, as quiet and discreet as ghosts. Vera took Tonie to help Lee pick up the clothes.

When John told her he had put money down for the house on High Street, she was deeply relieved. It meant that he had begun the punishment. At first his pain had been so great that he had been cauterized of the desire for retribution. That had been the worst part. Now he was becoming petty and vindictive. He bought the house on High Street without telling her.

She said, "People are going to wonder about you buying a house. They'll say you think you own the church and you're planning to stay forever."

"I do intend to stay. I have no choice. I am fighting for my professional life, and my only option is to stay in Galatia."

He was naked. He had just had his bath and was drying and powdering himself, and she was still in bed. It was the only time when they were alone that he would speak to her. There were certain plans that could only be arranged directly, so he spoke to her in the morning, while he was dressing. "It's the last house on High Street, next to the field. No one will bother you there when you decide to play dress-up." He lifted a leg to the bed and buffed his thigh with his towel. The hair dried short and curly.

Wanting the worst at once and finally, she said, "You should have consulted me before you bought a house."

He froze; he was delighted; he leaned over his leg. "I should have consulted you? After what you did to me without consulting anyone?"

"Yes. By rights. You certainly would have if you hadn't been so mad."

He smiled. "You forfeited your rights when you forgot how to act like a rational human being."

"Something came over me."

"Something came out of you."

She started talking rapidly. "I had a dream last night that I was on this long sunny dirt road and there was a terrible danger just over the hill and in my dream I couldn't separate myself from you, I couldn't tell if I was an I or a We. When I woke up, we were still in this fight, and it seemed so awful. You know what I did really had nothing to do with you, John. It had to do with how I always go a little crazy when I have to move. I've told you about that."

"The one thing I do believe is that nothing you do has anything to do with me. I do believe you never consider me for an instant when you do something, so now you can see how it feels." He had his pants on, his shirt and jacket in hand, starting for the door as if he couldn't bear to be in the room with her any longer. Some noisy part of her, just under the surface, said, Good, leave me alone. I'll go back to sleep and dream I'm safe.

He said, "I believe that I am nothing to you but something to guard the door and warm the bed. You'd do as well with a German Shepherd."

When he was gone, she smiled, imagining a windswept hill, a large dog. She could hear the girls moving around. Living up there near the fields they would get a dog, she decided. She hadn't seen the house yet, but she looked forward to it. It was the beginning of a good change. His buying the house was a good sign, an act of equalizing, to wrong her and bring them closer together. She thought she would iron all the shirts this morning and make a cake. Not that he could be bribed, but it would begin to accumulate over days and days. Enough white shirts, enough vacuumings of the den, enough chocolate cakes with boiled icing.

Chapter 3
John

He is in the pulpit, just smoothing open the great Bible. He glances out at his audience and has an odd sensation that they are too far away, that there are too many empty pews, that the dimensions of the room have increased. He is not sure he can see anyone out there at all, and he wonders if he might have come on the wrong day. He turns the pages of the Bible, pretending to look for his place, and from the corners of his eyes sees a bright mist veiling the room. He wants to, but doesn't dare, walk along the aisles to find his congregation, but that would be the style of a country Bible thumper. He wonders if he is going blind, and is so frightened that he begins to speak without making eye contact. He welcomes any strangers, says what a fine day the Lord hath made, even though he can't tell anything about the weather through this mist. He clears his throat. Something in the mist is keeping his voice from projecting; his words hardly reach the first empty row. Perhaps they will think it is their hearing instead of his speaking; he hopes they won't whisper. Worrying about his voice, he goes on too long with the warm-up. Weather is a little surprise from God every morning, he says. We never know what the weather will be, unless we listen to the radio, but sometimes even the weatherman is wrong.

He thinks he senses a tiny yawn out there somewhere, although up to now the audience, if there is one, has been very patient.

He must begin the sermon, he sees at once, if he is to hold their attention, and he reaches in his coat for his note cards. They are not in the breast pocket. Not the side pockets, not in the trousers. He tries to remember where he put them, in another jacket, on his desk? But this morning is as lost in the haze as the walls of the sanctuary. He will have to extemporize. But the sermon topic has evaporated too.

He thinks he hears the yawn echoing in the back of the room. He strains to recapture the kernel of what he wanted to say. Make no mistake, it was a strong message, something to get under their skins and keep them awake.

The yawn seems too loud; his voice can't reach them, but the yawn is coming to him as if it were amplified.

He says: Today's message is about the thing that lets us rise above boredom. Love is the subject of my sermon. He thinks: But didn't I just preach on love last week? He listens for an impatient shuffle, for a groan, but they are quiet. Cagily he says: My friends, Love is the one topic worth a sermon every week of the year. We all need love. We eat it up, gulp it down without chewing.

Now he can't think of much else to say about love. Sin would have been a better topic, you can always get your teeth into sin, but sometimes with love it seems like it is eating you up. Love is everywhere, he says; you can't grasp it in your hands, but you have to live on it.

He is sure now that the yawning has increased in volume. It lasts an inordinate amount of time, as if the mouth took a long while to stretch open. He is afraid of the yawn, and he is afraid he is going to yawn too. But on the other hand, he says, Love is like a mist in your nose, you can't get away from it. Love surrounds you and never ends. Something he says seems to enhance the Yawn, and the whole room vibrates as if they were all inside It.

He keeps on talking, though, even inside the Yawn: You have to watch out for Love, it's odorless, colorless, and tasteless, and it's all around. God is Love and He's all around too. God's yawn is a vast echo chamber. No walls, no ceiling, no floor. A bright mist in hollowness. He is very tired of talking, bored of his endless sermon with no one to listen but God, and God is bored too.

What he is betting on is that God will be too polite to close His mouth as long as the sermon lasts, so he preaches on and on.

Thirty-nine High Street was the first property John Scarlin had ever owned. He took a restless pleasure in the fact that it was the last house within the city limits of Galatia, and it had a view of the whole valley and town. It was a bargain too; the previous owner had been consigned to a nursing home and the next of kin wanted to settle fast. He was a little uneasy that he might have been hasty. One day he and his wife and children were nestled up to the side of the church, and the next they were isolated up here with a woods and a cow pasture on two sides.

He had bought the house as a commitment to Galatia. The crisis was his awakening, a bright sign that he was overambitious and his work at Galatia was not finished. People were sure to misinterpret, to see it as an act of pride rather than humility, but being misunderstood would be part of the humiliation. What he had to learn was how to continue with all the old relationships, the people he thought he had known for too long. He had to keep slogging among former mistakes and bad starts.

The house was old and drafty without having any quaintness to speak of. Four big rooms below, six small ones opening off a hall upstairs, dark walnut baseboards and door frames. Lingering stains and whiffs of the old person sent to the nursing home.

We'll have to trace that leak, he thought, lying in bed, watching an irregular stain roughly the shape of his own body. It's an old slow leak. It's been coming down for years. It frightened him that something could go on for years and never be fixed. Sometimes he tried to say that casual thing aloud to Vera, We'll have to fix that leak in the roof, to start them acting together again, but he couldn't squeeze it out from between his teeth.

People were right of course that he bought the house because of Vera. She was the immediate cause of everything—of his humiliation. She was the instrument by which he knew he had to stay in Galatia. The people of the congregation sidled up to him with knitted brows and concern welling from their eyes. Are you all settled now? Do the girls like having their own rooms? And (diving in at the meat) how is Vera? It was generally rumored either that she was drinking or that she had had a nervous breakdown. Oh, he would say, Vera likes the house very well. She has all kinds of plans for fixing it up. Ah, the person would say—Thelma Shinn for example, tottering towards a fall from her four-inch spike heels, pretending to balance on his upper arm but really pulling his face down towards hers—It gives her something to do. You keep her busy, John, keep her mind occupied. John accepted the advice gravely, but he preferred Emzie Wright's bluntness: "You better keep her in hand, Preacher."

"I'll take care of my own affairs, Emzie."

"See that you do," said Emzie, matching eyeball to eyeball, "or we'll all be in a fix." She took it personally, as she was an in-law through her son's marriage to John's sister, and John shared her appreciation for the threat to the family. So far his congregation had been almost purely sympathetic, swollen with sympathy, in fact. But you never knew. Poor young Reverend Scarlin, they said, his wife is quite a cross to bear. Nothing vicious, but when he preached on Sunday morning he sensed a bottomless curiosity and willingness to be entertained by his troubles. He would bear it as part of his humiliation. He would choose his sermon topics with great care. There were fewer calls for personal counseling than usual.

The odd thing was that Vera seemed to enjoy the new house at least as much as John told people she did. She set her sewing machine up in the unfurnished living room and turned out sailcloth cafe curtains and pillow shams and little drawstring sundresses for the girls. She made picnic snacks and took Tonie and the puppy up on the hill every afternoon. John winced at the irony, the hypocrisy, of Vera being gay and normal in the midst of all this drugstore gossip about her nervous breakdown or was it alcoholism?

He sat with *Newsweek* in his lap in his corner of the den. The rest of the room was still piled with boxes of books and winter clothes and toys. Everything waiting for Vera to finish her decorating spree and get the shelves and closets filled. She was hemming something now, sitting on the floor in front of the fireplace rolling the puppy's tight pink tummy back and forth between her bare feet. The puppy snarled at her toes.

"You're going to turn that dog mean," he said.

"Oh he likes it." Vera rolled him once more, then shoved him away. The puppy skidded into the mantel of the fireplace and then scrabbled back to bite her hard on the big toe.

"You see? I don't know why you want to go around barefoot anyway. Tonie came down this morning with no shoes. There are pins and nails all over." Vera quieted the puppy and held it on her lap, stroking it and letting it chew her thumb.

He tried to finish off his complaining. "I just don't want Tonie picking it up from you."

She kissed the puppy's ears. "I go barefoot because I like to look like some hillbilly from up on Hawksnest."

"That's not much of a joke."

"I like to feel with my feet. I never used to do it, down at the parsonage. Down there any moment Emzie or Thelma or Mrs. Bodkin was likely to pop out of the laundry basket."

She let the puppy go and leaned back, braced on her arms, legs stretched out like a bathing beauty. A safety pin held the house-dress together over her breasts, and they were spread and flattened by the tight bodice. Each breast individually defied him. Her bare feet were too small for a grown woman. "I don't want the girls getting tetanus."

"Or hookworms like a hawksnester. We don't have to worry about Lee, anyhow. Whatever I do, she does the opposite."

A childish voice in him wanted to say, And you do the opposite against me. To hold that voice in line and to keep her breasts from filling the room, he made up a lash of meanness; she had been grinning and teasing him too much. "It's true, you have been letting yourself go a little lately."

She covered the safety pin with her hand.

"It isn't the safety pin I mean."

"I'm making curtains. I haven't had my bath yet."

"You make the curtains but you don't put away the dishes. You play with Tonie but you don't unpack her dolls—"

"She has her favorite!"

"Lee goes to scouts or sleeps at her friend's house or goes anywhere to get away from you—"

Vera started to cry. Her eyes filled up gently. Be nice to me, oh be nice to me for pity sake! Sometimes she actually said it aloud. He thought she was saying it now, but he was hearing things. Waters rose in him too, scalding floodwaters to drown her whimpering. When his jaw began to twitch, he got out fast, ran for the porch to catch his breath.

Even when he was a boy he had run out-of-doors. It was the Preacher then who tried to overwhelm him then. John was a person who had to have space; he could never have lived with tall buildings where you couldn't get a good look at the sky. He liked the perspective from up here on the hill. It was an unseasonably chilly day with many low fast rain clouds, and all the colors were gray. Galatia tumbled down the hillside and one red roof halfway down stood out. There was a good sermon opener in that, if he could just get his lips and jaw to stop moving nervously against his will. He found a toothpick in his pocket and began grinding the sweet wood flat between his molars, nearly swallowing it, then thrusting it forward again. That spot of color you would never notice on a sunny day.

Mary Katherine tried to explain everything by saying that Vera had a problem. No, said John, I have the problem and its name is Vera. She's the one who stopped me from getting the church. A psychological problem, said Mary Katherine; Vera had an unhappy childhood. I know all about Vera, said John. Mary Katherine said, She needs understanding. No, thought John, she needs to get ahold of herself. Just like we all have to get ahold of ourselves. She needs to stop acting like she never grew up. What did Mary Katherine know about psychology? He had had courses in counseling; she read *Ladies Home Journal*. If it came to difficult childhoods, he and Mary Katherine could top anyone hands down. Mary Katherine was just looking for a way to excuse Vera. Everyone always wanted to excuse Vera because of her big eyes and because she made them laugh, and herself laughed and cried so easily. Everything easy and instant and emotional with Vera. If you don't want to move to Parkersburg, you don't discuss it rationally, you explode and strike out and destroy all chance completely and utterly. She no more thought of consequences than a baby throwing a tantrum. There was no outwitting her, no way of finding out in advance what she might do next.

His fury came back now. He couldn't get Vera in perspective. He saw against the clouds his own fist shoot out in a long trajectory that landed with satisfying impact in her mountain-sized breast. Drew the fist back and sent it out again like a long-distance cannon. He saw her face fall apart and then reconstitute itself just in time to be smashed again.

His shoulders ached as if he had been really punching, but he finally got control and quashed the image on the far hillside, just in time too, because the door opened behind him. He saw out of the corner of his eye that she had put on pedal pushers and a striped jersey. She leaned her stomach on the porch railing. If the widow across the street happened to be peering from behind her pink nylon curtains, they would seem companionable, a couple taking a look at the weather.

He said, "I have to go down to the church. I can't work here."

"Do you want lunch first? I put on tomato soup and I have cheese sandwiches ready to grill. I already started one for Tonie."

"What about Lee?"

"She called. They're staying for lunch. It must be the longest slumber party in history."

"I'll skip lunch."

"I'll make you a sandwich to take with you. I'll put up some coffee in a thermos. Or the soup. How about the soup in the thermos?"

She had on anklets and saddle shoes. That was about as mature as she would ever get, he thought, she would always be a volatile teen-ager.

He said, "What do you want from me with all this attention?"

"I want things back to normal."

"That would make it easy for you."

"And for you. This is no fun for you either is it?"

She wasn't wrong, of course, but she underestimated how important it was. How he could not at will go back, how he had to wait for the right moment. For a sign.

She had turned her right hand palm up on the porch railing, and he found it bullying him for attention: the little pink roll of muscles that worked the thumb, the color of the fingertips. To make her go inside, he said, "I guess I'd take the coffee. A cheese sandwich would be okay too."

This pain, he thought, looking out over the gray expanse of daylight again, at all the shapes of houses, the bridges, the river, the bell tower of the church. He wondered what it was a preparation for. Even the terrible tension as they lay in the bed coldly side by side, the pain that shot out of his clenched jaws and down his spine. He was being tempered for some purpose. He had thought the church in Parkersburg was his object, but now he had to wait again and suffer.

The first time he knew he was being prepared for something was

60

after an argument with the Preacher when he was about ten years old. It was something about reading a book instead of toting coal for the stoves, and one of the stoves had gone out. The Preacher started yelling at him, and John quoted him chapter and verse of the Bible where Jesus says that study is the better part, chores the lesser. The Preacher had always let them talk, encouraged Bible quotation and dispute, but this time the Preacher turned John over his knee and beat him while Mary Katherine jumped up and down and howled and the Preacher yelled at her to shut up or she was going to get it too. John had been the only quiet one, although he felt tears run out of his eyes.

When he was released, he refused Mary Katherine's hug and took out of the store without a coat—and without going for the coal. It was November and stormy, and he had headed up over the hill through the woods to the nearest place with a view, the fifty-foot slag heap mountain, flat on top so the trucks could dump. People dumped garbage down the steep sides too. John stood on the rim and stared in fury up at the lowering clouds, piles and piles of them, and a nasty edge of wind cold enough to be bringing snow.

"I was right!" he had shouted. "I quoted the Book and the Preacher hit me!"

In answer to his shout, the impossibly thick clouds parted, and for just perhaps fifteen seconds, a shaft of absolutely golden sunlight came through and landed on John. The hills, the tipple, the dump truck thirty yards away, were all as leaden as before, but John was standing in a quadrangle of light.

"You see!" he shouted. "You see! I got a sign—I'll get you for it, Preacher!"

And then he received the second half of his sign, the terrifying part. He was moved—he was lifted—and flung over the edge of the slag heap, slapped against the side, bounced in a gully and rolled over and over in spite of his screaming at the sharp little black coal stones of pain every time he landed again on his arm. When he came to himself, the dump truck driver was coming to help him. Later he told them that John's first words were, "God struck me with lightning." He was proud now that he had understood so clearly when he was so young.

Sometimes he thought that was the high point of his life: the broken arm in a sling, the sidelong respect of the Preacher, and his own serene confidence.

The public stairs that cut down the hill from High Street passed backyards and vegetable gardens. Whole sections of galvanized pipe railing were missing, and the concrete of the steps had crumbled. No one used them much except the mailman and the paperboy. Sometimes John would almost stumble over some child's toy trucks lined up on a step. He liked the stairs, the rear view of Galatia. He walked for the exercise too, for fresh air, and the private time between duties. Every step away made it more possible to think of Vera. We'll get ahold of ourselves soon, he thought.

Living up on the hill helped him get the church in perspective too. Living next door to it he had begun to see only the cracks, the painted concrete in the new building where they had run out of funds for plastering, the peeling of the mountain stream mural in the baptistry. As he came up to his church, he did a mental exercise, pretended to be walking into it the way he had the morning of his first tryout sermon. After almost no sleep he had slipped out of Emzie Wright's house that day before anyone else was awake, walked over the bridge, down Pike Street, past the red brick Methodist church, and up to the Galatia First Baptist itself. It had been built after the First World War on the scale of a large private home, a mellow-colored church without a spire, a church of the golden mean.

He walked in the front door today although ordinarily he would have gone directly to his office. He tried to remember the light of that other morning, how spacious the high wide space had seemed, the pentagonal sanctuary with ten-foot-high stained-glass Jesuses on either side, identical except one had a blue robe, the other a green; the brass-tiered chandelier; the magenta carpet strips; the gilt organ pipes inset in blond wood arches. He liked to touch the carved wood, the communion table, the baptistry bar, the pulpit. The pulpit still fit him as irreproachably as his ten-year-old suit. The sanctuary lay open before him now, familiar as the palm of his own hand. He could touch every corner with his voice. He still loved this church house, equally when its life was all of light and glowing wood and when it was full of his congregation creaking and coughing and singing a half beat behind the choir.

"I'm very happy to be here today," he spoke aloud, feeling a sermon at hand. Something about moments of rededication, the diamond in your own backyard, and you thought it was lumps of coal. He could feel its shape and he knew before making a note or looking through the concordance for an appropriate scripture that this could be one of his best ones, one of the ones where his thoughts and people's needs and the truth all come together in one brilliant blossoming. Today is not a great religious holiday; today has nothing world-shaking in the news, but as I look around our beautiful sanctuary I have a feeling of possibility, of fresh starts. He said to his empty church, 'This is the Lord's day, a special day because the Lord hath made it for us to rejoice in."

From behind the choir box there was a shrill giggle. "Practicing? Practicing your sermon?"

He had to clutch the pulpit to keep himself from turning in anger. Just when his imagination had begun to work, just when he was on the verge of finding his way into a sermon. How dare they set off anger in him again? He turned slowly, as slowly as he could in the circumstances, to give himself as much time as possible to get a handle on this new anger. Woman, he thought, you don't know what I am saving you from. It was Rosemary Pickett, always called Roe, the choir director, also his daughter Lee's science teacher. He had known Roe all his life. She was a friend of Mary Katherine's. There was a mutual recognition among them, himself and Mary Katherine and Roe, how they had all raised themselves up from ugly beginnings.

He said, "I'm running late, I don't have a sermon for tomorrow." He expected her to wish him a good day and leave with her armload of music or whatever she was here for. She understood business.

But she didn't go, she hesitated and came down the several platform levels of the choir to join him on the stage. "I won't keep you," she said. "The last thing I want to do is bother you. I've had enough of being in the wrong place at the wrong time. Sometimes I think this whole town is the wrong place at the wrong time the way they talk about me." She was close enough now that when she opened her mouth he could see the rot on her incisors. Why would a woman who obviously spent money on clothes, who had her hair done in a beauty parlor, why wouldn't she go get her teeth repaired? She said, "I left my music down here. I'm getting to be a regular absentminded professor. I'd quit teaching before I became too absentminded, though. The kids would get too much pleasure out of it. I had to talk to you, John."

"Shall we go back to the office?"

Roe's eyes got big. "Oh no, not that kind of talking. What makes you think I need counseling?" She laughed a little shriek again, and he couldn't help himself from glancing around the church in embarrassment, to make sure no one was listening to her. You could whisper in here and in the back no one would miss a word. She said, "I've been elected county delegate to the National Education Association convention in Cleveland—"

"Congratulations."

"Oh it's nothing, they just couldn't find anyone else willing to pay their own way. But I'm going to have to miss another weekend on top of my summer vacation."

"Well, we'll work something out, Roe."

"I'll have the choir prepare a couple of anthems they can do without me. The congregation will be delighted no doubt not to —see my—face—" And her face twisted into more than ordinary homeliness, eyes popping in self-pity. "Probably—the choir too—"

His professional machine ground into action; he laid a hand on her shoulder and said, "Roe, I think it would be good if you came into the office with me. I think it would do you good to tell me what's on your mind. I believe it would relieve you."

Her giggle was surrounded by a bubble of sobbing and she withdrew from his hand, stumbled, dropped into the large carved chair behind the pulpit and wept. He glanced around the empty church again, then pulled one of the other heavy chairs close to hers. He felt his spiritual second wind coming on; now that she had begun, he didn't mind so much. It reminded him of what he could do well, of what did not frustrate him.

Roe said, "Don't think I'm crying over anything he does to me."

She lifted her head craftily. "You know who I'm talking about of course. The whole town knows. The whole town knows Roe Pickett is stuck on drunks. Well, you should know he wasn't always like that. They say you marry your own father, but that's the one thing you won't catch me doing, marrying Joe Bob. I haven't fallen that far yet."

The thing Roe had risen above was her parents, the drunken, brutal Picketts and all their crazy rickety children. Except for Roe, who worked, studied, put herself through college, did everything right except fix her teeth and stop seeing Joe Bob Farley.

"I'm having dreams," said Roe. "I'm sitting in the middle of town under the traffic light sucking on a bottle of wine and everyone is watching and laughing of course and little by little they get blurry, but what is awful is that I can't see clearly who's mocking me."

" Your dreams are your fears, you know that."

"I have a master's degree," she said. "And not in education either, it's in science."

"You could get a job in any state in the union with your credentials, Roe."

She sat up and blew her nose, looking terrible, so he concentrated on the rows of lace and buttons on the front of her dress. Her full bosom and small waist. "You think I should leave Galatia."

"I don't think you should, but I always wondered why you didn't, with the burden of the past, when you could have gone somewhere and started brand new."

"You left," she said. "But you came back. At first I was determined to show them all, I wanted to show something different named Pickett.

That never stopped them from talking about the Picketts, which would have been okay, but they talk about me and Joe Bob and that gives them a lot of laughs. I could still go, but I stay for him now too. I can't give him up; there's something wrong with me."

He wasn't paying his full attention to her words anymore, but to how she was quieting down, fumbling in her bag for her compact. He thought the main thing was over, she had done it herself. They always do it themselves, he thought. Or, I should say, God does it through them.

"You could try going out with other men."

"In this town? Please. Who would I date in this town? I would never talk down to some dumb farmer to make him feel big. Joe Bob may be the world's most worthless drunk next to my pop, but he attended college. He never finished his degree, but you can't take away even a little education from a person. That stays."

She did her nose now, powder, powder. It occurred to him that no one had ever done that up here behind the pulpit. In her own way Roe did as she pleased. He said, "No you can't take education away from a person."

"No one ever gave me anything and no one ever will." Snapped her compact shut.

"Would you like to say a prayer with me?"

She shook her head. It was just his minister machine going through its paces. She said, "I don't pray over Joe Bob Farley, not to get him and not to get rid of him. He's my own weakness." The words were in his throat, lying on his tongue even, What else do you need to pray for except your own weakness, but he just nodded and sniffed her powder. Vera never used any perfumes or makeup. Bad or good, Vera's odor and color were her own. He approved of Roe snapping the compact closed, insisting she hadn't come for help, refusing to go to the office. He watched her compose her face, purse her bitter lips. He supposed he should be moving her toward humility, but instead, in her, he admired the pride.

Chapter 4
Tonie

Their voices seemed to have been discussing her for hours. Sometimes they would take a detour and discuss her sister, but they always came back to her. She sat in the centermost circle of the rag rug beside Rastus Smith the dog and turned his ears inside out. He groaned and kicked his hind legs. Their voices had unrolled through lunch, then out of the kitchen into the den. Her father sat in his reclining chair with a newspaper on his lap. Her mother, barefoot, looked out the window at the side of the hill. It was Easter vacation, and Tonie had been up there with the dog all morning. She wanted to leap over her mother now and fade through the glass, take up the side of the hill again, only this time she and Rastus Smith wouldn't come down; they would hide out permanently. The wild girl and her dog.

"Every year," said her father. "Every Easter you do a play, no matter what I say."*

Her mother's toes were half-buried in the rug. "This is so simple, honey, no props, nothing."

"Nothing but Lee."

They were talking about the Easter play her mother had made up for Lee. Tonie went to rehearsals sometimes, on her father's hospital nights or when he had meetings. She wrapped herself in the velvet curtains around the baptistry or lay in the dry tin tub itself and listened to Lee practice saying over and over, "He lives! The one who forgave even me, Mary Magdalene! He lives!"

"John," said her mother, "you should see Lee. She is so good—"

"I suppose I should be thankful you aren't building towers and trap doors in the sanctuary this time."

"I never put a trap door in the sanctuary. You'd understand what I'm so excited about if you'd just come to a rehearsal once."

"How can I come to a rehearsal? I have to cook dinner for Tonie."

Tonie listened closely. Just so they stayed on Lee and the play. She didn't mind when her father cooked: they had nice quiet dinners, reading while they ate, *Life* magazine for him, comics for her, and for dessert, big bowlfuls of ice cream. He never started in on her when it was just the two of them having dinner together.

As if he were reading her mind, her father suddenly said, "And if the play wasn't enough, there's Tonie. Nothing is ever simple with Tonie."

She thought, It wouldn't be hard to live up on the hill with Rastus Smith except for learning to eat groundhog because that was the only thing he could ever catch.

Her mother said, "Tonie just tries to be honest." The bare feet came toward her and the dog: the soles were yellowish and there were veins across the tops. They rolled Rastus Smith's loose skin back and forth across his ribs. He grunted and looked mournful, then moved to the patch of sun under the window.

Tonie was left alone in the bull's-eye of the throw rug. She whispered, "You told me never tell lies."

Her father said to her mother, "Are you her coach? Whose side are you on?" He had a beautiful deep voice; you could hear every word he spoke.

"You said never lie."

"Stop repeating that!" His fingers flew up in the air. "What does that have to do with your getting baptized?"

"Oh, John, you understand very well what she means."

She wanted her mother to stay out of it. It made too many to watch. Her mother suddenly squatted and laid her hands on Tonie's shoulders, then her neck, and rubbed the skin on her cheeks and twisted her ears the way she did to Rastus.

"Don't, Mama, leave me alone."

"Oh dear," said her mother. "I can't keep up with them. Now Lee's my best friend and Tonie can't stand me to touch her. You used to be such a little nuzzler, Tonie."

Her father did not tease, and she didn't look at his face, but there were these huge spaces between his fingers as he gripped the chair. "She still has to explain to me why she doesn't want to get baptized."

Her words squirted out: "I do too want to get baptized."

"You see?" said her mother,

"I don't see anything."

"I want to get baptized but I don't want to promise!"

"She understands exactly. She doesn't want to promise to go and sin no more when she figures it's impossible. I think she's very sensitive."

He wasn't looking at her, she saw, but at her mother. And one finger, the forefinger on his right hand, began to tap. I'm making him nervous, she thought. She wished he would yell at her and get it over with. Get to the spanking even.

"Vera," he said, "I cannot deal with both of you at once."

"But she's right, John. She doesn't want to make a promise she knows she's going to break—it seems so reasonable."

"It is not reasonable. Eight other children are ready to promise. Including my sister's son. Why is no one else balking? Why is it only Tonie who refuses to recite the declaration of faith? And what about all the dozens of other children I have baptized over the years, including Lee? Why have none of them found the declaration of faith so pernicious?"

"I don't mean she's really right. Just that her motives are good."

Tonie did a thing with the insides of her ears; she made a pressure that blocked off some of the noise and unfocused her eyes. She made her father into a smear, made his gray suit stick to the green reclining chair, and she couldn't see his finger tapping anymore.

He leaped to his feet. "What's she doing? Stop jiggling, Tonie! I refuse to lose my temper over this nonsense."

Her mother tried to hug her, but Tonie ran out of the house after her father, chased him as far as the sidewalk in front.

She yelled, "I can explain!"

He stopped, he turned. "Tonie," he said, "we won't have this. We'll talk about it later when you and I both have calmed down."

A little later, the phone rang and her mother said, "It's for you, Tonie."

She approached it suspiciously, held it slightly away from her ear, but his voice still bored into her head. He said, "Tonie, I've had an appointment cancelled. I want you to come down to the office and we'll finish this discussion."

Her mother was in the kitchen polishing something. Tonie said, "I have to go down to the church."

"That's good, honey, you two will work it out better without me. Look at your baby spoon shine. I should be doing the dishes instead of shining baby spoons. I'm such a terrible fiddler and time waster."

Her mother was always changing odors, different foods, different detergents, silver polish. "Do I have to change clothes?"

"It's just your daddy, Tonie. I doubt he would recognize you in anything but overalls."

To Rastus Smith she said, "Stay. It's dangerous downtown." To her mother, "I'm going."

And her mother said, "Haven't you gone yet?"

Going down the hill she kept hoping to have to stop and talk to someone, but she didn't see a single person she knew and only one dog, who sniffed for Rastus on her hands and then trotted on his way. There were trees all along Church Street, with fat brown buds on every twig. There was the parsonage where they used to live and now no one lived. We never could have kept a dog as big as Rastus there, she thought, but just the same she didn't like the look of the spot of bare dirt where her swing set used to be.

She wasn't really afraid of her father; he spanked her sometimes, more often than he did Lee, but Lee was practically a teen-ager. She liked wandering around the church, too, but not when her father was there. Her father-in-the-church was the preacher and you had to be careful not to expect him to act like your father. Once some kids said, I wish I was the preacher's daughter, I'd play in the church all day long. And Tonie said, You'd get a whipping too.

She heard a rustling in his office. Once she had brought his lunch down and heard a grown-up sobbing inside; deep sobs, unstoppable, each one like a pit opening in the ground, and she was terrified of seeing who it was and so she hid. She did that now, passing his door on the dark side of the hall, slipping around the corner into the old part of the church. There was a back door to the office here, and a wardrobe full of old choir robes. She ducked into the little bathroom where they would all drip and dress the night of the baptism. Her father's rubber baptizing boots hung on a hook there, black and stiff as if a topless man were filling them. She stared at the boots until she heard her father call someone on the telephone, then she went in.

He waved at her. and she climbed into one of the upholstered chairs facing his desk. He kept his office very clean. At home they had piles of stuff everywhere: magazines and baskets of clean clothes and in her room her collection of horse statues and her dirty clothes.

He was talking to Miss Juliet Bodkin, the church organist, about music for a funeral. She liked the sound of grown-ups talking about practical matters to one another, and her father always spoke especially respectfully to people like Miss Juliet or Miss Pickett who worked at the church. Miss Juliet had shiny gray hair and she wore pale dresses with hand crocheted trimmings. But when Miss Juliet took the huge organ with four keyboards, all the daintiness fell away and she lunged from side to side, her dresses hidden under a black robe. She flung organ music all over the church, and at recessional just when everyone was standing up and stretching to leave, she would open the stops and play something joyous and so loud that people complained they couldn't hear to have a conversation. Once Tonie had wanted to take organ lessons but found out you had to take piano first, and piano seemed so tinkly compared to what she wanted.

"You took your time getting here, didn't you?" said her father. But he wasn't mad yet, only letting her know she wasn't getting away with anything.

She looked at her shoes and waited to be convinced. She knew he would win; she had known from the time he called that he would convince her and she would get baptized the same as her cousin Jimmy and all the others.

"I want to explain this to you, Tonie," he said. "Without any yelling or interference. I understand that you're afraid of breaking the promise." His hands lay one on top of the other, as relaxed as sleeping kittens. "Let me begin by telling you about the two kinds of Christians. There are those like Paul who are blinded by their great conversion experiences, and then there are those who grow up in the faith in Christian families, like yourself, like Lee and Johnny and Jimmy. For you, baptism is like saying to God, I'm not a little child anymore; I'm ready to take responsibility for my own actions."

In Church Membership Preparation Class he had said, It's like a young person committing a crime. When you're sixteen, the law won't hurt you, but at eighteen you can go to the Chair. He had said it softly, and suddenly they had all leaned forward to listen, and Tonie began to think about things that could commit her to Hell.

She said, "What if I promise to try not to sin?"

A shadow passed over his face. "It isn't something you can bargain over."

"But if I promise," she said, "and I know I'm not going to keep it, what if I die before I have time to get forgiven? Then I'll go to Hell won't I?"

"We're talking about your dedication to a Christian life. You're a healthy ten-year-old; you aren't going to die."

She saw the others, but especially her cousin Jimmy, in their white junior choir robes. Jimmy was rising up out of the water and floating toward heaven—one by one they were all floating out of the water, only when her turn came, something inexorable pulled her down into the deep. "What if I drown while I'm getting baptized?"

His hands flashed through the air and pounced on the edge of his desk. "You're doing your best to make me lose my temper, aren't you? How many have I drowned? How many baptismal candidates have not made it out of my baptistry alive?"

Something blinding was happening to her, as if her brows were lowering and blocking the light. He was not convincing her fast enough; she wanted him to stop fooling around.

"How many have I drowned?"

"None."

"How many have refused to make the promise?"

"I don't know."

"None. No one has ever refused to make the promise." He began to pace around the room, but she was stuck in her chair, following him with her eyes. A sullen ball in the pit of her stomach.

He took a deep breath. "Now listen: this is a happy occasion, a celebration. I designed this little promise for the families because they always like a little recitation, like one of your mother's Easter plays."

"It isn't a promise?"

He whirled and came at her, and his head seemed as far away as the top of a great pine tree. "Oh it's a promise, little girl. Don't try to get away with that. It's a promise and you are going to make it if you want to get baptized in my church." The top of the tree was swaying over her, and she was tightening and shrinking, ready to spring away if it should topple. He backed off a few steps. "It's an event for the rededication of families. Emzie Wright has planned a reception following the service. You have to see the whole picture."

"She's just doing it for Jimmy."

"Don't mumble at me."

"It's easy if you have a grandmother. It's easy for Jimmy."

"What are you talking about? You're not making any sense!"

"Jimmy is my cousin and he has a grandmother why don't I have a grandmother!"

"Take that imperious tone out of your voice before I slap it out."

But she was imagining a surge, a tidal wave of music controlled by a tall skinny grandmother like Miss Juliet Bodkin who would take hold of everything and carry Tonie forward through the promise in one rush of music and power and no fear and part the waters for her.

Tonie felt she could move again. "I want a grandmother," she said, getting up on her knees. "Promise me a grandmother and I'll promise for you!"

He whispered, "As I live and breathe Tonie Scarlin you'll never be baptized in this church unless you make that promise. And I'm going to wale the hide off of you if you don't."

She began to jiggle. "Give me a grandmother! Give me a grandmother!"

He lunged at her, and she rolled over the arm of the chair and leaped for the door.

"I promise!" she shouted. "I promise I promise I promise!"

She slammed the door between them and ran halfway down the hall where she waited for him to come and spank her. But the door never did open. He had never let her get away with so much before.

Tonie sat on her bed and played with her white nylon net dress. Lee had teased her and said it was a Catholic dress, but Tonie insisted on buying it because it seemed to fit with how good she had been all week. Tonight for instance, the night of the baptism, she didn't so much as look out the window at the hillside and be tempted to run away. Softly she sang "Up from the Grave He Arose" and made the dress march across the bed and be dipped down into imaginary baptismal waters.

Lee sauntered in and leaned against the doorjamb with her arms crossed over her chest. "Are you baptizing the dress?" But it wasn't a tease, just something to say. "Listen, Tonie, I hope this is okay to wear tonight." She had on a polished cotton shirt dress, dark blue with little red and yellow flowers all over it, a full skirt. "I'm asking you because it's your baptism and I could wear my Easter suit, but I'm supposed to help Mom and Aunt Mary Kay in the drip room."

There were only three years between them, but somehow Lee always seemed to use the years to better advantage than Tonie. She remembered when Lee was ten and she was seven that Lee had seemed just the same, with prettier clothes, knowing how to talk to people. "I like that dress," said Tonie. "It's got nice buttons."

"That's what makes a Better dress," said Lee, "details. But listen, Tonie, what I wanted to say, was about your dress. I really like it. I think it *was* supposed to be a Catholic confirmation dress, but so what? I always did think they were prettier than the colored dresses. Maybe I was just jealous that you went ahead and got one." She dropped her arms briskly and said she would set the table and Tonie should stay up here and take her turn tomorrow.

Tonie thought to herself, Lee is being nice to me. It was true and she was glad, but it seemed to complicate things too. One of the reasons she had been able to be so good this week was that she had had no one to fight with. Lee was wrapped up in her play and their mother was too. Their father had been down at church with one kind of Easter week service or another. It had not been a fair test. No homework to shirk. The only kids on High Street to play with were little ones who love to be ordered around. All week she had organized them into platoons and brigades and posses and commanded them to attack each other. She wished her mother would call up and order her to dust her collection of horse statues. "Right away, Mom!" she would yell. She had it all planned that she was going to get home as soon as she could after the service and say her prayers on her knees instead of in bed where she usually fell asleep before she finished. After she was baptized, she was always going to say her prayers on her knees.

She could smell dinner frying, and she was still hoping that her mother would shout up a job for her to do, so it made her jump when her mother suddenly stood in the door, just where Lee had been. Her mother half-dressed, wearing her good silk blouse, but no skirt, just an apron over the blouse and slip. She had on pink cheeks and lipstick, and smelled of onions.

"Do you want to dress before dinner, Tonie?"

She shrugged, then was sorry because her mother immediately started gathering up crinolines.

"Do you think one crinoline's enough since we have to take everything off before you go down in the water? Let's not forget your dry underwear and a handkerchief for your nose."

Something alarmed Tonie; she wanted to be left alone to be good. She said, "I read the Bible today."

"That's good, honey."

But her mother was looking at the dress and aiming it at Tonie. She put her arms up just in time to receive it. While her arms were still caught in the bodice, her mother rested her chin on Tonie's shoulder. "Listen, Tonie," she whispered. "I had an idea about the Promise."

"I told him I was going to do it. I already told him."

"This is my idea: when you all line up to say the promise, you face the congregation and Daddy is still in the pulpit, so he's behind you. He doesn't see your faces. All you have to do, Tonie, is breathe in when the part comes to say 'I promise,' just swallow those two words. You can say the whole thing with the others except for those two words."

Tonie tried to get away. Her mother wouldn't let her go, but kept on buttoning and tying. "It isn't cheating, you see. He's doing what he thinks is right and you're doing what you think is right. That's fair enough, isn't it?"

"You aren't supposed to fool the Preacher."

"He's your father too, and he should have a little more consideration."

"I'm going to be good."

"I know you are. You already are good."

But she didn't believe her mother, and like a terrible miracle all the stored-up goodness of the week was slipping through her fingers, out the corners of her eyes, through her lips. To stop it from happening, she tried not to move.

Her mother began to back out. "Well, just think about it. It's up to you. Maybe it's a bad idea."

She listened to them downstairs for a while, Lee and their mother talking back and forth in the kitchen. She heard his voice once from the den, and when Lee shouted up that dinner was ready, she heard his footsteps heading for the kitchen, and she didn't think she would be able to look at him. She dropped onto her knees to pray, but as soon as they touched down she hopped back up. "I can't eat!" she shouted. "Do I have to eat?"

They didn't answer at first, then she heard him at the bottom of the stair, in his soft daddy voice. "Tonie, are you okay?"

"I'm okay, but I don't want to eat. I don't feel like eating."

"Well, all right. She doesn't want to eat, Vera. Why should she eat if she doesn't want to?" She heard her mother whispering something to him—whose side was she on?—and then he said, "Well, just give her some time to herself, that's all."

Moving carefully because of the crackling of her dress, she went down the stairs, quickly around the staircase and away from the kitchen entry. There was the sound of them eating, their calm voices. They were still talking about her. Her father saying it was such a big day for her. She meant to go to the den and get Rastus, but someone's chair squeaked at the table, and she ran for the front door and outside into the twilight and gathering clouds. Almost at once she began to cool off and then to chill and she realized that her sweat wouldn't last through a cold night up on the hill, especially in this thin dress. She thought of slipping back inside and going to dinner, but the goodness had gone and her badness was not satisfied.

She headed down the public stairs, then trotted through the back alleys, ducking behind fences when she thought she heard voices. Chafing at her arms, so exposed in the dress. All the way to the church, and then through the double doors and up to the sanctuary, down the main aisle, past the communion table to the baptistry with its carved wooden bar and the velvet curtains. There she wrapped herself up to get warm and looked down at the water, all ready for the service, black water and no tub bottom in sight. She dipped one finger in, and the warmth made her shiver. She lowered her whole hand in. Her father's church was perfectly still and perfectly ready. Only a few lights on; the stained-glass windows reflected light like brown and gold metal. Wrapped in magenta velvet she felt already baptized and a part of the church. A member saved and in good standing. She waited, increasingly peaceful and drowsy, for her father to come and find her. They must be looking for her by now. She imagined that her father and mother would come in together and without a word they would each take one of her hands and lift her into the water; they would all three go into the water together and duck their heads under and play.

She heard a clumping on the stairs; it would be the custodian and she didn't want anyone to find her until her parents came, so she slipped backstage quickly and up into the rarely used attic storeroom that used to be the church office. She moved some dusty old hymnals and lay down on a three-legged couch.

A great thrust of organ music rolled her off her bed and stood her upright. She stared into darkness, trying to guess what day it was. There were voices with the organ under her feet, and she remembered where she was. They had started church without her. She ran downstairs and through the back hall right to the minister's stage entrance but stopped there because the singing voices had been replaced by one deep thrilling one saying a prayer. She sat on the floor with her eyes wide and unblinking, trying to figure out what had gone wrong. How they could have started without her. They must have looked for her; they would have had to have looked for her. People would have asked where's Tonie, so they couldn't forget. Her father would have gotten so mad, though, that he would want to forget. There was still plenty of time to go around the outside and come in the church from behind the audience. There was still the whole sermon yet to go. He was preaching the sermon about the baptizing, and all the kids were out there in a row, her cousin Jimmy, and all the families, her mother and Lee sitting there and Aunt Mary Katherine and Uncle Earl and Johnny and her cousins' grandparents Emzie Wright and Uncle Everett and Miss Juliet Bodkin at the organ and all the other people she could name if she could see through this curtain. But they couldn't name her. She thought suddenly that she could walk right out on the stage behind him as he preached and no one would see; she could go right up and touch his back and he wouldn't feel a thing. She was like one who had never been born. If she had been, they wouldn't have started church without her.

She cried for a little while, and then the organ started again, and she knew something was wrong for sure because the sermon shouldn't have been so short. Even now the kids would be lining up in front of the communion table to say the promise. So she wouldn't have to hear them, she ran back to the wardrobe opposite the little bathroom and climbed behind the robes, leaving herself a tiny space to see through.

They were singing again, and it was too late now because she felt the floor shake; he was coming back to get ready. She thought of stepping out in the hall in his way to see if he could see her, but he was huge and he passed like a billowy black angel, a tower of darkness.

She drew back into the closet because of the welter of whispering children that came next, pastel girls, plaid sports jackets and grease-slick boys' hair. They headed the boys off to be dressed in the study; the girls went to the little bathroom opposite Tonie. Her mother was there and Lee too, helping Ruthie Rogers with her coordinated anklets and gloves. Everyone was changing clothes quickly, at a terrific speed, in a single clenched breath of Tonie's. They lined up in their white robes, Jimmy in the lead. She could have reached out and pinched him. Her father passed and whispered something to her mother and Aunt Mary Katherine. Then it was true; no one had noticed her absence. The children passed her by too, and Aunt Mary Katherine. Only her mother and Lee stayed in the little bathroom hanging up dresses.

Tonie's legs were going to sleep; she had to stretch. She struggled, lurched, and thumped against the wall. The curtain of choir robes parted and her mother's face was there, finding her. Pulling her out, dragging her quickly across the hall into the bathroom and setting her on the toilet seat.

"Tonie!" said Lee. "We looked everywhere! Where were you?"

Tonie started to cry; the light was too bright, she couldn't stand to see, but she had been lost, and now she was found.

"Leave her alone, Lee, let's just get the dress off and find her a robe."

Lee took a dramatic step backwards. "Aren't you going to tell Daddy?"

"He's up to his waist in water! We'll slip her into a robe and send her on with the others. The whole thing was my fault anyhow."

Jimmy came down the hall, puddling. He was baptized already and grinning like an idiot. "Hey, Tonie! Where were you?" As if she had missed dessert. She looked away. Her mother was lifting her, Lee was pulling off her shoes and socks. She let herself go limp as if she were already saved and a dead angel. It was all taken care of at last. Her mother and father were going to baptize her. Her mother rushed her down the hall and squeezed through to the head of the line, pushing Ruthie Rogers to one side, and Aunt Mary Katherine too. Her mother lifted her and swung her over the ledge and stood her feet on the first step in the water.

The water was warm, and it made her grin foolishly. She didn't look at her father's face; she looked at the bellying of his black robe on the water and picked her way down step by step. When the water oozed around her thighs, it was so warm she thought for a moment she had wet herself. When it was to the middle of her chest, she finally looked at his face. His eyes were stern, but she had been frightened when she was little too, and he used to throw her up in the air and catch her; he always caught her, but she was always frightened and she always loved it. She extended her hands, and he reached out too. She let him pull her through the water, parting it with her chest, and she expected him to pull her right out of the water and lift her into the air, but he murmured in his formal church face, "No handkerchief? Well, you'll have to hold your breath then." He raised his voice to reach the people out beyond the spotlight. "Do you accept Jesus Christ as your personal Lord and Savior?" And she kept smiling, because he was going to baptize her; she remembered once they had been in the water together before, at Maple Lake for a church picnic, and he tossed her up with the sun in her eyes and water shimmering all around them, and he told her he was going to throw her in the water, and she laughed at him.

"Then I baptize thee my little sister," he said, "In the name of the Father, and of the Son, and of the Holy Ghost, Amen!" And he pressed her under the water and she was still struggling with her mouth open and grabbing at his wrist, bony, covered with wet hair, and she grabbed it with both hands and kicked his leg, and then he lifted her out, heavy and shocked. He set her on the steps. "Amen," he said. "The Lord bless you and keep you in His path."

Her mother dragged her up the rest of the way, streaming from the nose and mouth.

She said, "I better go back, I don't think my head went under—"

Her mother said, "You're completely baptized, Tonie."

He spanked her in his office. He held her by a handful of crinolines and each whack nearly knocked her off his knee, but she cried mostly out of tiredness. He said, "I should have done this when you first started this nonsense," but she thought she could tell from his voice that he was glad she was baptized too.

Then her mother came in and stood by the door. "Isn't that about enough, John?"

"I was just finishing up," he said, offering Tonie a tissue.

"They're wondering where you are downstairs, both of you." They both sat down, though, and gave Tonie a chance to catch her breath.

Tonie licked a tear off the side of her face. Their faces were obscured by shadows, but they waited patiently and politely. She didn't listen to what they said. They would all go downstairs together when she was ready, and she didn't care if her eyes were still red. Her daddy would shake hands with people and her mother would laugh. The kids would say, Where were you Tonie? How come you're crying? I hid, she would say, because I didn't want to make the promise. And I got whipped for it too.

Chapter 5
Lee

For Lee everything always seemed to come back to the four of them at dinner. She could work up a sweat at dodge ball, and she could worry through the morning about the algebra test and then feel better after taking it, and she could go into town with some girls to the bakery for lunch and stuff herself on cream puffs and gossip about who was pregnant, and she could even get two glimpses of the boy she only named to herself on her pillow at night, and then suddenly it would be five-fifteen with her family at the kitchen table.

The plates, a gift from the old ladies' Sunday school class, were plastic and each one had a big rose in the center. Scattered around the table were little leftover dishes of applesauce and cottage cheese, canned peaches, and a reheated portion of mashed potatoes with Velveeta cheese. Her mother brought over a tin saucepan of green beans that she dropped on their plates beside the hamburger patties. Lee served herself a large portion of potatoes, feeling that she needed to fill some hole inside her with pale, heavy foods.

"Tonie," said her father to her younger sister, "while your mother's busy, why don't you get us the ice water."

"I forgot it," said her mother. "I'm sorry."

Tonie started to pout. "Why do *I* have to do it?"

Lee leaped up. "Oh for heaven's sake, I'll get the ice water." By the time they had all stopped popping up and down, the potatoes with Velveeta cheese were cold, but since they were still filling, Lee ate more of that than anything else.

Her mother said long before their plates were empty, "I didn't have time to bake today. We had a missions meeting, so there's nothing but ice cream for dessert."

Her mother was still wearing her gray jumper, but she had unzipped the side and her blouse tailed out. She had a headache, Lee could tell from the way her eyes looked lashless and her mouth as if it had no lips.

Lee said, "We're better off without a cake for once." Taking care of her mother made her very tired.

Her father began to talk about his day. She tried to think of what to tell when her turn came round.

She needed something funny, a wisecrack from some boy in the back of study hall, something from gym period. Her father's story was about an oddball salesman who had tried to convince him, a lifelong Baptist!

to buy purple vestments and clerical collars. That amused everyone except Tonie, who was in a mood, staring and sneering.

In the last couple of months Tonie had been getting taller and vaguely thicker without being fat; she had herself cut off her pigtails and she always wore corduroy dungarees. It reminded Lee of when Tonie was just a baby and said No to everything you asked her.

"I don't eat hamburgers without buns," said Tonie. She wasn't cute anymore, though. She seemed to tip the table and all of them with it in her direction. "I'm going to make myself a fried egg sandwich."

Their mother said, "Oh, don't dirty another frying pan!"

"She won't," said their father. "She'll eat what's here or she won't eat." Lee felt an awful nervous grin stretch over her teeth. She couldn't stand the obviousness of Tonie's moods. She couldn't stand the way her mother rubbed and massaged at her forehead.

Tonie said, "Can I be excused then?"

"May I, " said their father. "Yes you may, but if you leave now, you don't get dinner later."

Tonie stalked out of the kitchen into the dark dining room that they almost never used except to store bicycles. She muttered just softly enough that they could pretend they didn't hear her, "I don't know why it matters if I do it myself. It looks like I should have the right to make my own dinner if I'm willing to do the work."

"It isn't really much of a dinner," said her mother.

He said, "It seems like these girls could do more to help out when you're busy in the afternoon. Not that I'm complaining about the dinner. It's fine with me."

Lee said, "I had pep club after school. They nominated me for secretary-treasurer."

"Speaking of elections," he said, "what ever happened with your cheerleading business?"

She should never have mentioned elections. She looked toward Tonie sitting on the floor in the dark, sulking, but she, Lee, stretched her mouth out of shape into a smile again. "Oh, I never really expected to get it. There were thirty girls trying out and they only chose two, you know. The odds weren't very good."

"You spent enough time practicing for it if you didn't think you could get it. It seems to me you haven't done anything for a month but jar the dishes off the shelves jumping around."

Maybe, she thought, it was that she hadn't jumped high enough. Or maybe that people down deep thought she was a little strange, being a preacher's daughter. Maybe it was that her hips were so straight up and down that her chest looked top-heavy.

"Don't make her feel bad, John."

"Oh, I'm over it now, Mama! They posted the results this morning so I've had all day to get used to the idea." Talking too fast, looking from one of them to the other. Her mother with her brow knit, making tsk-tsk noises of mournful sympathy, and her father looking a little amazed as if he still couldn't believe that his daughter could work so hard and yet fail. It didn't matter all the other things she *had* won, the unusual nomination of a freshman to be an officer of the pep club, early permission to take speech and dramatics. All that mattered was that she had tried for something and failed and soon he would be wondering what was wrong with her. "It really is okay," she said.

"Still, honey," said her mother. "You must be so disappointed."

Her mother, on the other hand, was surprised when she *did* win something. "It's over, Mama. I'm over it."

I could have won too, she thought, if it hadn't been this week. I'm as good at cheers as the rest of them, and just as good-looking. And three weeks out of the month she had that special extra something too, the spirit, the pep, the smile that didn't stretch your mouth out of shape.

Tonie is right to resist, she thought, Resist, Tonie, don't admit it when it happens to you, don't let anyone know that you're turning into a woman. Don't let them give you cramps and holes in your gut so you feel like you could cry forever inside and never fill it. Or better still, be like Rastus Smith, with a face like a bloodhound and spots like a beagle, better to be a big lazy giant lap dog and wag your tail all the time but never do anything that isn't for fun or to eat.

Tonie sauntered into the kitchen after they had gone and she was still clearing the table. She sat down at the plate with the dried-up hamburger and laid the meat on a slice of bread, blanketed it with ketchup, and pressed another slice down on top hard. Rastus rested his muzzle on her thigh and begged for a bite.

"You never go up on the hill with me anymore," she said so softly that Lee thought at first she was speaking to the dog.

"I've been busy." Out the window she saw to her surprise that it was still light; she felt they had all been in darkness for a long time, but the top of the hill was alive with horizontal sun rays.

"Is that your way of saying you want to go for a walk?"

"Only if you do."

"I wouldn't mind getting out."

They went out the back way, leaving the dishes unwashed, and climbed the short wall that someone had built to keep the hill from eroding into their backyard. The dog ran ahead with no effort, but Lee liked the effort; she leaned forward to stretch the back of her calves even more. Cold air hit her lungs like snow balls, and she liked that too, and the frostbitten dirt.

"This is the first time you went hiking with me since you started high school," said Tonie.

"You know something, Tonie? You are never satisfied." But she wasn't mad; she liked being able to talk back safely to someone.

Tonie pulled ahead and reached the crest of the hill first, and shouted, "Hey, Lee, let's climb the tank!"

Galatia had two water tanks set on hills on opposite sides of town. Theirs was the East Tank, and it was shimmering in the sinking sun, except for the dull ten-foot letters that spelled GALATIA WVA.

Lee shook the ladder. The tank always seemed bigger and more swollen than she expected, and so close behind their house. She said, "Look at the rust coming off on my hands. It's a wonder kids don't get killed all the time fooling around up here."

"Climb it, Lee!"

"You climb it."

"I will if you will "

She looked deep into the perfectly blue sky: a giddy instant of gravity reversed and falling up. "Too cold. The ladder's rusty and it's freezing cold and windy as anything at the top." She gave the ladder a good shake, and it rattled so hard she scared herself. "Besides, you're scared to death of it, Tonie. You always chicken out."

"I'm going all the way to the top this time."

"Good, go ahead. I'll watch."

"I want both of us to climb. It's no fun unless both of us do it."

She didn't seriously mean to refuse very long. She liked to be begged a little, to have the fun of dragging her feet because climbing was Tonie's idea, not hers. But the familiar challenge felt good. The hill fell away so fast that you felt you were hanging out of an airplane. It was dangerous to have Tonie behind you too, because sometimes she froze and had to be coaxed down, but Tonie was sticking with her tonight. Her hands got cold and stiff from the metal, and her stomach began to heave a little with each rung. It had been a long time since she had done this. She stopped halfway up and leaned backwards. Better to fall up into the blue than be sucked under the garbage.

"Don't do that," said Tonie.

Deliberately, because she had been nice for so many weeks and smiled at so many people, she shook the ladder until it wavered and clanged along its whole length. Tonie pressed her forehead against her rung but didn't whimper. She's going to make it to the top this time, Lee thought, a little sorry because Tonie's courage put her under obligation to go further herself. The one thing she had never done was to step off the ladder onto the roof of the tank. There was a narrow rim along the edge of the steep dome where you could hook your heels if you kept your weight back. Making no promises to herself, and keeping her eyes off the ground, she contorted herself through the ladder supports and slid out along the roof. She was in a sweat, but leaning back, her body arched with the dome, she wasn't too uncomfortable. She touched the ladder perfunctorily with one hand.

She said, "You came to the top, and I came out on the roof. Look at the view."

Tonie shook her head and kept her cheek against the ladder, her shoulders hunched.

Feeling proud and regally generous, Lee said, "You should look, Tonie. It's so beautiful you may never see anything as beautiful. No place in the world could be so beautiful." The hills south of Galatia were darkening to ambers and dusky blues, and at the same time there was still this uncanny azure overhead. "The hills look like they'd feel stubbly if you touched them with your fingers." The river was orange, greenish where the sewers dumped under the old bridge. "I see all those cheap houses on stilts down by the river and there's washing hanging out and junky old refrigerators on the back porches. I'd like to run my thumbnail along the bank and scrape them into the river. The cars too. Just chuck everything that isn't beautiful into the river." Chuck the high school and the football field too, she thought, but was shamed by her lack of school spirit. Her sweat heat was gone, and she was beginning to get cold. Even as she watched, a gray film seemed to dull the sky. The sun had long since disappeared.

She rapped hard on the dome of the tank, and an enormous distant boom spread through it, something bigger than life. A creature inside made of water, roused, dripping and thrashing. Konng, konng.

"Lee," whispered Tonie, "what if there was a crack in the tank?"

Lee laughed out loud. A flash flood, she thought. Knocking the houses out from under the roofs, uprooting the trees and telephone poles. People clinging to floating sofas, the high school cleared out to house the refugees. "In one fell swoop," she said, "the town of Galatia washed away. One out of every three persons missing." She laughed until her laughter turned into shivers, and then she had a passing fear that the shivering would take away the strength of her youth and transform her into an old person with arthritic hands. "Let's go," she said.

All the way down Tonie kept stopping to talk. "We could stay up here and hunt with Rastus Smith and live off the land. Just suppose we never went down again."

Lee thought, It would be cold, terribly cold, and then colder still. Tonie's fantasy was of meat roasting over an open fire, but Lee thought of not getting the fire started, of shivering and feeling desperate. She wished they were still up on the tank. She had loved the flash flood washing away the trash. "Tonie," she said, "I'm going to take you on my last great adventure."

"What do you mean your last great adventure?"

She meant, Before they turn me all the way into a woman and I have to spend all my time keeping my knees together. She said, "I don't know yet what we're going to do myself, but you're invited to come if you stick by me."

"It's going to be dark—"

"Then go home."

"No, no, I want to come—"

Lee nodded. Tonie was good and loyal. She strode out along the ridge until they were out of sight of the tank and town. "Look down at the old Farley place. From the road it looks like a mansion, but from up here it looks like an old abandoned farm." They had come to the apple orchard, and they stood side by side.

Tonie said, "Mama danced up here in this orchard once."

"When did she ever do that?"

"Right after we moved. She used to bring me up here all the time."

That summer. It would be something out of kilter, something embarrassing.

"She sang hymns up here and danced."

"What hymns?"

"I don't remember. 'Amazing Grace' and 'Sweet Hour of Prayer.' You know what happened? Joe Bob Farley was here. He'd been asleep in the tall grass, and he sort of sat up and stretched."

"That stinking drunk! Did he leave you alone?"

"Well, he scared us, and Mama started yelling. I never saw her so mad. She stood there and waved her arms and yelled at him for spying on us. He said he was just watching the dance, and besides, it was his aunt's property and we were the ones that woke him up. Mama got even madder and said that nature belongs to God, not Mrs. Farley."

That was when she loved her mother, when she stood up to something with her arms spread out looking twice her size. She said, "Joe Bob Farley should be locked up. He must have something pretty awful in his past or he wouldn't be such a drunk. And the old woman too, there must be some reason that she's a recluse and he's a drunk."

"Like what?"

"Oh, families have secrets."

"Not ours."

"I wouldn't be so sure. There are things they don't talk about in our house too. But that wasn't what I meant. I meant something like how I read in the paper once about this family of fundamentalists up on a mountain somewhere and people kept hearing howling up there and they got the sheriff to come up and in the attic of this old farmhouse on top of the mountain they found an idiot chained to a bed frame. Five years or so earlier the young daughter of the family had got herself pregnant and they were so ashamed that they hid the baby in the attic and never spoke to it or touched it except to feed it and never let it see the light of day. It was blind and retarded and couldn't say a word."

"What happened?"

"The man had to go to jail. The idiot was carted off to a mental institution because there was nothing else to do with it, and the woman and the girl went to another town where they live to this day."

Tonie thought it over. "You think there's something like that down there?"

"I don't think anything. I just have an urge to go down and take a look at them. After all, Joe Bob spied on you, didn't he?" Lee started to run with big, easy, dangerous leaps.

"But Lee!" Tonie was chasing after her. "Rastus Smith ran off!"

"He'll find us!"

"But Lee! What if they have a gun?"

"Run broken-field. It's harder to hit a moving target!"

There was a vast openness between them and the next range of hills, there was still some orange and blue sky at first, but as they came off the hill they were running into the dark. I dare them, thought Lee, I dare them to try and stop me!

They caught their breath against the rough stone below the back windows of the Farley mansion. Tonie kept whispering between breaths, "What if they saw us? What if we get caught?"

"What's it to you? You're still a kid. I'll get all the blame."

"They'd spank me, they'd never spank you."

"A spanking is nothing. They would never trust me again. You don't have to come any farther, Tonie. You can go look for Rastus and go home."

"You know I wouldn't. You know I'm with you."

Lee felt a brief floodlight of peace as she explained her plan. "We'll work our way around the house till we find a lighted window we can look in."

They followed the dirt between the wall of the house and the row of evergreen bushes. About halfway around, just at the beginning of the brick half of the house, they saw one lit window.

Lee chinned herself on the sill, holding her breath, and eased her face around the sash to look: a small living room, old-fashioned, a cabinet model radio, a whatnot shelf. She took her weight on her elbows and stared in full face. Antimacassar on a plush chair, a ceramic elephant with ivy growing out of his back, brass-framed photographic portraits. But most engrossing, not four feet to her left, a cage with a parrot. He was green with yellow chops and long pink feet. He hunched over his wooden perch, cocked his head to look at her with one eye, then the other. "Brr," he said softly and fluffed his neck ruff. He took a sudden heavy leap at cage bars that shook the whole cage and walked up and down, unfolding one pink foot at a time, keeping up the throaty gurgles and brrs.

Lee dropped down. "Tonie! There's a parrot in there—you've got to see the parrot!"

She grabbed Tonie around the thighs and lifted her up. Tonie began to giggle and Lee lost her balance and they both fell flailing into the evergreen bushes. Lee covered Tonie's giggling mouth with her hand, but giggles kept slipping through her fingers. "It wanted to bite me, " Tonie said, her whisper disintegrating into belly chuckles. "That parrot was so mad because it couldn't get out and bite me."

"Shut up, Tonie, shut up!"

The bush made a cradle for them, and gradually Tonie was lulled; they were kept warm by one another, Tonie's cold cheek next to hers, bouncing gently under the sky, by the parrot window.

After a while she whispered, "Tonie, you know, if there was no window, I would reach right in and steal that parrot. I would wear that parrot on my shoulder to school tomorrow."

"To school?"

She imagined it croaking gently in her ear, spreading its yellow and green and touches of red over her shoulder. Setting her apart from other people. She felt already different from other people, but now it was more like she wore a filthy gray chicken squatting in its own droppings.

Tonie said, "Maybe the window isn't locked."

Lee jumped to her feet, shocked by Tonie's literalness. "And steal it? Don't you know when I'm babbling? Don't you have any judgment?"

She led quickly up onto the porch that surrounded the front of the house, making Tonie be absolutely still, stopping and listening even though the windows were all blinded and some covered with plywood and chicken wire. She glanced back and found Tonie's face featureless in the gathering dark.

Around the corner of the porch they saw another lighted window, and a shadow crossed it.

"Shh. Don't even breathe deep."

She made them both get down on their hands and knees and crawl on their bellies off the porch and inch by inch in the dirt to the window, scraping their palms on the frozen ground. Lee passed under the window crawling and carefully drew herself to her feet. This was a low window, a wide open view into another little room, not mansion-sized at all, a small kitchen with a white enamel cupboard and white table and chairs and Joe Bob Farley sitting with his back to them, eating supper alone. Light-colored stubble grew all the way down the back of his neck. It shimmered when he moved his head. He reached for his glass, turning his head just enough to expose the hairless red skin under his ear. There were crevices in that skin, and as he chewed, the crevices stretched flat. He was drinking milk. He chewed in silence, then they heard his fork ping as it passed through the potatoes to the plate. He cleared his throat, put apple butter on his bread and folded it into a sandwich.

The man was somehow not Joe Bob Farley, that drunk, but a clean object alive like the percolating coffeepot and the white mug on a tray with a yellow apple beside it. These things were droplet ripe to her like blackberries, like the town of Galatia seen from the tank, so close you could reach out and pluck what you wanted.

She wanted to taste the life in the little kitchen. She felt her way along the wall of the house for another corner and continued to scratch along the wall impatiently until she found a door.

Tonie whispered, "You left me back there!"

"Shut up, we're going in."

Tonie gasped, and Lee thought, That's right, no pretending. I don't make up stories about going up on the hill to live off the land.

It was a screen door with plywood nailed over the screen to keep the winter out, and it was not locked. They stepped into a short hallway crowded with coat racks and boxes, rakes and rubber boots, and a lighted doorway, and the smell of coffee and frying grease. Lee immediately knew she had gone too far. The kitchen odors were more real than she wanted, their richness choked her throat. Her forward motion ended at a hat rack where she clutched the coats and Tonie squeezed in behind her. It was a mistake, she thought, the whole thing was a mistake.

At that instant something began to thump on the stairs above them, and a vision came to Lee, of being held by the scruff of the neck and asked, Why did you do this? She tried to form a defiant face like a bad boy who has been caught over and over, but she had never mastered that expression.

Tonie started to jiggle and whisper, "Lee, Lee, there's someone coming, there's something on my leg—"

With her shoulder she pressed Tonie into the wall and tried to shrink herself into the coats. But Tonie wouldn't stop gasping unvoiced sobs, "There's something. Oh, Lee, there's something—"

She jammed Tonie with all the strength of her arm, trying to hold her until the shuffle had passed into the kitchen, if she could just hold her that long, but it was such a slow thump and shuffle. From the kitchen a clear perfectly sober voice said, "Aunt Josephine, what are you doing down here by yourself?"

They never found out because Tonie moaned, "It's after me!" and thrashed free, thundered toward the door. In the struggle to hold her, Lee tipped over the hat rack and it was like a crack of thunder too, and Joe Bob yelled something from the kitchen and Lee herself stumbled on the moving live thing as she burst out the door and leaped into the darkness. The live thing started barking, and Joe Bob was yelling and the house seemed to explode in noise and lights as she rolled under the barbed wire fence and slid through the weeds and bushes down into a deep drainage ditch.

"Tonie!" she shouted, "It was Rastus! Rastus Smith followed us into the house and we didn't know it." By now they couldn't stop their momentum and even when they came to the bottom of the squishy half-frozen streambed they kept running and Rastus jumped up at them and tried to give them kisses. When they were well out on North Avenue beside regular people's houses and yards, Lee said, "Stop running, Tonie, we don't want to look like we did anything wrong. Rastus Smith, you were a bad dog."

He wagged his tail.

"No he wasn't. He came in the house behind us and didn't make a sound so he wouldn't give us away."

"Joe Bob Farley thought he was having the d.t.'s I bet. Every light in the house was on and they were running around like a couple of chickens with their heads cut off."

"I bet he got his gun out."

"They're saying, Oh it's those bad boys again! They would never in a million years guess it was Lee and Tonie Scarlin!"

Tonie giggled and Lee felt wild and courageous, as if she had gone back to a happier, freer time without losing any smartness or strength. "Maybe they'll buy some German police dogs now for protection. And that could be the death of them. Maybe one night Joe Bob will come home late, drunk again, and the dogs, really murderous mean dogs, will turn on him and kill him and old Mrs. Farley will fall and break her hip and she'll wait and wait for Joe Bob but he never comes and she'll sort of dry up into a mummy and the dogs will howl and howl."

As they came to the next street, Tonie stopped and lifted her left hand. "I got hurt." On the fat part under the thumb there was a big gash where the blood was turning black. "I don't even know where I got it."

"Probably in the gully from one of Joe Bob's bottles."

Tonie nestled the cut hand in her good one. "It doesn't hardly hurt."

Lee wanted to put an arm around her sister to somehow make a perfect end of their adventure, but she was afraid Tonie would shrug it off. But even imperfectly she felt a contentment. "We're really late," she said, "and I never did finish the dishes. We're going to be in trouble with Daddy, you know."

Chapter 6
Tonie

Tonie came home for Everett Wright's funeral and Lee did not. It was early spring 1970, and even at the little Baptist college where she was a freshman, a few students had been protesting the war. Tonie didn't know which side she was on: she tended to think the protesters' side, but she didn't know them well enough to join in. She stopped going to classes, though, and sat in the cafeteria smoking and drinking coffee.

Lee should have come home for the funeral too, Tonie thought. Everett was the closest thing we had to a grandparent. In his will he left four Series E hundred dollar bonds, one each for his real grandchildren, Johnny and Jimmy, and one each for Lee and Tonie, all equal.

When she was little, Tonie used to spend far more time with him than the boys did. She would squat by him in his garden for hours, learning how to farm, she always said, but she really was there because she felt at ease. He kept rabbits, black and white ones, big heavy lumps that never struggled to get out of your arms, they just twitched their noses. She thought now that he probably raised them to eat because he was a practical farmer even though he'd had to work in the mines all his life. One of the rabbits would turn up missing from time to time. They ain't pets, you know, he would say. Sometimes they light out for parts unknown. Let's you and me go in the house and make us a butter pie; I know Emzie left a pie shell around here. His butter pies were constructed of layers of brown sugar, butter, and canned milk that formed a crusted syrup. The two of them once ate an entire pie at a sitting with glasses of milk and Everett chased his with beer. He winked and gave her a taste and made her promise not to tell Emzie or her father.

A few days after the funeral her father asked how she could stay away from college so long. She said it was a special study week with no classes before midterm exams. Then why don't I see you studying? he asked. Because you're at church all day.

She lied with unexpected talent. She liked the sensation of lying so well that she didn't even try to fool herself. She had decided she wasn't going back to Alderman-Davis at all. There was an immobility in her, a hunger to sit in one place. She didn't want to go out of the house, clammy as it was with sealed-in winter smells. She got up, zipped herself into blue jeans, put on a tee shirt and a sweatshirt over that, and went to the kitchen. Her father's cornflakes bowl was in the sink, and his coffee cup and spoon. Her mother, she supposed, was still asleep; she was working on one of her plays, volunteering again. Up at that high school, said her father, they don't know what they've got, a free director. They'll use you up, he said, but her mother didn't notice anything, her mother was staying up at the high school till all hours every night, sleeping all day. Tonie put on the kettle and leaned on the stove to warm up. She heard a sound, but from the den, not upstairs, and her mother came in wearing a flannel nightgown, barefoot, shoulders wrapped in a plaid blanket. A long wing of unbrushed hair rose from her forehead like a banner.

"You see, Tonie, I do so get up at a decent hour. I've been up since six-thirty. What do you think about that? I couldn't sleep, so I got up and started to work. I'll make the coffee. Do you want some toast? Or how about oatmeal, you used to like oatmeal and oven toast with the butter melted down inside and brown sugar lumps for the oatmeal. Do you remember how you and Lee used to fight over who got the lumps?"

Tonie didn't want anything but coffee, so her mother insisted on making up a tray with the sugar bowl and creamer. "I don't take sugar," said Tonie.

"Neither do I," said her mother, getting out a sugar spoon anyhow. "Let's drink it in the den. I've got to tell you what I'm doing."

Tonie almost blurted out I have something to tell you too, but frightened herself out of speaking because she couldn't remember what it was she wanted to tell.

The den was as full as ever of her mother's half-finished projects. The couch she had started to upholster, getting as far as one self-piped sailcloth pillow, the rest in its original bald plush. There were origami birds tied like blossoms to the old snake plants that no one remembered to water; there was a dusty basket of needlepoint, and now, on the end table pulled up to the couch like a desk, the typewriter and papers strewn all over the couch. So Tonie took her coffee and sat on the floor beside the dog. She began to pat him, but he paid no attention, asleep on an afghan that had slipped to the floor, probably off her mother's shoulders, she thought. He's getting old, she thought, like Everett got old.

Her mother pushed aside some papers, pulled her legs up on the couch, and folded her hands in her lap like some kind of little girl. It was the kind of little girl Tonie had always avoided playing with. "I'm going to burst, Tonie, I'm so excited. I know everyone thinks I'm a sucker to have taken on the play. The English department at the high school certainly does. But I don't care, I love it, I love those seniors. The only thing in the world that was bothering me was that they had already picked out the script when I got involved and of course they chose the play with the cheapest royalties and this one was absolutely awful, about getting permission to have boys for a dance at a girls' school. And who in Galatia has ever heard of real people going to a private girls' school? Anyhow, I've been rewriting it, and I just thought up the ending." She began to draw something in the air. "In the original play there's a legend that the building is haunted and people keep thinking there's a ghost but it turns out to be somebody's boyfriend. You know. So first I added a lot of extra hands coming out of closets, creaking doors, all the Halloween props we can think up. Then it came to me—in my play, the handsome young man is going to turn out to really be a ghost. There's a human boy who loves the heroine too, but she chooses the ghost. The scary thing is that they can't touch because they're different substances—I mean she haunts him just as much as he haunts her, but they choose to be together for all eternity. What do you think?"

"I think everyone is expecting a comedy like always."

"Oh, it's funny, especially the start, but little by little I want the audience to leave off laughing until there's maybe one joker out there still guffawing, and then his laugh will die away too and they'll all feel the other thing, the horror."

Tonie gave her a little sidelong glance. She didn't look like a little girl anymore but not like a mother either. "Who's in it?"

"My best actor is your friend Eddie Salerno. He's the ghost and he can send shivers down your spine, I mean it. But they're all good."

Tonie had never dated Eddie or anything like that, he was a year younger than she was, but she used to ride around with him sometimes in his uncle's Camaro, especially last summer; they'd go get a hamburger, they'd sit around and talk. He used to tell her his problems. It had been a lazy summer and she realized now that she had been counting on him in the back of her mind. That in a day or two she would run into him and they would ride around and talk some more. She had forgotten of course that he was a senior and how busy they were. She would never have guessed he'd be tied up in her mother's play, though. She said, "Those seniors never get a minute to breathe."

"They're wonderful! What a group. They rehearse on their lunch hour, they beg the custodian to keep the building open late for us—I love them."

Well, thought Tonie, that takes care of old Eddie. Who was she going to hang around with now? Where were her classmates anyhow? None of them had gone to Alderman-Davis, that was for sure. Some to the university, one friend still in Galatia was married and already had a baby and fifteen extra pounds on her thighs and butt. Tonie said, "You didn't direct the play even when Lee was a senior."

"No one asked me to. They may never ask me again either, after this one. Do you think the ending is too depressing for teenagers?"

"You can tell the teachers that the ending is ambivalent. That's the only thing I learned all year at A-D, if you don't know an answer, you talk about the elements of Ambiguity."

Her mother nodded. "How is everything at A-D, honey? You haven't said much."

Tonie thought to herself, I wonder how long I've got before she floats off to ghost land again. She got to her feet, disturbing Rastus, and he wagged his tail heavily once. "Old A-D is fine. Same old Hell Hole, pardon my French. I think I'll go for a walk." She headed for the door. "Yeah, A-D is just the same crummy uptight place it always was, but they'll have things a little easier now because I'm not ever going back there."

"Tonie!" Her mother tried to get up and follow her but knocked a lot of papers on the floor.

"See you later, Mom!" she shouted. "Tell Daddy I've decided to drop out!"

She went for a long walk; she had meant to go up on the hill, which was just turning green, but she had started off in the wrong direction, down into town. She walked through the alleys ending up on North Avenue, heading out towards where Mary Katherine lived, but she stopped along the way to sit on the wall in front of the old Farley mansion. There was a big fir tree there that supported her back, and she gazed across the field to where they were building some new houses. The air seemed to pick up the hammer cracks and toss them over the empty land, threatening the new grass. She didn't like them building in the fields where she used to play. She became a little drowsy as the sun came through the fog, and she pretended that Uncle Everett hadn't really died; that she had found out he was sick in time to come home and ask him how to set up a farm. I'm serious about this, Uncle Everett, she would say. I want to raise my own food, and no more nonsense about not eating the cute bunnies. Tell me what I need to know.

She heard the gravel crunch and peeped around her tree trunk. Joe Bob Farley was coming down the driveway from the big house. No one else in Galatia had that particular lanky stoop, the familiar long body that you sometimes saw lying beside the road late at night. It was not quite eleven A.M. yet; he was going to make it to town just as they folded open the iron gates on the State Liquor Store. I bet he follows a schedule as tight as Daddy's, she thought, disgusted with middle-aged men. He paused between the pillars to light his pipe.

"Morning, Joe Bob," she said.

High school boys boasted, Last night I was as drunk as Joe Bob Farley. Sober, though, he seemed ordinary in his plaid flannel shirt and poplin work pants. He had a bristly homemade crewcut that gave him the look of a child plunked down into unearned age. She said, "Do you know me?"

Tamping his pipe, he strolled along the wall and rested an elbow at her feet. "Let's see, the face is familiar."

"Tonie Scarlin."

"Ah, the preacher's girl. Now I know." He seemed absolutely comfortable to be standing there, sucking on his pipe, passing the time of day. He didn't seem surprised that she was here either, in the middle of the morning, where usually nobody sat but boys hitching rides to Black Run. "I know your aunt real well. She and I were in school together. And Earl—Earl and I were good buddies. We played football."

"What were Mary Katherine and Uncle Earl like then?"

"She worked in the drugstore after school—"

"I know that, I mean what were they like?"

"Pretty quiet, both of them. But Earl had her picked out from the very beginning. She didn't say much, but I think she picked him too. She didn't have much to say in favor of me or Bill Rogers either. She thought we were a bad influence on Earl."

"Did you know my father?"

"Oh sure. He was ahead of us in school. He was smart. He didn't play football."

She had an urge. She said, "You won a lot of awards when you graduated, didn't you? You were Most-likely-to-succeed."

"Who told you that?"

She started to say, Everyone knows that, mothers say to their little children, See that heap of rags? That is a kind of a man, a Joe Bob Farley. He was once voted Most-likely-to-succeed. Beware of strong drink. "My uncle Earl."

"I hardly ever see Earl anymore. We did everything together then. We hung out in Bill's dad's drugstore, teasing Mary Katherine. The good old days."

"Uncle Earl's father died."

"I heard about that. I always liked old Everett."

"Then why didn't you come to the funeral?"

His chin snapped up and something sharp passed through his eyes.

"How old are you?"

"I'm in college."

"You talk like someone a lot younger. Don't take offense. Most women like to be mistaken for younger."

"I'm not like most women."

She wasn't prepared for his grin, not armed against it. It was a live thing, and she was shocked by how it sprang out at her.

"I guess you're not," he said.

She had been easier when they were just jawing politely like a couple of old-timers. It had been a lot like being with Everett Wright, not too much talking, but what was said was clear as a bell and solid as cabbages and fat black rabbits. "Actually," she said, "I'm dropping out of college."

"That's not a very smart thing to do. Believe me, I know, because I dropped out of college myself."

"Did you drop out of college for drinking?"

Like an animal considering flight, he sniffed at the air. Finally he grinned again. A tamer, more calculated grin. "What if I said it was none of your damn business?"

She leaned back against the tree and stretched her legs, trying to decide if he might be flirting with her. She was a little scandalized, not sure how middle-aged men flirt, and not sure that a derelict had the right to. She didn't know much about alcoholics. For all she knew, a complete souse like Joe Bob might be so rotted from the inside that he had no sex left. She took out her cigarettes.

"You shouldn't smoke."

"What if I said it was none of your damn business? You should talk about bad habits. Besides. you're smoking a pipe."

He knocked out his pipe on the wall near her foot and glanced towards town; he had already missed the opening of the liquor store. What was it like to know that people really do laugh at you and it isn't your imagination? She wasn't ready for him to wander off yet.

"Hey Joe Bob, do you remember what you had for dinner one night at the beginning of November 1962? You had a slice of meat loaf, mashed potatoes, and stewed tomatoes and milk. You don't remember? I do, because my sister and I spied on you. We made a terrible racket—we were sure you'd shoot us."

He seemed a little stupid, as if this didn't mean much to him. "We used to have a lot of trouble with vandals ."

"It was us! My sister Lee and I. Well, one time it was. We just wanted to see what it would be like to be bad."

"Funny to think of someone knowing what I ate for dinner eight years ago."

"Meat loaf, mashed potatoes, stewed tomatoes, and bread with apple butter."

"That's me all right, apple butter's my favorite."

His wide hands had a healthier tan than his face, and the soft hairs around the wrists were almost the same color as the skin. Her father's hands were white with black hairs and his nails were always perfectly manicured; her mother pushed back the cuticles for him every Saturday night. "My father loves blackberry jam," she said. Then, as he started looking around again: "Are you going to town? I think I'll walk along with you."

"Walk along."

She kept an eye on his profile, on his humorously low-tucked chin, and thought she must have been mistaken about the flirting. "What would you have done if you had caught us that night?"

"I suppose I would have sent you home. What else would I do with two little girls?"

"Lee wasn't very little," she said, but he seemed to be getting more and more distant, to be fading away. What was she to him? She made one last try. "Are you going to go start drinking now? I don't mean to insult you."

"I don't insult so easy."

But he didn't answer.

"I remember something else about you, Joe Bob. You gave me a hot dog once. At the Halloween parade."

Joe Bob said, "I guess I've done a lot of things I don't remember in my life."

Joe Bob gave her the hot dog the Halloween that their mother dressed them as the Tin Woodman and the Scarecrow. They were really little then, Lee too, because they were still living at the parsonage and Galatia was still having the annual Halloween parade. They would block off Pike Street and the Galatia High School band would march, and people set up tables selling hot pepper sandwiches and hot dogs. It was all going on just a few steps from the parsonage, so Lee and Tonie went alone, Lee wearing her tinfoil-covered boxes, Tonie with a broomstick across the back of her shoulders and straw trailing out her sleeves. The straw itched, and her pillowcase mask kept slipping to one side, and her hands were incapacitated by the broomstick, so she would yell at Lee to fix her eyes and scratch her nose and find the straw that was tickling her. When the parade was over, the wide street flooded with children waiting for Mr. Hebert Shinn to announce the best costumes. Children played crack-the-whip all over the street and when they were cracked off kept careening wildly, ricocheting off the crowd. Tonie's costume was too awkward for running, so while Lee played, she began to whirl around all by herself, banking her broom arms, ducking her head as she whirled, trying to see out the corner of one eyehole. "Lee!" she called, "Lee! Fix my face!" The air and the street lamps were blue; she had a glimpse of boys with soot moustaches and girls clattering with gypsy jewelry, all tipped to one side.

Lee didn't answer, and she didn't hear her voice, or the voices of Lee's friends. She wrenched her head around, trying to get at her eyeholes, but the mask slipped again and pulled the skin tight across her forehead and distorted what little she could see. Everyone was jumping and screaming, and Tonie screamed for Lee but it felt like all her crying and screaming were lost in the squeals of laughter.

Someone said, "Don't cry, scarecrow," and she turned around twisting and stooping to see who it was. "Don't cry, scarecrow," he said, "eat a hot dog."

She said, "My mouth isn't there, it's all twisted." He straightened her mask for her and stuck the hot dog in through the mouth hole and she took a bite, seeing through her tears that it was Joe Bob Farley. Her mother had always said, Stay away from drunks, especially when they're giving things away, but he was very helpful, giving her another bite. He said, "You take it, scarecrow, I'll get me another one."

"I can't hold it," Tonie started to sob. "I don't have any arms." Joe Bob fumbled in the straw in her sleeve and pulled out the broomstick and she took the other half of the hot dog. A little boy in a cheesecloth superman suit asked Joe Bob to buy him a hot dog too, and Joe Bob bought hot dogs for superman and his friends too.

Lee came out of the crowd. "Where were you, Tonie?"

"Where were you?"

"Didn't you hear the announcement? We won! We have to go up on the platform and get our prize. Put your mask on, where's your broomstick?"

Joe Bob had it over his shoulder like a toy soldier's gun. He was lining up the giggling children to go get hot dogs.

"Did you get that hot dog from him? Well, you're taking it right back."

In shiny silver foil with a silver hatchet in her hand, Lee stepped in front of Joe Bob Farley with the remains of Tonie's hot dog. "Excuse me, Mr. Farley, but my sister needs her broomstick. And we have to give you back your hot dog."

A thumbnail-sized tail of wiener and a fingermashed bit of bun.

"No, no," said Joe Bob. "That one's for the scarecrow. For the fat little scarecrow."

"She isn't allowed to eat between meals," said Lee. "She's on a diet."

"I'm not fat," said Tonie. "It's the stuffing!"

"Shut up and get away from him. And don't you ever take food from Joe Bob Farley again. Don't you know he's a drunk?"

"Will I get drunk?"

"He doesn't know what he's doing. He doesn't have control of himself."

Tonie let the broomstick be rammed through her sleeves again. She didn't mind not being able to use her hands as long as Lee stayed close. "You let go of me and lost me. How was I supposed to know he was a drunk? I couldn't even see."

They tramped up on the platform and people cheered for them and they got three dollars each. Tonie kept getting her stiff arms caught in people's coats and bumping things. All the people seemed to move in different directions at once without going anywhere, and she thought maybe she really had got drunk.

Going down the steps she buzzed and dive-bombed Lee. "Look out! I can't control myself!"

Tonie made her pilgrimage up on the hill the next day. It was an extraordinarily hot day for so early in the spring, and Rastus Smith disappeared right away on a private rabbit hunt. She got as far as the apple orchard before she stopped and took off her shirt and tied it around her waist even though all she had underneath was a green tank top with no bra. In the shimmery distance earth movers were tearing up the fields to build more houses. Down at the mansion Joe Bob Farley was puttering in the garden. All her good intentions to let the wind blow away the laziness in her went tattering off as she focused in on the man. She was still curious. She headed down the hill to see how he spent a hot afternoon.

She liked herself as she strode along, brown-armed, picking up speed, hair flagging behind, her chest free. She climbed through some rusty barbwire.

Joe Bob leaned on his hoe and shaded his eyes. "It's you again," he said. "I couldn't figure out who would come down off that hill. I don't guess two people in ten years have come to the house from the field."

She stalked around him, sinking in the dirt between his leaf lettuce and his scallions, waiting for him to ask what she wanted, to make a joke. Finally, she said, "I never knew you kept a garden."

He started hoeing again and she had to step over the lettuce to get out of his way. The back of the mansion looked like it needed repairs to the window frames. He made no effort to talk as he scratched at the surface of the dirt. He stumbled once, and it finally occurred to her that he was drunk. She was disappointed; no wild singing, no lavish gifts. Cloddish silence. He won't remember tomorrow that I came by.

There was a rusty pump on a wooden platform, and she sat there with the pump for a backrest, alone after all. Joe Bob was stooped over scrawny lettuce and uneven rows of onions. She was right about him the first time. The hillside was rich and green; weeds were springing up, insects beginning to buzz. Higher up, the new leaves, the fringed orchard. The next field north had fat calves and cows munching along the fence as steadily as buzzing. She closed her eyes on the cows and let the sun seep into her; she wished he would come off the hill, a spirit of horses, the spirit she used to worship as she groomed the real horses up on the hill. I'm just a horse thing, she used to say. Nobody kept horses anymore, but she thought that the spirit might still exist. It filled you like the sun, warmed you from the inside out.

Joe Bob had stopped hoeing and was looking at her. He pulled a pint bottle out of his back pocket, drank, and capped the bottle. He brought it with him to the pump. His tee shirt bared most of his big-boned stringy arms: he seemed able to stare indefinitely. He sat beside her on the pump, drunk and not responsible.

She said, "Can I have a drink?"

"Go ahead." When she hesitated, he grinned. "No, you didn't come down here half-naked to have a drink."

She hugged her knees to hide her chest. "I was just walking and I saw you back here in the garden!"

Joe Bob turned his head toward her ever so slowly and grinned, and she realized that he was not doing nothing at all. "Don't get huffy," he said, "I never make the first move. I'll just sit here in the sun and rest. Enjoy the scenery. If you want something, just ask."

"Ask for what!" She felt she couldn't get away because it would mean standing up and letting him see her breasts. "What do you think I came down here for?"

"Don't ask me." A reptilian narrowing to his face, the snide cunning she hated in old country boys.

"I was bored. I got bored and came looking for something to do. That's all you mean to me."

He muttered something. She was pretty sure it was "And showing off your tits."

Now she had to jump to her feet, and she stomped in the general direction of his fingers. "You're trying to spoil everything!"

He shaded his eyes as he looked up at her, and all she could see was his mouth sneering on and on.

"I was having the nicest time talking to you. I can't stand a stinking hypocrite!"

"I'm not laying a hand on you, not a finger."

"And you better not. Don't think I wouldn't kick your teeth in. You were a human being yesterday—you wouldn't be this way if you weren't drunk. The only reason I'm not long gone already is that you're drunk and not responsible—"

"Don't fool yourself."

She really did want to kick in his grin, and she couldn't stand not seeing his eyes; her feet were beginning a little dance back and forth there on the hollow pump base when doors in the house started crashing and slamming in time to her fury.

"Joe? Joe?" The old woman in wrinkled cotton stockings and a man's buttoned-up sweater brandished a broom. "Here! Let's have none of that!"

Joe Bob said, "You bounce when you're mad," and hurried to the old woman.

Tonie froze where she was. She couldn't let him get away with that.

Joe Bob reached for the broom, but the old woman wrenched it to one side. "Who's that?

"Just a friend of mine, Aunt Josephine. Let me take you back upstairs for your nap."

Gently, using the broom, he pressed her backwards, but she kept peeking around his shoulder at Tonie.

"Tonie, would you mind coming over here? She likes to get a close look at people."

Tonie took her time approaching them. The old woman reached a spotted hand over Joe Bob's shoulder to touch the top of her head. "Who is that, Joe?"

"Tonie Scarlin."

"What's she here for?"

"Just to visit."

"Is she coming around here often?"

He laughed, with his back still to Tonie. "I wish she would, but I don't think so. She's pretty mad at me."

"What? You been drinking, ain't you?"

"I always have a drink in the afternoon, Aunt Josephine."

"You drink too much."

"I'm going to take you up for your nap now."

She finally let go of the broom and worked her mouth in and out. "That hair's pretty," she said to Tonie. "You tell him he drinks too much."

Joe Bob had softened again, as if the lecher had been a disguise he put on to prove something to her. "I have to take her upstairs. If you feel like waiting, I'll make you some ice tea."

"If I wait, are you going to start that stuff again?"

He grinned. "Maybe."

She sat on the wooden steps and listened to his soothing voice and the old woman's skittish one going upstairs. She leaned her forehead against the bannister and tried to figure out what to do, but kept listening to the buzzing and the hot wind instead. After a while she saw his muddy-soled gardening boots again.

"I didn't think you'd stay."

"Do you know why you do what you do?"

"Some things." He touched her head just the way Aunt Josephine had. He said, "I'll make ice tea."

They talked for two days. He had a thousand stories, a few about when he was in the merchant marine, but mostly about things he and Earl and Bill Rogers did years ago as boys. The time they dragged a goat to the top floor of the mansion for a circus.

On the night of the second day, she came to him after dark, when he was drunk and wet-mouthed. He cradled her against his chest, and she felt safe with him, but she also felt she didn't have any alternative. Her father had, she thought, thrown her out.

She and her father had begun that evening in relative harmony, the two of them alone at dinner with her mother off at a play rehearsal. It was their old truce, to read magazines as they ate. She made his coffee and he smiled and told her how pleasant it was to have her pour his coffee. He said, "And what are you doing this evening?"

An unexpected blood blister of fury welled up in her head. "What do you care?"

"It was a polite question."

"I'm going to go out and pick up boys."

He seized his own wrist, as if to keep a grip on himself. "Tonie, that kind of talk is destructive and crazy." He made his voice be sonorous, placating.

He was right, of course; she was the one starting a fight, and not even sure why. She agreed that she was destructive and crazy too, but the fights had their own momentum, and they plunged on, her father as eager as she, like struggling cowboys who don't even miss a blow as they drop into the river. They skipped quickly to the part where he demanded what she intended to do with the rest of her life, and how did she dare sit here after wasting his money on an unfinished semester of college and how did she intend to live because he would not support her forever. He spoke much more than she did. Her strategy was to be bad. Nasty short remarks and sneers. She became less crazy, more quiet as his hands went flying through the air, as his voice began to shake.

"I can't stand to see you sit here day after day in that same pair of blue jeans. You're living like a vegetable. Riding in cars at all hours with a bunch of high school boys. Doing Lord knows what."

"What?" she said. "What do you think I'm doing? And how many with? Besides, that was last summer anyhow."

"That's enough!" he shouted. That's enough, she thought, for it had become boring, not enough blood seemed to flow, or else the blood had flowed and then clotted too soon as they swam in it, and they had begun to choke. He says, I can't stand to look at you! She says, I can't stand to be in this house! The implied agreement: she had to leave, at least for this evening. And as she left, the thing that infuriated her was knowing that he would pace twice around the kitchen and then go to his den, turn on a cone of light over his reclining chair, and in a few minutes be comfortable with his *Time* and *Newsweek*, living his unchanging life that nothing could disturb for long. Whereas she had no idea what to do next. She was just beginning, she was supposed to be thrilled by the prospect of all her life before her. Oh to be young again, they all said, oh to have my life before me. Her life was before her, and the rest of this evening was before her, and she saw a long slide into darkness.

It was not, after all, the worst fight they had ever had. It was perhaps the quickest, and that made her sad, how faultlessly they had run through it. He floated in her mind now in his cone of light, like one who had died, his back straight, wringing his hands, clasping them. She saw her mother too, in the dim stale stage light at the high school, watching them practice her silly play over and over. All of her family located in spots of light scattered at great distances from one another, little galaxies separating inexorably on a vast plane of darkness.

She needed shelter; she could not go to her mother; in the night mothers slip out of your bed and go to your father. So she went to Joe Bob. She sought his long body, the sweet smell of liquor and chewing tobacco and pipe, the interlaced thighs. He held her fingers and made noises over the nicotine stains. She said, Do you think I'm fat? He said, Do you think I'm old? And there was the safety of his chest, the perfect hardness of his breastbone, the rubbery give of his chest muscles. She would keep her face there.

Later, while he snored, she slipped downstairs and went home.

After that, she went every evening, sometimes in the afternoon, slipping in the side door, going down the hall to his little room. But on Wednesday, she found the side door locked and went around to the kitchen where she saw a light. Aunt Josephine was sitting there as stiff as death, gripping her broom to her chest. She jumped when Tonie knocked, but let her in.

"I ain't scared when there's a young person here," said Josephine. "I ain't scared anyhow except I'm so old. But he ain't here tonight."

"Where is he?"

The old woman put the stove on. All the white kitchen enamel was yellowed, cleanly with great age, not grease. They didn't do too much cooking, Joe Bob said. What comes from a can mostly, Campbell's soup and applesauce. Josephine braced herself on the stove and shouted as if Tonie couldn't hear either, "Sit down there! Postum?"

"I wanted to know—"

"No, no, young people like spicy milk."

Working her loose lips to their own private rhythm, she began to move around the kitchen, milk from the sparely furnished refrigerator, honey from a cabinet. She had to prop herself by the belly on the lower cabinet to reach the honey in the upper one. Tonie jumped in to help, but she shouted, "I said you sit down! You go look in his room, and see if he's here."

Tonie was pretty sure he wasn't in the house, but she went down the back hall anyhow. She thought maybe Aunt Josephine wanted the house checked for burglars. She glanced into the room with the empty cage where the parrot used to be, at the big dining room with brittle yellow sheets covering the chairs. She went as far as his room and stood in the doorway. Of all the dozens of frugal little bedrooms in the vast house, Joe Bob slept in the tiniest, near the back door, with a single bed squashed in beside an easy chair. Pipes and little pouches of tobacco on the windowsill and empty whiskey bottles lining the baseboards. She couldn't remember the reason, but Joe Bob had explained why he slept in such a crowded room. He had explained too why his uncle built the house so big with such little rooms. There were supposed to be lots of children and visitors and boarders. There was a time when Joe Bob brought crowds of friends here. When he was in college, he once had a huge raucous party on a weekend with people sleeping in bathtubs, and someone started a little bonfire in the attic. He had any number of stories; they lay one whole afternoon in his narrow bed, her face on his chest, and he sweetly, with slightly slurred consonants, telling what fun he had as a boy. Tell me about the parrot, she said. It always called for women named Rosie and Frances and Mae and his aunt used to talk back to it: If you shout for Frances one more time, I'm going to bake you into a Frances Fricassee, I mean it, you old green chicken.

The old woman was mixing hot milk with honey and cinnamon. She served it to Tonie in a glass on a saucer. She sat back down and watched Tonie. "Not here, is he? You like that stuff? Joe Bob likes it. He does most of the cooking these days, but I still make him his spicy milk every now and again."

It was too sweet. Tonie wet her lip with it up to the nostrils and didn't take her face away from the glass, drinking steadily without breathing.

"Where is he? "

Josephine held her mouth still for several seconds. "Is it Wednesday? Wednesdays he does his sparking."

Tonie, not sure what she meant, blinked. "Sparking?"

"I used to be a real hand at baking and making candy. He does most of the cooking now, and he ain't a bad cook for a man, but he won't bake. A man won't put in the time to bake. I won't put in the time anymore either."

Tonie had never heard her talk so much. "Do you know where in town he might be?"

"No, you can't ever really trust a man in a kitchen. They'll stir everything up and then leave it for you to clean up."

"I'm going to look for him in town. I'll tell him you're waiting."

"I'll make more milk. You drank that right down."

"No, no," Tonie hopped up and ran to the sink; she rinsed out the glass before Aunt Josephine and her broom could get upright.

"In the Depression," said Aunt Josephine, following her to the door, "I used to make it without milk. Just honey and water and cinnamon. A little lemon juice perked it up, if you could get it. We still called it spicy milk, though."

Galatia seemed closed for the night. The streets rolled up and put away. With a car you could move fast enough and far enough to find people, but walking was slow and invisible. She stood in the dark doorway of Rogers Rexall, where the clot of men lounging on car hoods across Pike Street couldn't see her. They were the only living souls in sight, taking the fresh air in front of Nuzzi's Pool Room and Cold Beer. Big guys with beer bellies blocking the sidewalk, letting out thick laughs and hard-to-understand gestures. She knew them; they had all been a few years ahead of her in school: one of Eddie Salerno's married brothers, a Riley boy, Johnny and Frankie Gallo, sons of Fat Frank who owned a small mine. She came at them in the dark like a little commando, scurrying across Pike Street and approaching obliquely, then stopping suddenly as if it had just occurred to her they might know,

"Listen, I'm looking for someone."

The biggest and most bearlike stirred. "Is that Lee Scarlin?"

"No, Tonie. Her sister."

"Her little sister? Hey, I'm Frankie Gallo, I used to go to school with her."

"Up to first grade," said one of the others.

"Naw, Frankie made it to second before they threw him out."

"Nobody threw me out, and I never flunked out either. I quit when I had enough."

They were a pack of animals, but she had always got along great with animals. "Has Joe Bob Farley been here tonight?"

"Joe Bob Farley!" said Frankie. "What do you want with him?"

The others said: "That's her business" and "Well it sure wouldn't be mine" and "Naw, Joe Bob's okay."

Tonie's ears began to get warm. These were the real bums, she thought, not good for anything but weighting down the sidewalks. She didn't care if they did laugh.

Frankie Gallo said, "I guess he's down at Waterbridge Alley."

"What's down there?"

They all said different things and laughed: "The bridge." "Salerno's warehouse." "Roe Pickett's place."

Tonie didn't trust them, especially not enough to turn her back on them and hear them make like hyenas at her expense. She turned to Frankie because he seemed kindest-hearted. "Lee always talks about you."

"Oh yeah?"

"She used to talk about the time you threw the chair at Miss Pickett."

"I never," said Frankie. "I never threw anything at any teacher. I just broke it in front of her, to scare her."

"That's why they threw him out of school."

"They threw me out, but Miss Pickett, she knew she had pushed me too far. She made them let me back in."

"She called him retarded."

"I never minded her calling me a bum, or lazy, or useless, but she didn't have any right to insult my intelligence. She was out of line."

"I never liked Miss Pickett much," said Tonie.

One of them laughed. "Some do and some don't."

"Listen," said Frankie, "you ask Lee if she remembers me."

"I know she remembers you, she still talks about the chair."

"You ask her again. She was good looking for a smart girl."

Tonie backed away and Frankie raised his voice.

"You hear? Ask her if she remembers me, Frankie Gallo!"

She went to Waterbridge Alley, looking for one of Joe Bob's drinking nooks. To him, she thought, Galatia was a sort of pasteboard facade concealing alleys and stairwells and bridges to drink under. She thought of going back and saying, I'm not really looking for Joe Bob, you know, I'm sick of someone irresponsible like a drunk. She couldn't recall why it was Joe Bob she was looking for instead of, say, one of the high school boys, Eddie, or even Frankie Gallo himself. Joe Bob is just for sex, she told herself, pleased by the hard-boiled sound of it. But of course she knew all the while it was something else. She just couldn't recall anything else good about him. She had given up on Waterbridge Alley and started toward home when she saw his shadow ahead of her on the grade school hill.

She ran, invigorated by her annoyance. She really was sick of Joe Bob Farley. How dare he let her wander around town alone all night? "Joe Bob! Where were you? You've got a suit on!" She hesitated at the smell of sober dry cleaning.

He only paused long enough to see who it was. "Are you spying on me, Tonie? Because if you are, I don't like it." He walked with great purpose and none of his usual meandering looseness.

"Listen, Joe Bob Farley, don't get nasty with me. I've spent this whole blessed evening traipsing around town looking for you. I've been to Nuzzi's and I've been to your house. I was just down under the bridge—"

"I go out on Wednesdays."

"That's what Aunt Josephine said. Are you sober?"

"Like me better drunk?"

"Maybe. And you didn't say you were busy tonight." He lurched to one side and fumbled behind someone's garbage can and came back drinking from a pint bottle. "You should have told me you weren't going to be home so I didn't go scare poor Aunt Josephine."

"Can you shut up a minute? I've had all the women jabbering I can stand for one night."

"Who are all the women?"

"If you don't know, why did you go looking for me down there?"

"I told you, I went everywhere. The people at Nuzzi's said to look for you on Waterbridge Alley—"

"Jackasses."

He was still moving too quickly, heading out North Avenue toward home. She had never seen him so sharp, with straight edges, blade edges.

"You're a different person, Joe Bob." She was so interested in the change that she wasn't even angry anymore. "Are you always like this sober?"

"I had a bad time. And I don't like it when people accuse me of things. I'm a free man. You really don't know who I was visiting down there?"

"Is there a whorehouse? In Galatia?"

He started laughing so hard that he had to stop walking, and while he was stopped, drank again. "You really don't know? I figure when the boys in Nuzzi's know, the whole town knows. I always supposed you knew too. She knows about you all right. And lets me know what she thinks about it."

Tonie breathed shallowly. It was the one thing she had never expected, a rival for Joe Bob. "You're dropping me for someone new?"

"New? Tonie, I've been going to her place every Wednesday evening since May of 1950."

"May 1950! That's before I was born! You've had a girlfriend since before I was born and you never told me?"

"Your daddy knows well enough. She goes and confesses to him."

"Someone from church then. Who is it?"

"I can't tell you."

"You said everybody already knows!"

"That's not the same as telling. She always wanted it kept a secret. She has never been exactly proud of me. Not since I didn't finish college."

They were beside the wall now, under the giant pines in front of the grounds of his property. Tonie was extraordinarily awake, as if she had found what she had been looking for all evening, something to do, a mystery to solve. "Tell me, Joe Bob. How can I get jealous and all that stuff if I don't know who she is?" She thrust her hips in his way. "Come on, Joe Bob. For all I know, it's my mother." She pulled his hips toward her, rubbing his with hers, making him chuckle, working her hands into his shirt, pulling it out of his pants to feel the loose skin over his ribs. He was leaning her farther and farther back over the wall, and suddenly he lifted her off her feet and rolled both of them belly to belly over the wall and under the bushes, over the knotted roots. She pulled his bottle out of his jacket pocket. "Tell me who it is or you don't get it back." He grabbed her hand with both of his, holding her body down with the weight of his thigh, and took a leisurely drink. A car passed on North Avenue. She was excited by the cold ground, the roots pressing her back. He laid the bottle aside in a nest of moss and began to pull off her sweatshirt. "You get undressed too," she whispered, "I want to feel your chest." She unbuttoned his shirt, tugged his undershirt high so flesh would touch, but he was in a rush, using his hand to give himself force, using his hands under her, lifting her by the buttocks and

106

to her surprise, her guts were responding, quickly, heavily, of their own volition, without elaborate play, almost against her will. The tight ball rising like a bubble in honey, expanding thickly, bursting slowly, leaving a tingle on the surface of her belly, her cold thighs. She was surprised by the way her body took over and carried her with it. And when they were quiet again, she was wakeful and alert. Eager for what would come next.

"Oh, God, I'm tired," he said into her breasts. "Women wear you out at my age."

"Go to bed then. Aunt Josephine is waiting up for you." She wriggled back into her pants, pulled her sweatshirt down.

Joe Bob put his head in her lap. "I suppose it would be better if I told you. I never meant for you to be in the dark."

About what? she wondered for an instant.

"It's Roe Pickett. I've been with Roe off and on since we were in high school. But I told her it was all over. I said you weren't ashamed, you didn't refuse to look at me if I'd had a drink—"

"*Miss Pickett*? Honestly? She was my science teacher. She was everybody's science teacher. She's as old as the hills!"

"Don't start insulting her, Tonie. She deserves a lot of respect—"

"I'm not insulting anyone. I just never imagined Miss Pickett— doing it with anyone."

She felt infinitely cheerful, imagined Miss Pickett furious: Joe Bob Farley, you aren't worth the powder it would take to blow you up!

He said, "I shouldn't have been so mean when I saw you. But she was hard on me. I thought, goddam it's starting again with another one. Tonie is going to try and run my life too. But from now on, you can have my life. Wednesdays too." He kissed her lap. "Let's go in and I'll make you some cocoa."

"Cocoa okay, but no spicy milk. Aunt Josephine is under the impression I like it."

"She'll go to bed as soon as we go in."

He would walk her home through the field later if she wanted, and they would get dew on their feet. He would do anything she wanted. She wondered what he did for Miss Pickett. "Is there anything to eat in there?"

"Saltines and Velveeta."

She hoped Aunt Josephine would sit up awhile with them. "So you would give up Miss Pickett for me."

"If you want me to."

"I'll think about it."

She imagined saying, Look, what I really need him for is coziness,

Miss Pickett. You can have him for love. I like to sit around and hear him talk. He is always the same. He walks me home in the fog, even if he's drunk. But I really don't want him for love.

When her period didn't come, she was mostly embarrassed to think what it might mean. She smoked more. She took swigs of Joe Bob's whiskey. She tried to will a certain fullness in her abdomen into cramps. She tried through mindsweight to wrench the bloody nest loose, but the vague shiftings never tightened into pain. The period didn't come.

She was at Farleys', and Joe Bob had taken Aunt Josephine outside, but Tonie obstinately refused the sunlight. Even the patch of sun on the floor of the room made her wince. It pointed up the yellow in the streaked old sheets, it glinted off the hedgerow of Joe Bob's bottle collection marching along the baseboards. It glared on the lithograph of old-fashioned children gamboling on tiny feet.

Joe Bob said that the old picture had always been in the room where he slept. I hate it, said Tonie; Look at their sappy little smiles. I guess I just like children, said Joe Bob. Tonie said, I hate children; I hate childhood; and adolescence hasn't been so great either. He went out then, saying he didn't like to see her smoke so much. I'm quitting, she said. I'm finishing this pack and I'm quitting. When I make up my mind to do a thing, I do it.

To make quitting easier, she smoked cigarette after cigarette, collecting butts in the ashtray cradled between her thighs, and ashes in her mouth. Today everything was suffering. Church, she thought, seizing on a reason. No wonder I'm in a mood, after going to church. Why she had gone was another matter. She had told herself that she had as much right as anyone to appear in public. Even if she had been sleeping over at Joe Bob's.

She wondered who knew. Did Mary Katherine and Uncle Earl know? She doubted it because at church Mary Katherine had given her a big hug and told her she looked wonderful. It's because I washed my hair, Tonie said. Her mother had practically been in tears; her father with perfect slim dignity had passed his eyes over every part of the congregation and had not seen an atom of Tonie. But to make up for his cold ignoring there was Miss Pickett in the choir box, eyes fixed on Tonie. You should have seen the looks she was giving me, she told Joe Bob, and he said, Let's not talk about Roe, that bridge is burned as far as I'm concerned. But Tonie felt they were too powerful for her, you couldn't mess around with Miss Pickett, and her father could make her disappear anytime he wanted to.

All that danger was more than equaled, though, by this weight crouching on her chest. Maybe my period isn't really late, she thought, maybe I just lost track. "All right," she said aloud, "this is it. I'm going to sit down with a calendar and I'm going to figure it out."

But she didn't need a calendar. She could suddenly see the receding days and weeks. Left school on a Thursday, Everett's funeral was Friday, Joe Bob for the first time a week after and that was five weeks ago. All the information had been filed and organized in her mind waiting for this moment.

Grimacing she laid aside the ashtray and ground her fists into her abdomen, not to hurt herself, just telling her organs to beware, the giant was awake. She had, of course, never been late in her life. Her body had a purring regularity that she used to boast of when her friends complained of bending-double cramps, iron pills, debilitating flows of blood. She had a nearly invariable twenty-nine-day cycle, an hour of discomfort, a day of heavy flow. The healthy, conventional, dependable, inexorable dumbness of her body: This happens, that happens, therefore the following must happen. Why must it happen? Her breasts sweated where they lay on her ribs.

She imagined the consequences. Her father's frozen fury, her mother taking the blame. Joe Bob all happy and promising to stop drinking. Nudges of elbows at Nuzzi's. Worst of all the possibility that incipient motherlove was already flushing the systems of her body like a widespread cancer. She would begin to spew at the mouth with talk about women's organs, women's offspring. Baby rashes and gynecologists.

As she fingered her rib cage, her belly, the answer came to her. She would go to Lee in New York, and Lee would know where to go to get rid of it. Lee would have the phone numbers and know the laws. Had there been something in the paper? It was legal in New York now, wasn't it? Lee would be with her when she started to bleed to death. A vast well-being spread around her. She knew what to do for the next hour, for the next day. She would tell everything to Lee. Tell about Joe Bob. She figured she would vomit from terror and shriek that she didn't want to die, but while she screamed. Lee would take care of the details like a mother.

She put her church outfit back on Joe Bob waved from the corner of the garden. Tonie squatted beside Aunt Josephine. She loved the old woman's ability to be still. If you didn't look at her mouth, you could think it was a mummy or a doll made out of a wig laid on a wooden darning egg.

"Nice day!" Tonie shouted.

Aunt Josephine pointed up. The hill was completely green now, and wind patterns constantly shifted the grass. Some children and a dog passed along the ridge, the dog leaping the tall grass like a rabbit.

"All summer they go by, twice a day sometimes. Children, children."

"That's the path," said Tonie. "It goes from Tank Hill to your orchard and then on up to the rock quarry. We used to play up there too."

"Where do they go, all those children?"

"Maybe it's always the same ones."

When she was a child, she had known what to do every day after school. Get the blue jeans, get the dog, go up on the hill. Look for horses.

Joe Bob wiped his hands on his handkerchief and came towards them, politely putting his shirt back on. He had been very polite lately, very sentimental, always wanting to hold her hand. Sometimes she thought she liked Aunt Josephine better than she liked Joe Bob. She supposed Aunt Josephine must have something to do with him being a drunk now, but she could never blame old people. They were so finished. So impressive that they could still sip tea and swat flies. You could be easy with old people.

Joe Bob squatted close to his aunt and looked at Tonie. "You look good today."

"Get a good look, you may never see me in a dress again."

He grinned. "No dress is fine too."

"Good, I'm glad you think so, because you won't have me around to corrupt you much longer. I'm going to New York to visit Lee."

The change went over his face very slowly. "Is something wrong?"

She leaped to her feet. "Why does everyone think that anyone going to New York—" Aunt Josephine bent over to catch the excitement—"that anyone going to New York is in some kind of trouble. I'm going to visit my sister who is smart enough to have gotten out of this stupid town."

"Do you need some money?"

Including her savings account and the bond Everett Wright left, she decided she could afford to be proud. "Not unless you want me to buy you something."

"I've been to New York City. Nothing in any city I want—until you get there."

"Oh, Joe Bob, I can't stand that sentimental stuff!"

"Hey, Aunt Josephine, Tonie's going on a trip and she says we're not allowed to miss her. She's going to the big city."

Aunt Josephine gave Tonie a long look and then sniffed and narrowed her eyes, turned her face away.

"I'll be back, Aunt Josephine. I don't like big cities either. I couldn't live without a hill to climb."

"I may be dead too," said Aunt Josephine.

He walked her around the house to the driveway and slipped his arm around her waist. "Don't stay away too long."

"Why not? You'd never notice. You've got Miss Pickett to court. I know you went and saw her last week because Aunt Josephine told me."

"I wasn't sneaking. It's just harder to let Roe down easy than I thought it would be."

"I hope we aren't all giving one another diseases."

"Don't talk like that, Tonie. I'm ready to start a new life with you." He had shaved this morning; his chin was softer than his upper cheeks and his eyes were crinkly. Sun and shadows from a multitude of new leaves speckled the two of them. "If there's ever any trouble, Tonie, you know what I mean, I'd marry you in a minute. I'm free. I'll marry you any time you say. I leave it up to you."

She glanced past him at the house: at this moment in sunniness and green, not looking deserted, but appearing to be truly a mansion set against her hill. And what would you do here with your whole life before you? Can the vegetables he grows in his garden? Have sex six times a day? Grow babies? What would you do anywhere?

"Have you noticed?" said Joe Bob. "I haven't had a drink yet today. That's because of you. I can change."

She recoiled from growing and changing. She had thought Joe Bob would hold still for her. "Oh Joe Bob, you don't want me. I won't wash dishes and I refuse to have babies and you'll be drinking again within the week and we'll have fights." He was reaching for her. "You'll be brutal and try to hit me and you know how it will end up? I'll get a gun and shoot you and then where will we be?"

His hands were all over her face, choking her with the odor of earth, of their bodies pressed on the bed. She let him stroke her cheeks and her ears, and ruffle the skin of her scalp until she had had enough, and then she kissed him good-bye.

Chapter 7
John

John lusted after these moments in his life when he was alone in his office. He had hospital visits in the afternoon, and the phone might ring at any moment, but for now he had this wonderful silence of morning light, and his girls were coming home this evening. Even if Lee's influence had not gotten Tonie a job or a decision to return to college, he was still looking forward to seeing them. He thought with love of a delicious bite-sized Tonie, Tonie as she used to be when her little hands always seemed to be outstretched to get hold of something to hug or something to eat. He had been good with babies. People commented on it. Babies are easy, he used to say. I put them to sleep by practicing my sermons.

He decided on a family dinner to celebrate Tonie's return. He imagined it without sound, everyone bathed in white light, food being passed, each one serving the next one. Gradually the sound came up, but never so loud that you could hear the words. A choral piece for laughter.

He decided to add Family Responsibilities to the no-thank-you letter lying before him on the desk. He had been drafting it off and on for a week, not eager to let it go. It was a job offer. His secret hobby, to which there were no witnesses, not Vera, not Mary Katherine, was applying for jobs all over the country: teaching positions in tiny Baptist colleges, chaplain in hospitals. He even inquired into military service from time to time. He made his applications and often had interviews offered, but this was only the second time there had been an actual call based on nothing but his resumé and references. A prison in Montana invited him to become their Protestant chaplain. He assumed it must be a miserable place if they made the offer without meeting the applicant. He imagined a vast gray big-sky, a long stone wall with turrets, gray earth: a grim cleanliness. A world with no elderly ladies, though. Sometimes he had too much of the ladies, aging roses and giant peonies. And Hebert Shinn was an old woman too. But a low-paying isolated job in a tiny prairie town with winters at thirty below was of course a job for losers, preachers who couldn't speak in public, pastors who philandered.

It was not that he could not have left Galatia if he had wanted to. There had been calls, but never a chance again like Parkersburg. He should have been allowed to go to Parkersburg. He cherished the memory of himself as he was then, drawing young people to the church, building the educational building. Then the shadow, the taint of spoilage. He didn't draw the crowds anymore. People were used to him. The old people especially would vote for any project he wanted, only he didn't have that many projects anymore. The price of their support, the cost of having Galatia as long as he wanted it, was never to unplug the telephone, to be available to hear them complain equally about church finances and arthritis. Some of them limited their time; Hebert Shinn still had the funeral home to attend to, Gladys Shingleton was scrupulous about having something particular to discuss so she wouldn't appear lonely and pathetic. But Emzie Wright could talk for an hour on end and never draw breath.

Her legs were bothering her, the swollen feet, and she was having trouble breathing. "Oh Preacher!' she said, her voice wavering, the groan starting as low as a stomach growl. "Oh Preacher. It seems like Mary Katherine does nothing but gallivant from morning till night."

"Gallivant," said John.

"She is never here. I don't know what I would do if it wasn't for the telephone. What if I was to fall? I'd just lie in my agony till she got back. Where does she go all day long?"

He didn't listen too closely. It had been the same legs and feet swelling thirty years ago when he boarded in her house. Perhaps she was more querulous now that Everett was dead.

"The boys are at school—what does she have to do? She runs around for the pleasure of it."

He let Emzie talk on and on and toyed with his letter to the prison in Montana.

He was just waiting at the light to cross the street when Bill Rogers called him from the door of the drugstore. "Did you go to my house?" said Bill. "How's everything up at my house? Nobody up there is speaking to me."

Bill was grinning so widely that John almost took it as if Bill were a good friend making light of a personal problem, but there was something else in his manner, something had been sanded off. "Very well, I'd say. Ruthie is almost as good as new."

"I don't want to talk about Ruthie. Nobody has any conception of what she's been through except maybe me. Not her mother either." The smile was sucked away rapidly. He's crazy about Ruthie, the wife had said, he talked about killing himself if anything ever happened to her.

"Ruthie's a wonderful girl, Bill."

"I mean it, I don't want you or anyone else talking about my daughter. Talk about your own daughter if you want to carry tales."

John thought that maybe Bill had been drinking. They had always got along before, without any particular sympathy. John had no interest in the crowd Bill and Ruth ran with: the landscaped fieldstone houses on Elm View, the cocktail parties on the patios. They didn't participate in church activities. Then Ruth started calling him after this business of Ruthie running away, latched hold of him, demanded visits, cried every time. The girl was sullen, whining for cold drinks and new record albums. If Bill was drinking, it would hardly be a surprise. They were self-pitying, self-indulgent people.

Bill leered. "And how is my little woman? As I was saying, she doesn't talk much to me."

"Ruth's fine. They're both better every time I see them. Things will be back to normal in no time—"

"Normal! Nothing normal at my house is normal!" Bill had begun to be loud. "What do you know about normal at my house?"

John waited, giving himself plenty of time to find the right way of handling this, but he waited too long and Bill pressed his face closer to him.

"And how is your little daughter, Preacher? And how's your little woman?"

"Vera's fine. We're expecting Tonie and Lee both home tonight."

"Tonie's all right is she? Been to New York has she? Listen, John, you go calling on all the ladies, don't you? How is Roe Pickett these days?"

"She's fine as far as I know."

"I'll tell Ruth you said that. It'll break her heart, make her cry, but don't feel too bad because everything makes Ruth cry."

"Maybe she's unhappy."

"She's happy, although it's none of your damn business. It makes Ruth happy to cry. That's normal for us, you see. I only cried over my little girl, though. Would you cry over your little girl?"

What John disliked about the Rogers family, Ruth and Ruthie as well as Bill, was that they seemed to need an audience for their feelings. He had heard a lot of grief, seen a lot of people break down, and he knew performers when he saw them. The girl lounging on her bed with dungarees and boots on, drinking a forty-eight-ounce Coca-Cola, and eating a Mars bar. You'll get fat, he joked, and she said, It doesn't matter, nothing matters anymore. And the mother fluttering here and there with tears streaming over her cheeks saying, Oh you don't mean that, she doesn't mean that! And he did not feel so neutral about Bill either, to be honest with himself. Not since the night of Vera's play when Bill had laid his big arm on Vera's shoulder and left it there.

"I always thought you preachers were too special to have family problems. I always thought you preachers pissed cologne, pardon the expression."

He said, "I'll talk to you another time, Bill," and started across the street again.

Bill followed him. "This is normal for me. You hear? Hey, Preacher, tell Vera that if she wants a house call, I'll be happy to oblige. You hear, Preacher?"

He concluded in the end that there had been no good way of handling it. It had been an attack, and the best thing was clearly to get away and not go back to see Ruth and Ruthie. What had Bill meant bringing up Roe Pickett? And had he really made some kind of a pass at Vera? John had been shocked at the way they all gathered around her that night, teen-aged boys and old men alike. The principal and the county superintendent of schools. John had stayed in his seat in the auditorium as the people crowded around to congratulate her. She had on a new dress, blue, with folds of shiny material fitted to her waist and behind, a deep cut neck with a blue rose. Every time she moved, a different plane of her body gave back light. He understood why they gathered around her, why Bill Rogers put his arm on her shoulder, but he wouldn't go up and join them. It was her moment of glory, he told himself, but mostly he didn't want to go up and only have a share of her.

She still annoyed him with great regularity, her sneakiness. The way she hadn't told him Tonie was going to New York to visit Lee. But for all that, he felt that they had together passed through their darkest valleys.

He touched her hand as she cleared the table, made her pause just a moment. "It's nice to have you back."

"You mean from the play?"

"You were pretty wrapped up in it." He didn't enumerate the nightgown days, the papers-all-over-the-den days, the 3:00 A.M. leaps out of bed to write down an idea. "It was a good play too. I enjoyed it." Many things pleased him tonight: a big cake for dessert, the girls coming home. Vera's back as she worked at the counter. "I saw Bill Rogers today. Bill and Ruth are fighting again."

"Those two! No wonder Ruthie wanted to run away."

Vera's cake had fluffy pale icing that swirled artistically. She held it in front of her and frowned.

He said, "Ruth was a runaway herself. Did you know she ran off to marry Bill? She gets me to come over there to counsel the girl, but she's the one who wants a shoulder to cry on." Ruth always wore short flowery shifts with ruffles around the bottom and pink leather mules. Vera went barefoot around the house or wore old wool socks for slippers. "I think she's terribly lonely."

"Well, Bill sleeps with everyone except her. That's what people say, anyhow."

"I sometimes think she asks me over there—"

"Listen here, John, look at this." She set the cake down in front of him like a birthday. "We don't have anything else for dessert, but I was saving the cake for when the girls get here. What do you think?"

"I can do without dessert."

"No, you want it. You always like dessert. It doesn't matter if part of the cake's gone. Lee will probably be dieting anyhow. I just never know the right thing to do. I wanted something special and festive when they came in."

"Save the cake! For heaven's sake, Vera, I can wait for my dessert till they get here."

"No, no, I should have made something for you too. Look, I'm already cutting it."

The big cake wedge lay in front of him, fat and selfish. He had always been possessed by a secret, dirty, almost sexual craving for sweets. He and Mary Katherine used to eat nickel cakes out of the old Preacher's store-church for breakfast. He had no resistance to the way icing between layers seeps into the texture of the cake.

Vera propped one knee up against the table and rested her coffee mug on it. "So you think Ruth Rogers flirts with you."

"I didn't say that"

"I think the best thing that could happen to Ruth would be if you or somebody took her up on her offer."

"What is that supposed to mean?" He decided he didn't like the shadows of the Rogers family lying around his house. He wasn't going to say anything else about Bill. He reached over and touched the calf of her leg. He was addicted to her, he thought, the way he was to sweet cake and strong coffee.

"Don't, honey," she said. "I'm thinking."

He said, "Why do we have instant coffee for supper? Why don't you ever brew coffee for me anymore?"

"I do, in the morning."

"Why not for supper?"

"Because I'm lazy. I'll brew some now. I'll put the pot on." He should have stopped her, meant to stop her, but let her fill up the electric pot.

She murmured, "Let's see, there's the ham, and Mary Katherine gave me a big bowl of potato salad, and there's the cake, and a lot of ice tea in the refrigerator. That should be plenty if they're hungry when they come in, don't you think?"

He shrugged, closed his eyes, letting himself be surrounded by her small clatterings, the soft closure of the refrigerator door, the rush of water. It did not matter so much anymore that she was a bad housekeeper, as long as she made a cozy nest of kitchen noises for him. He had been denied a mother; he felt a great debt of attention was owed him.

A strangely distant and inappropriate car door impact, far to the front of the house. There were light voices, scrapings on the porch. He and Vera bumped shoulders passing through the kitchen to the hall. The door opened, they were here, Tonie and Lee. For an instant he could not distinguish one from the other, or either of them from the babies they had been. I'm glad it's a girl, he thought, a girl will be tender. No one ever had more beautiful babies, more beautiful girls. He was hugging the prodigal Tonie, groping for Lee and Vera at the same time.

They began talking all at once, adult women with interchangeable pie-wedge faces, enormous eyes. How did you get here? Was the bus early? Why didn't you call us to come and get you. Let me take your things. So glad to stretch my legs.

Tonie was better, he could tell at once. She had decided something, something had happened to her. Lee was a puzzle, though, nervous, wearing bizarre green leather sandals that laced up the leg. New York, he thought. The three of them together formed a full organ chord lingering in the air. "How good it is to be together again!"

Lee gave a little laugh, not in the same key as the chord. "It's not just us, though. Tonie brought a friend."

"Somebody drove us down," said Tonie. "We got a ride from Pittsburgh, and I told him he could probably stay overnight here."

"Who is it?"

"It's a brand new friend of Tonie's. She just sort of found him in the Pittsburgh bus terminal. We sent him out to buy gas while she finds out if he can stay." Lee was pacing in front of the sealed fireplace. "He has a Volkswagen and a guitar and no place to go. He thinks a college education is irrelevant."

Tonie was sending up a screen of cigarette smoke. "I don't care if you don't want him to stay. He's nothing to me."

"They're just friends," said Lee.

It was strange that he had expected the discord from Tonie, and here it was Lee who was irritating him, and so soon too. He said, "Is that thing you're wearing a dress or a tee shirt?"

"This is the longest I have, Daddy, wait till you see my short ones."

Vera said, "If he drove all the way down here, the least we can do is offer him a bed."

"Oh yes, of course. It was just that I had wanted to be—by ourselves, just family."

"I'll send him back," said Tonie. "I'd be just as happy without him."

"Now she's happy," said Lee. "Now that she's back in Galatia."

"Bad as this town is, it's better than that city. As soon as the bus got on the Pennsylvania Turnpike and I saw a hill, I started feeling human again."

"There's nothing wrong with New York. You just had a bad experience there."

Vera made a little noise. "What happened?"

"I don't like it, that's all. You never see anyone you know."

Lee's hands flew around like angry birds protecting their nest. "Of course not. You can look at eight million faces and not recognize a single one because you don't know anybody who lives there!"

"Did you see the sights?" asked Vera.

"The sights! She wouldn't leave the apartment!"

"Isn't it dangerous?"

"I'll never get used to it," said Tonie. "People talk harsh."

"Am I harsh?"

"Yeah, you too."

"I'm harsh!" Lee had the floor; she threw up her arms, appealing to the gallery.

"Take it easy, Lee," he said. "Take it easy, Tonie." Lee was high-strung, Tonie probably was right. New York seemed to have done something to Lee. There was a line for a sermon in his mind: These times have been hard on our daughters. On our children. He was confident, though, that Lee would quiet down.

The car pulled up outside, and boots stomped on the porch. The intruder was hardly taller than Tonie; he had the long hair, of course, and a certain thickness around his middle that suggested his pants and tee shirt were likely to separate. His hand was sticky.

John didn't like it. It was not what he had planned. You never get what you expect, that must be one of the chief laws of the universe. "Well," he said to the boy, "what do you do?"

The boy was definitely overweight; sweat seemed to form on his face as soon as he was spoken to. "I'm right now out of work," he said.

"Looking around for a college for this fall, are you?"

Vera and Lee glared, but Tonie didn't seem to care. She sat in the chair farthest from the rest of them, making smoke and more smoke. Vera and Lee gathered in close on either side of the boy, protecting him, giving him their attention.

The boy said, "I'd like to be a songwriter, but I've been looking into electrician's school too."

"Electrical engineering? Yes, there's always a need for a good electrical engineer."

Lee said, "Be a songwriter. I've never met an engineer I liked, or an electrician, either."

Vera said, "I went to the University of Pittsburgh for a while."

"I sort of live outside of Pittsburgh." He had an ingratiating stupid smile and no eyelashes. Vera attempted to talk about Pittsburgh, but it seemed she and the boy had never been to any of the same places. They all got quieter and quieter

Tonie said, "I'm hungry."

Vera slapped her thighs. "Oh I've got all kinds of things in the refrigerator!"

"I've got a craving for a Burger Chef hamburger."

"She couldn't find a place in New York that made hamburgers to suit her either."

"Hey!" said the boy, leaping to his feet far too eagerly. "Let's go get hamburgers! We'll bring some back for everybody. I'll treat! Mrs. Scarlin? Reverend Scarlin?"

"But I have a refrigerator full of food!"

Tonie ground out her cigarette. "My parents won't let you give them anything. Let's go."

When the two of them were gone, Vera said, 'That's how it's going to be. She won't stay in the house for ten minutes. We couldn't even sit for half an hour together."

"How could we be together when she brought her boyfriend?"

Lee said, "I was certainly impressed by Daddy's performance."

"What did I do?"

"You get the alienating-young-men award."

"I talked to him!"

"You made fun of him."

Vera said, "I think I'll go slice some ham."

Lee didn't offer to help. "Well, Daddy, here we are. You never have thought much of our boyfriends, have you?"

"I trust your good judgment to triumph in the end."

He remembered Lee's real self, her gentle smiling self as she had been when she worked in the office for him: a horseshoe of golden light caught in the top of her hair as she bent over addressing envelopes.

Her triangular face lifted to his.

She curled up around her legs. "Poor Daddy. I expect we'll always disappoint you."

"I was just thinking how proud I am."

"Don't. I can't stand it. I can't stand this whole thing. Mama has been sneaking around behind your back like you were senile or something. She thinks she's protecting you. I can't stand it when people pretend they know what's best for other people. I wish I smoked, I'm so nervous. I told Tonie I couldn't stand it. I told her to tell you, and she said she wasn't going to be the one to start trouble. I said, 'He should know and you should respect him enough to tell him and if you don't I will' and she said for me to go ahead. No one ever takes responsibility!"

Lee went on and on, and he nodded sympathetically, working on the beginnings of his sermon. How we have failed the children of this decade.

"Daddy," she said, "Tonie was in New York to get an abortion."

He managed one more understanding nod, and then he could feel the shaking begin with his hands. "Your mother knew?"

"Sure. A lot of people knew or figured out."

He could feel a black wave coming at him, but Lee raised a hand and stopped it a little longer, let it gather more force.

"That's not all, Daddy. There's a little more. You don't know who she's been going out with since she's been home."

"One of the high school boys."

"Joe Bob Farley."

At first the name didn't mean anything to him, and then the face popped to the top of his mind amid other things, dirty bubbles. Roe Pickett's silence, a look from Mary Katherine. Bill Rogers grinning and laughing: I thought you preachers pissed cologne. He found himself watching the drunk touch his baby daughter with his damp fingers, and he realized that all these other people were watching too. But that's not Tonie, he thought; something had happened to Tonie.

The knowledge spread around him like pee in your bed. He had got caught in a place where voices were laughing at him but too far away to make contact and fight his way out.

"Vera!" he shouted out of darkness. "Vera!"

She came running with a plate of ham. "Oh no!" she said. "Lee, you had no right—"

He was trying to place himself, fumbling for the lights. "Who knows? Tell me exactly who knows?"

"That's right, Daddy," said Lee's voice off to one side. "Plan a strategy. That's first; find out which flank is exposed." Lee was laughing at him; he could not see her, but her laughs hit him like splashed acid. He could not see, so he left the women in possession of the house and ran away.

It helped to be in real darkness; he could distinguish better which blindness was real. He started for the church first, but changed his mind and went to the dead end of High Street instead, through the barbed wire and into thigh-high weeds, and after thrashing through them for a little while lay down and looked straight up into a moonless sky.

It helped that there were no stars either and that the legs of his pants were wet through and now his shirt was getting soaked.

He throbbed from running.

Everything helped. Some clouds shifted and he saw one star.

He heard his name spoken in the old Preacher's voice and knew he was about to get a sign.

John, said the old Preacher's voice in his head, You've worked this vein long enough.

He said, If I leave now, it will look like I'm running. They'll all think I can't face the church.

The voice said, Go to Montana.

He lay until his breathing was entirely quiet and his body grew cooler and the star closer. There was no more; the message was over, but it could not have been more clear. What Galatia thought, what the First Baptist Church thought, was not to be his concern anymore. He was to take up a duty to men who weren't free. To free his daughter too. He would in turn be free of Hebert Shinn's shock, Bill Rogers's leers, Emzie Wright's disapproval. It made him calm deep in his stomach.

He decided that he wouldn't tell anyone quite yet. He had plenty of time, once he had officially accepted the job. He would live on the strength of his secret for a while.

He was a man alone on a wide windy plain, able to see in all directions, and thus whenever anyone came at him, he would have plenty of time to mount his defense.

Chapter 8
Lee

All the time she was in Galatia, Lee had dreams that took place in two cities, a dream New York and a dream Galatia. In the dream New York buildings were made of wood; there were porches on every floor and lines of wash hung across the porches and between buildings. The other, the dream Galatia, seemed like a suburb, or sometimes like a ghost town out West, a flat treeless place with low houses at great distances from one another. Houses, roads, and sky were yellow; there was no overweening heat, but no shade either; she was always exposed, out in the open. In the dream Galatia she was weighed down by a terrible conviction that the dream was waking life. She would stand in the middle of this yellow desert and hear her voice saying to herself: You just dreamed you went to the university, you just dreamed you live in New York. You dreamed it all. She was relieved to wander back into the pseudo-New York, even though it was damp and ramshackle and dangers lurked in the alleys and doorways. Sometimes she would duck into one of the dark places until some footsteps overtook her and passed on by. She felt lithe and confident, a hero, as long as she kept moving. The dream New York was an adventure, not a nightmare. The nightmare was returning to Yellow Galatia.

Lee was the last one to get up, and no one else was in the house. She wandered around with a mug of coffee clutched to her chest, finding evidence of several breakfasts in the kitchen sink. The sewing machine was set up on the dining room table. When she was a teen-ager, she used to slam the door to her room and sob to herself that she needed solitude, but now the empty house frightened her and she wanted nothing so much as to be engaged with someone, laughing or arguing politics. No one here even seemed to know the students had been killed. She wanted to say, Kent State, and now Jackson State, have someone know what she meant. Anything to bring her among the waking. She had been in such a deep sleep.

She had nothing to do in this town anymore, no friends here. She was here for the Scarlins and there were no Scarlins in the house. Where was her mother? And why hadn't she waited for Lee to go with her? Her father would have escaped to the church of course. She had a chance at a dinner theater job for the summer, she was going to act. She was never coming back here.

She stuck her head in the den where the guest Rick's sheets were still spread over the couch. His shirts were draped on her father's chair, and her father had been avoiding the house ever since Rick came. He had been sympathetic and kind to Tonie, to everyone's surprise, but he focused silent anger on the guest, the easy-chair-usurper

From the living room window she saw Rick playing catch with a little boy from down the street. Rick looking fresh and clean, his long blond hair drying softly after a shower, his face as blank and cheerful as the child's. No, not like the child's at all; the little boy was determined and taut with effort. Rick was loose and soft.

Her mother played Scrabble with Rick all day long because Tonie ignored him until after dark when she used him and his Volkswagen to go out and run up and down the highways. Lee played Scrabble with them sometimes, to help her mother. Everyone was waiting for Rick to leave. She went out and sat on the top step with her coffee mug on her knee.

"Hey!" said Rick, immediately deserting the little boy to come and sit beside her. "Nice day, ain't it?"

It was a pure West Virginia morning with the light falling from over the hill behind them on the brick houses in the valley, on the greens of the other tank hill. The sky was pale, but becoming bluer and bluer. There were no words, really. And if there were, Rick would never be the one to find them.

The little boy, already in spring tanned and wearing only a pair of red plaid shorts, called, "Hey, throw me one! Hey! Where's the pitch?"

"Want to play ball?" Rick asked her. He didn't care who helped him pass the time, Lee, Tonie, their mother. It was all the same. He said several times, thinking he was paying a compliment, that he was strung out from all the beautiful women. Lee made a face, but he took everything in good humor. The problem was that he didn't allow them to themselves. Scarlins can hardly talk to each other in the best of circumstances, and one stranger living in their den made it impossible. Rick said, "I was thinking about a picnic. Is there a place around here to go swimming?"

She made a noise in her coffee cup and pretended her mind had been so occupied with something else that she hadn't heard him. "Where are Mom and Tonie?"

"Mrs. Scarlin went for groceries. I offered to go along and help, but she wouldn't let me."

"Play ball!" shouted the little boy.

"Now I can't find Tonie. I know she's up. I've looked all over. I think she's avoiding me."

Well yeah, thought Lee. Maybe you'll finally get the message.

The boy seemed to have given up on Rick temporarily, and he tapped Lee on the thigh. "Who are you?"

"Lee Scarlin. This is my house."

"Naw, this is Tonie's house."

"Mine too."

He looked like he didn't believe her. She said, "I wish I was a kid."

"Come on and play," said Rick. "Be a kid." He leaned on his elbow closer to her.

"No thanks. I have to go clean my teeth and get rid of this cold coffee. If I see Tonie lurking around, I'll tell her you're looking for her." She moved away fast, and paused inside the door just long enough to be sure he had gone back to playing ball and wasn't following her. Then through the house and out the back door to the patio where she squinted up at the steep swell of the hill. After a little while Rastus Smith came out from behind the laundry outhouse. He wagged once, then disappeared again.

"Tonie? Are you back there?"

Tonie was lying on the ground with her feet braced against the side of the washhouse. Her arms were back to cradle her head, and between her halter top and jeans her midriff was bare and pale.

"Rick's out front playing ball with the little Salerno kid. He's been looking for you."

"I heard him. I put my hand over Rastus Smith's face so he wouldn't bark."

"That's real polite."

"Nobody believes me, but I'm tired of having Rick around. I want to have some time to myself. He tries to hold my hand all the time. He always wants to hang on."

"Well why don't you get rid of him then, because Mom and I have been entertaining him for a week for you."

"You don't have to do that. Maybe he'd leave sooner if you stopped being so nice to him."

Lee wondered what made men want to hang onto Tonie. Would she herself if she were a man? It was a ripe body, too much like her own though, top-heavy. Tonie had better bones, could take more weight. She supposed it was a body men would want to get their hands on, bury their faces in. Their mother had it too.

Lee's face had always been better, though. Or was it only better trained? Not to be sulky like Tonie. A photogenic face, a cheerful flag that followed a camera shutter like a sunflower after the light. Whenever a camera was pulled out, Tonie would duck or drop a curtain of hair.

Their mother never did photograph anywhere near as pretty as she was, either.

"Tonie, do you remember arguing about who resembled which side of the family? I photographed well like Daddy, but I had Mom's big earlobes. You got car sick like her and turned green and had to suck lemons like she did. Do you remember? The object was to pile up evidence that you were the one most like Daddy. I guess we were neither one very happy about being girls."

"Why should we be? All that happens is you get your period or else you get pregnant. And Rick wants to hold hands."

"Poor Rick. He's so patient with that little kid."

But why was she defending Rick, she didn't even want to think about him, or about being a woman, although that was closer to what she wanted. No, she wanted to get back to New York. She had to go to auditions. She had to see about getting someone to take her share of the apartment while she was away for the summer. She had to apply for graduate school. Or not. Why was she spending all this time here?

Tonie said, "If you like Rick, take him."

"Tonie, I hate to be the one to tell you this, but boyfriends aren't like hand-me-down dresses."

"He'd be just as happy with you."

"Tell him to go home. Or West. He's heading West, isn't he?"

"As long as he stays, it's nice though having someone to go to the Burger Chef with me."

"You have your other friends. Eddie Salerno."

"They're all busy. I don't mind having Rick to talk to, as long as he's here."

Without planning to, Lee said, "What about me? You could spend some time with me if Rick left."

"You spend all your time in the kitchen with Mom or helping Daddy out at the church."

"Tonie Scarlin! The only reason I came to West Virginia at all this summer is because of you. I had promised myself I would never see a coal tipple again. Something happens to us here. It's why I don't like to come back. You start pouting and whining and when I walk into this house it gets dark around the corners of my eyes and everything narrows. Do you know what I mean? And you and I had been doing so well in New York." In the dark, over Lee's spare bed, a prick of light from Tonie's cigarette ash, and Tonie's voice floating. "Why don't you come back with me to New York."

"New York makes me want to throw up."

"Oh, Tonie. Not everything?"

"The clinic wasn't as bad as I expected. They treated me nice. But I was sorry you had to spend the whole day waiting for me."

"I loved it." She had missed an audition that day, thus making it a genuine sacrifice. She had read magazines, had conversations with mothers and husbands and boyfriends. Tonie's counselor came out with regular reports: Tonie was in the procedure room; Tonie was resting and recuperating; Tonie was drinking orange juice and eating vanilla wafers. "To tell the truth, I envied you. You came out looking so clean. They really did vacuum you out."

"I liked your apartment pretty well too. And your room mates. You had some nice plants, and I liked the red paint in the kitchen."

"I liked the way we talked at night. I felt like I knew something about you for the first time in years."

The voice in the dark had told the story about a boy at Alderman-Davis, about Joe Bob. About not knowing whose side she was on.

And Lee had explained it to her, the students, the war.

She said, "Are you going to see Joe Bob?"

Tonie began to stroke and tug at Rastus Smith. She hugged him suddenly, and he struggled to his feet and wagged uncomfortably.

"He's nice in his own way. But he isn't anything to me really." Tight mouth, not wanting to talk about what she had reserved for midnight confidences. But I want to talk now, thought Lee.

She smiled at Tonie. "Sometimes I'm jealous of you. Rick follows you down here. Joe Bob wants to marry you—"

"One thing for sure is that I'm not marrying anybody. Maybe I'll get my tubes tied. I asked the doctor about it. You'd see what they'd say when they heard that, Joe Bob and Rickie."

Protection, thought Lee. Protection from doing what women do when they can't think of anything better. Protection if it turns out they go to audition after audition and find out they are spending more and more time waitressing or working in boutiques. Ending up back in some kind of graduate degree program. "What do you intend to do, Tonie?"

"I'll tell you if you won't tell anyone else. No one is going to believe me. I intend to buy a farm. I may go back to college first, but I intend to buy a farm eventually."

"I believe you," said Lee. She had always suspected that Tonie could in the end do whatever she wanted to and that she, Lee, was doomed to fail. She had a private superstition that there was a magic rope underground attaching her and Tonie, and if one of them rose, the other would have to sink back into a hole.

All I want to do is act, she thought. To get out of this town and act.

The summer dinner theater. A stage, experiences, new people to be among, fall in love among.

To hell with the Scarlins.

Tonie said, "Daddy got me in a corner yesterday and said he wants to help me if I'd just tell him what to do. I may ask him to invest in a farm for me. But he means college."

Everyone wanted to help Tonie. In their own way they were all available to her: Rick sitting around waiting to go to the Burger Chef when she was ready; Mom feeling guilty; Joe Bob Farley off in the wings making proposals of marriage. It seemed to Lee that Tonie wandered through a life-landscape rich with people bending towards her, to offer help.

"I wouldn't mind if someone worried about me," she said.

"Get pregnant," said Tonie. "They all like that."

Lee decided to give a family party. When she was in Galatia, she usually found herself waiting around for her mother to start things, to suggest a shopping trip, to say Let's call up Mary Katherine and get her over here to drink coffee with us. It was just like being little and depending on her mother to organize time, to give it life for her. "Mama," Lee would ask, "what can I do?" "Read," Vera would say. "I already finished my library books." "Play with Tonie." "She doesn't have anything to do either." Then Vera would turn off the iron or put a lid on the stew, and ceremoniously open the suitcase of dress-up clothes or drag out the old catalogues and start Lee cutting out. When her mother opened the book or the suitcase, the things inside became full of possibility. Even Tonie always seemed better at shaping time than Lee. If she didn't have anything else to do, she would declare a birthday for the dog or the parakeet and spend an afternoon making invitations and sending little neighborhood children around to deliver them. But Lee always waited for someone else to do the inviting, until she went to New York. Now I can invite people too, she thought. This was going to be the first social function she ever organized in Galatia, and she had a clear vision of what should happen. She wanted to create a perfect memory of family life, a perfect balance and harmony of generations and sexes. Her cousins Johnny and Jimmy couldn't make it, but Rick would be the substitute young man. Emzie Wright was not a grandmother by blood, but she was as familiar as one. Aunt Mary Katherine for dignity and loyalty, and Uncle Earl for his crew cut and bad jokes. Her father would be on good behavior in front of the Wrights.

She got up before anyone else to do the sweaty work, brown the meat for the pot-au-feu, wash the dishes she had left from her midnight cake baking. Then she went back to bed till they had all gone off to church. When she had the house to herself, she dressed slowly in her green smock dress and lace-up sandals, and she wove two thin braids to hold back the rest of her hair. She dressed the table as carefully as she had herself, blue linen napkins she gave her mother for Christmas once, the price tags still stuck to them. She went outside and cut a couple of early roses and some irises. She opened all the windows her mother insisted were stuck to let the damp smells from the hill mix with her simmering meats. She loved the power of tasting and adjusting, and she dashed in a little of the wine they'd sent Rick to the State Liquor Store to buy. Her mother never moved without a recipe book, and even when dinner was well underway, she used to panic and open an extra can of beans or pull out some cottage cheese just to be sure there would be enough. Lee's dinner, however, was planned in advance. She only wished she had courage to serve the rest of the wine with the meal or to drink a small glassful herself, but she couldn't imagine giving her daddy his after-church kiss with wine on her breath. A limit to what you could do in Galatia.

He came in first, his face still set in its wide open public lines. To thank him in advance for being sociable for her dinner, she kissed his cheek high on the bone near the eye where the skin is more sensitive. "How was the crowd, Daddy?"

"Not bad, not bad. Not like the old days, but it takes a fresh face for that."

"It's harder to do what you've done, isn't it? To stay on?" Usually he practically purred when she said back to him something he'd been saying for years, but today he shrugged and grinned as if it didn't matter one way or the other.

"Something smells good."

"Pot-au-feu. Pot-on-the-fire. I cooked the best cuisine of all, hearty French peasant. Except that we have to settle for Italian bread."

Tonie stepped in, already out of her church clothes and zipping up jeans. "Do you want wild flowers?"

"I already got some of Mama's roses and irises, but we could have wild flowers too."

"I'll send Rick out."

Rick stuck his head in too, jeans and striped tee shirt, just like Tonie. "I enjoyed the sermon, Reverend Scarlin! I'm not usually a sermon freak, but I enjoyed that one!"

"Let's go, Rick," said Tonie. "We're picking wild flowers. Rick volunteered to clear the table too, didn't you Rick?"

"Are you letting my sister push you around again?"

"I'm at your service," said Rick. "Both of yours."

Her mother came in last. "Well, you look pretty, honey. What can I do?"

"You can leave your dress on so you'll look pretty too."

"I always liked this dress, but it's getting old now."

"The only reason your clothes last as long as they do is that you take them off as soon as you walk in the door."

"Not when someone's coming for dinner."

Lee almost said, but you never have any guests, do you? but instead told her, "There really isn't much to help with. I'm beating up some French dressing. I guess you could wash the cucumbers."

Quickly, efficiently, Vera scrubbed. "I'm so thankful you're an organized person, Lee. Not like me."

She had taken the point precisely; that one could, that Lee could, serve something more complicated than meat loaf with ketchup sauce, but now that she was saying it, Lee didn't want to hear. "Oh Mama, please stop badmouthing yourself."

"But it's true, Lee, I always start to do one thing and then remember something else and end up finishing nothing."

"You must have finished two dozen plays and pageants. You ran a girl scout troop for years."

"Well, anybody can do things they enjoy."

"You've always hated housekeeping, haven't you?"

"I just never was good at it."

"You've always hated housekeeping. It's the one role you always sounded phony in: 'Oh I left the iron plugged in! Oh! I smell something burning on the stove! Oh the world will go up in flames if I don't get the washing done!' "

Vera shook the cucumber to get the water off. "One thing that never changes is you criticizing your mother. You've always known my responsibilities better than I have." She was smiling as she spoke, as if she were saying something light and charming. "When you were six years old, you told me I wasn't supposed to go barefooted, and when you were eight you told me you didn't like the way I sit in a chair."

"You should have set me straight. You were the grown-up."

"When you didn't approve of me, you used to throw fits!"

Lee had a brief apparition of a fury, of a time when she wanted to stuff her mother in a trunk and slam the lid, but she rejected it, she wanted her mother, she had always wanted her mother. Big strong arms and delicate wrists and hands that could make anything. What Lee always wanted was more of her mother.

Mary Katherine came in then, just in time maybe. She had brought three covered dishes, in spite of Lee insisting she wouldn't need anything extra. A mixed vegetable au gratin, a tin box of cookies, and a marshmallow salad. Lee stared at the salad with particular distaste. She intended pot broth as a soup course and a lettuce salad as a palate refresher after the entree. She swished the pale sweets and mandarin oranges and thought of dropping the bowl. "Listen, Aunt Mary Kay, I think I'm going to serve your fruit salad as a dessert, if you don't mind."

"Sure," said Mary Katherine, turning on the oven to warm her casserole as if it had been her own kitchen. "Now what else can I do?"

Vera said, "Lee didn't want anybody to do anything except herself. She's cooking New York style."

Mary Katherine said, "You'll have to forgive us Galatians, Lee, we don't know any better than to share the work. Especially kitchen work."

Vera said, "You can help wash the lettuce. She said we could do that much."

"It isn't as funny as it sounds, you two. Flavors have to be matched. With all respect to the marshmallow salad, it would spoil the pot-au-feu."

"It has wine for flavoring," said Vera.

"Oh my goodness!" They both giggled, as if wine were a racy joke, then Mary Katherine said, "I'm feeling giddy today. Good news always makes me giddy. Johnny called last night—he got the early acceptance into medical school. And that's not all, Jimmy's grades came and he got all A's except for one little B in his phys ed, isn't that a shame? For phys ed to be allowed to bring an average down?"

"That's great, Mary Kay. I'm really happy for you."

"Me too, Aunt Mary Kay."

But Mary Katherine drew her brows together, the Scarlin worry sign, the little vertical cut in the forehead. "I haven't told John yet. He's had so many things on his mind—"

Vera nodded, but Lee said, "Wait a minute, you mean Daddy will feel bad because his nephews are doing so well? Why, because his daughters are doing so badly?"

"That's not what she means, Lee."

"What does she mean?"

Mary Katherine said, "I mean you have to be careful when you say certain things to people. John is sensitive."

"Yes," said Vera "You never know what he's carrying around inside him."

The two of them with their strong jawlines, her mother's all-seeing eyes, and Mary Katherine's loyal worry. Compared to them Lee felt unformed, soft, and a little silly. She said, "You act like he might break, you two."

"Lee!" they said. "He works so hard! He takes things to heart!" It sounded like something they had been practicing a long time.

She began to doubt she could make the dinner party happen the way she wanted. You needed strong women backing you up to do things, and she neither had one nor was one. Still, she did what she could. She told them all where to sit, she had Mary Katherine arrange Rick's handful of wild flowers or were they weeds with the irises and roses. Once she finally had them all together at the table, she felt better and began to smile down on them as she served. Surreptitiously Aunt Emzie pinched an olive from the salad plate, and while that one was still in her mouth, took another. Uncle Earl and her father tried to be hearty with one another. They had never really been friends. Daddy has never had friends, she thought. Didn't I ever realize that? She wished she could magically shoot a little alcohol into their bloodstreams, get everyone loose and warm-loving. Even sentimentality would suffice.

They did do one thing together, and that was to stare suspiciously at her soup course; she passed the bread wrapped in a linen napkin and the big plate of celery and olives.

"Very nice, Lee," said her father, reaching for the salt before he tasted. "Very unusual."

"It's soup, Daddy, broth from the pot roast."

Uncle Earl said, "This little girl's going to qualify for her Mrs. degree yet."

Vera giggled. "Earl, that's the wrong thing to say to one of my girls." But Lee gave him a nice hypocritical smile, and Tonie stared out the window.

Her father stood as if he were about to make an announcement and said. "We haven't offered thanks yet."

Everyone got up except Emzie. "I'll just stay put, Pastor, it's my knees. I'll explain to you after the blessing."

They had not prayed at the dinner table in years; they lost the habit sometime when Lee was in high school and everyone seemed to eat at different times. But even before that, Lee and Tonie always said the grace. Their father saved his resonance for church. He made a short prayer now for strength in all our new endeavors, and Lee wondered if it were a prayer for Tonie.

When they got to the meat and vegetables, Mary Katherine asked for the recipe and Lee glowed and said, Oh you just toss everything in. The serving platter went around again. How fast it slid down their throats— they were eating it, her whole dinner, just like it was food. While they ate, Uncle Earl and Rick discussed hunting, which it turned out Rick used to do and surprised them all. Emzie told her symptoms to John, and Tonie and Vera took turns slipping meat under the table to the dog.

I should have given them something really exotic, thought Lee. Chicken tandoori. That would have jarred them. Out of, into. Something.

She served coffee and the three kinds of dessert. Emzie said she was taking some of each, just a little to sample. Fat had kept her cheeks high and round, and Lee had a secret admiration for the way she never seemed to doubt her right to fill up space, the worth of her flesh. Her knees had felt like there were hot needles being stuck in the back of them yesterday, she said, and today it was like the fronts were caught in a vise. As Emzie talked, Lee watched her father's face; his patience was a wonder. The look was one she used herself sometimes, a horizontal smile, uncurved, appropriate to good news or bad, if you just shook your head a little and lowered your eyebrows. She supposed she must have spent a significant percentage of her life watching his face, at church, at dinner. She had once told someone, The reason I'm an actress is that I spent my whole girlhood and youth trying to be my father. She was watching him out of the corner of her eye and saw the exact moment when he left his sympathetic trance and began to examine the plates and coffee cups. How nervously he touched each piece and brushed cake crumbs into his napkin and shook it out on his plate. He interrupted Emzie; his voice became louder and louder until it drowned out all the other conversations.

"Well, Emzie, we are all called to something, aren't we? Some of us are called to preach, and I guess some are called to suffer. Some act, some stand and wait. We all receive new calls every day. I have just received a new call myself to a ministry at a prison in the state of Montana. The Big Sky State, they call it." He looked around mildly, just checking on their attentiveness. "I want to tell you all first that I've accepted the call and I intend to take up the chaplaincy there."

There was not a sound in the room as they looked at one another to be sure they had heard the same thing. He had an expression of gentle enjoyment, as if he had just shared some mild pastoral anecdote. Her mother expelled a breathy giggle and tried a couple of twitchy smiles.

"But John—"

"It's time," he said, "to move on."

Lee thought, He didn't tell her.

"I've never been farther west than Cleveland," said Vera.

Mary Katherine frowned deeper and deeper. "Who would want to? Why would anybody want to work in a prison?"

"The challenge," said Lee. "Right, Daddy? You need a new challenge."

"Mary Katherine doesn't approve," he said.

"I don't know if I do or not. I can't believe you would do something so spur-of-the-moment"

"Don't say that, Mary Kay. I've been wrestling and praying a long time in my lonely way."

"Maybe too lonely," said Mary Katherine.

Vera had finally found a smile that lasted, and she clapped her hands. "I've always wanted to see a geyser."

Earl said, "In Montana?"

Lee began to hate her mother the way she used to hate her when she did things that didn't seem right. She remembered the bare feet and broken zippers now, the safety-pinned dresses. She remembered the summer they moved up here to High Street. She said, "He isn't talking about a vacation on a dude ranch."

John opened his hands. "I present all this as an accomplished fact for only one reason; after all these years the decision has been so difficult, the break is going to be so painful—I wanted to make it quick and clean with no turning back, I feel I owe some apologies—"

He never got to make them though, because Tonie, who had been the quietest of all, shoved her chair away from the table, pinching the dog by mistake. He howled and the chair toppled, and Tonie shouted, "What about Rastus Smith? Do you think he can take a change at his age? Do you think he can stand the cold winters? Did anyone think about Rastus Smith?"

Lee would have run after her, but Rick was closer. No one spoke until the echoes of her anger had died away. Mary Katherine picked up the chair. Lee wanted to overturn a chair too. She leaped to her feet and they all cringed. "Why didn't anyone say anything? I forgot to put out the sugar bowl!"

From the kitchen she heard them start talking again. Her father said he was due there in a month. Mary Katherine said there were plenty of prisons nearer than Montana for heaven's sake if he was determined to work in a prison. Uncle Earl wanted to know what size the town was, and Emzie announced that a prison has criminals in it.

I really don't belong here with these people, thought Lee. I'm not being forced to stay here and see how thoroughly my mother is humiliated. I'm cutting out of here just as soon as I can. The next bus. Cutting out from under Daddy. I'm cutting out of Galatia and cutting Galatia out of me, with a knife if I have to. I'll scoop it out with a spoon. Gravity seemed mysteriously, monstrously, to have grafted her onto the things of the house. She had a cut glass bowl for a left hand and a teaspoon for her right forefinger. She walked as if she were ripping up roots. A hybrid monster: enameled-on New York hair and sandals, utensil hands. Flesh sticky and eager to fasten onto things. She avoided touching people or empty chairs as she circled the table and put sugar, one teaspoonful, in her father's coffee, stirred it for him. She looked down at the empty place next to her aunt and couldn't see herself anywhere.

"A month is too soon," said Emzie. "How do you expect us to organize a farewell dinner? I'll have to call Thelma this afternoon. We'll have to work night and day."

Mary Katherine said, "You aren't supposed to complain to him about how hard it is to organize his dinner, Emzie."

"He knows how hard it is. He knows what he's doing to us. And now we'll have to get a new preacher and the new preacher won't know us, and we'll have to get used to him, and who knows what you're getting in this day and age. I think it's a dirty shame."

Mary Katherine said, "What about Tonie? Is she going?"

He glanced at Vera. "It's up to her, of course. "

"What about Mama?" said Lee. "Is she going?"

"Why, Lee," said her mother, but her smile crumpled. "Well, I think I have to get up and stretch my legs too."

The others stared after her, keeping their reactions to themselves just as they had over Tonie. It's my dinner party, Lee thought. And I don't have to excuse myself. She trailed her mother through the kitchen, into the den, where she found her standing at the east window looking up the hill. "What are you going to do, Mama?"

Vera jumped. "What do you mean?"

"Are you going to go?"

"Why, what else would I do?" Walleyed, like a shying horse.

"You could come and live with me in New York."

"What would you want with your mother in New York!"

"I'd show you things. I do already—sometimes I catch myself walking around and pretending I'm showing what I see to you. I could tell people you were my older sister. You hardly look ten years older than I do, let alone twenty!"

"Would you support me too? I've never supported myself, you know."

"Did he really not tell you, Mama? You go around worrying about not hurting his feelings, and then he made an announcement like that. Without telling you. Listen, Mama, don't go with him. At least don't go right away. Tell him you'll come when you feel like it."

Vera's face came together, closed down, her mouth tightened to nothing. There was a harsh, skinny anger living inside her too. "Just leave me alone, Lee. Don't torment me."

"But Mama, how am I ever supposed to be anything when all you have ever done is trot along after Daddy like a bird dog? How am I supposed to be something if you don't show me how—"

Vera seemed to move in several directions at once. Her face tried to smile and cry; her hands to rise and fall. In the end Lee wouldn't stand it and said, "There are no grown-ups here. There are no grown-ups in this whole house."

She could forgive her father because he was tricking himself at least as much as he was tricking the others, but she couldn't forgive her mother. Her mother's absence wrapped itself around her throat.

There was no question that she had to leave. She was taking the first bus out on Monday morning, but she had these hours to get through in the house with them, and she had no Rick to drive her up and down the highway. The house was fearfully still, her father in his chair in the den reading, her mother taking a nap for a headache. Lee washed dishes and sat on the back patio and looked up the hill waiting for something to happen. She used to think someone would come down off the hill for her, a wounded enemy soldier, the vanguard of an alien landing party. She tried to work out ways of communicating that would be completely universal. Some gesture that would have meaning to any creature from any galaxy. When it began to get dark, she decided to go out and see Mary Katherine.

She would have preferred to go over the hill, it was the most direct route from their back door to Mary Katherine's, but she was afraid, so she went the long way, through the back streets of town, out North Avenue. The fog fell early that evening and she was acutely aware of how there were empty areas between the dwellings in Galatia. I never knew this town, she thought, I knew the church and the grade school, the high school and our houses and Mary Katherine's, and in summer I knew the swimming pool and Tank Hill, but never the town. Even the sounds were unfamiliar. The dogs barking, a car with no muffler and someone inside hooted. This is Galatia, she thought, a person should be afraid in New York, not in Galatia. But in the city the streets were never so silent, and the people were never so hidden indoors. She shivered walking past the foggy fields between the Farley house and Mary Katherine's.

But Mary Katherine's was a place she knew. She had always loved the big stucco house at the end of North Avenue. It had the fields in back of it, just like their house on High Street, but never seemed isolated. She and Tonie used to sneak up on it by going through the field. They would crawl on their bellies and try to catch Uncle Earl in his garden as if he were a foreigner, a Russian peasant, or was it German, and they were paratroopers dropped behind enemy lines. The question was, could they make the house without being seen.

On this night, she spied on the living room from the porch. In one corner, so far to the left that she had to press her cheek to the glass to see, was a bridge table and Mary Katherine holding a small book up to the lamp as if she were candling an egg. When Lee opened the door, she dropped the book into her lap hastily.

"Oh it's you! I thought it was Emzie home already." She brought the book back into sight but didn't tip it enough for Lee to see the title. "She ran right over to Thelma's, to plan the testimonial dinner, she said, but first they have to inform the whole church."

"What are you reading?" Lee wanted to get away from the whole warm, angry day.

"Well, it was supposed to be Plato. I'm trying to follow Jimmy's courses. I'm already a semester behind, but that's when I get the reading lists. I'm embarrassed by how stupid I am. No, really, I am stupid when it comes to things like this. The list starts with Plato, but they had to put him on order at the bookstore, so I bought the next one in line and I'm having a terrible time understanding it. It's Descartes' *Meditations*. Do you think it would make more sense if I read Plato first?

"Day-cart. It's pronounced Day-cart."

"You see?" She dropped the book as if it had snapped at her. "I can't even pronounce his name right. I didn't start life stupid, but it's been so long since I exercised my mind. A few years back, when you and Johnny started college. I read some of his English books. I read James Joyce *Portrait of the Artist as a Young Man*, and I read Dostoyevsky *Crime and Punishment* and *Doctor Zhivago*, and Franz Kafka *The Metamorphosis and Other Stories* —those were difficult, but you could miss something and not get lost altogether."

"I never knew you read all that."

"Your mother and I read them the first winter you and Johnny were down at the university."

"Mom too?" She saw her mother with scrapbooks and dried flower arrangements and little dishes of supper leftovers and directing the plays of course, but not reading James Joyce.

"Of course she read them. We read them together and had discussions. You shouldn't underestimate us because we didn't go to college."

"Underestimate you! Aunt Mary Katherine, in my heart I think you two know everything without having to read. I read to find out answers to things you already know. I think of you as the gods and the people who were adults when you were children, like the old Preacher, they were the titans, the ones who came before the gods—"

"Maybe I should get a book on mythology before Plato comes."

"Mythology is okay but the stories don't fit together. You might want Bulfinch or Edith Hamilton around for reference." Mary Katherine made her repeat the names while she wrote them down. Lee said, "I can't help you much on Descartes, though. He's mostly interested in religion. He tries to prove logically that God exists."

Mary Katherine threw herself forward and landed hard on her elbows. "How? How does he prove it?"

"Oh, I forget the details. He starts with 'I think therefore I am' and somehow gets from that to God. Somehow. I forget in how many easy steps, but it's all supremely logical."

"I never guessed he was getting at that. The sentences are so complicated I can't seem to make it to a period. But if it's all leading up to proving that God exists! Well, that's worth struggling for. Listen, Lee, can you stay awhile? I have to talk to you about something."

"About Daddy?"

"No, no, not that. I'm so irritated with him I won't be able to talk about that for days. No, I want to have a discussion about something. There aren't many people I can talk to about ideas. Earl, bless his heart, isn't interested, and the boys laugh because I'm their mother. I can talk to Vera, but sometimes that mile from your house to ours seems so long. What I want is a real discussion where people give each other their views and learn from one another."

There was only one lamp near them, and it gave an aura to Mary Katherine's features. Lee yearned to do what Mary Katherine wanted, to forget the nonsense about Wyoming or Montana or whatever state it was that her father had decided needed his services.

"Especially tonight," said Mary Katherine, "I would like to discuss something important. I think it would clear my head. It's something I've been thinking about for a long time, even before I read Descartes. It's the Virgin Birth." Jokes and quips flitted through Lee's mind like moths, and she brushed them away, annoyed at herself. Mary Katherine said, "Descartes talks and talks about having a clear idea of something, and how that's the test, whether you can have a clear idea of it or not. So many things are muddy in my mind, so I picked out one to practice on, and it came to me after a while that I don't really believe in the Virgin Birth. Most things in the Bible are perfectly clear to me, but the Virgin Birth comes out fuzzy. God didn't need a virgin birth. If He was going to let a woman be Jesus's mother, then why not an earthly father too? That was what was clear to me. It seemed unnecessarily complicated to do it without a human father. But Lee, listen, you mustn't tell anyone I don't believe in it. Not even your mother, till I make sure. I have to be sure my idea is clear too." She sat back out of the light, then leaned in again quickly. "Now tell me what you think."

Lee felt pale and dry. Young people are supposed to shine with ideas, she thought, middle-aged aunts are supposed to have settled into stodginess. "Well, I read somewhere that the whole doctrine is based on a mistaken translation from the Greek. The word just meant 'young girl'—"

"Where? Where did you read that? Is it true?"

"Oh, I don't know—I don't remember where I read it."

"But Lee! If the Virgin Birth is based on a mistake in translation! But what if other things are too? Well, I won't jump to any conclusions, the thing to do is to clear away the mess and find out just how much I believe in, just that and no more."

Lee imagined a lifetime of chaste disputation. I'll take the pro on the Virgin Birth, she thought, just for the sake of argument. She thought of the Brontë sisters nourished by one another and books, living in a fen or was it a moor and studying German, communing gracefully with one another. She would stay with Mary Katherine. In the mornings there would be work in the dewy garden, grit on the lettuce; they would can vegetables in the afternoon, talking all the while, in the kitchen, in the cool of the evening as they walked on the hill. All their activities purposeful, to the glory of God, if he was interested.

At that moment, when she was most caught up in her thoughts, a vague background noise ended, the TV, and here came Uncle Earl, stretching and yawning, wearing his Hawaiian pineapple shirt. He rubbed both hands over his head. "I thought I heard you out here." He grinned at her; he was a pleasant man, her Uncle Earl, and he had no part at all in the Brontë sisterhood.

Lee said, "I got in such a mood today, I didn't tell you all goodbye. I'm leaving first thing in the morning."

"That's too bad. You should stay around a while longer someday. You're always in such a hurry to get back to your big city."

Mary Katherine's worry line appeared. "Are you really, Lee?"

"My dinner theater starts in a couple of weeks, and I still have to get someone to cover my share of the apartment."

"Maybe we should have a little party, Mary Kay, with some cake and a little ice cream? To give Lee a send-off?"

"All right. You go back and finish your television show, Earl, and I'll call you when the coffee's ready."

"The show's over—oh, I get it." He winked at Lee. "Girl talk. You take her advice, whatever she says. Even if I don't know what you intellectuals are talking about."

"The war, Uncle Earl. We're going to solve the war."

"Can't quarrel with that. Well, you work it out between the two of you, and then I'll call up the president and let him know what you decided."

Lee followed Mary Katherine into the kitchen and sat on the high stool as she used to when she would come out here after school in preference to going home and sometimes Mary Katherine would give her a bowl of potatoes to peel and sometimes she would just sit and listen to Mary Katherine make kitchen noises. The boys would come running in and dash out to practice sports, and she would feel sorry for herself because she wasn't anything that counted, not a cheerleader or a majorette or even a dumb pom-pom girl. I wanted to be Jimmy or Johnny, she thought, and then, No that's not true, I wanted there to be no Jimmy or Johnny, or Tonie either. And I wanted you for my mother and my mother for my aunt. She would have made a terrific aunt.

Mary Katherine plugged in the coffeepot and took out cake plates. "I'm worried about Tonie," she said.

"She'll do all right. She always seems to find someone to take care of her."

"She seems to find the wrong person if you ask me."

"You mean poor little Rick? Because if you mean Joe Bob, she says that's all over."

Mary Katherine shrugged and made up a coffee tray. "I guess so. I'm going to ask her to stay here. I have the room."

"That's nice," said Lee, thinking, Why don't you offer it to me? I might never go back, everything might get a better start.

The phone rang, and Lee continued to feel sorry for herself, not listening to what was said on the phone, enjoying self-pity and the lily flower pattern on the vinyl tiles, and Aunt Mary Katherine's feet in old leather ballet-slipper flats. The kitchen hummed and percolated as it always did around Mary Katherine. "Yes," she said, "yes, yes, my niece Lee." And then of course Lee started to listen. At first she thought it was her mother or her father calling because of Mary Katherine's intimate but irritated tone. "Lee, not Tonie. No, I don't know where Tonie is. With her new boyfriend, I would guess. She brought some boy back with her, the one at church." She glanced at Lee, and Lee tried to figure it out, something funny, and then all at once realized who it was and at the same moment Mary Katherine said the name. "Roe," she repeated it several times. "Roe, that gets us nowhere. Roe. You know I won't listen when you start that. Roe. Roe, I'll call you back later, but I won't listen to that. Roe, listen to me, I'm going to hang up now, and I'll call back later, but you know I won't listen to that.

Goodbye now Roe, good-bye Roe, I'll call you later. Good-bye." She looked weary when she hung up.

"That was Miss Pickett?"

Mary Katherine went to the refrigerator for the cream.

"I know all about her and Joe Bob Farley of course. Tonie told me, but I knew years ago, in high school. The funny thing is that Tonie didn't know until Joe Bob told her. Why did you hang up on her?"

"Because she curses."

"Miss Pickett curses! Well I shouldn't be surprised. She was always very creative with her insults in school. She used to say to people like Frankie Gallo, 'I'm going to snatch your eyeballs out, you worthless piece of dogmeat!' She didn't curse in school, though."

"She says everything to me. She calls up and I don't recognize her voice at first. She gets out of control. She calls me almost every night, Lee. But don't tell John and Vera. They don't need to have that added on. It's like a stranger calling up—she hisses some awful little scrap about who saw Tonie somewhere with Joe Bob and what they were doing—"

"Well, she's lying if she says that."

"Oh, I think she makes most of it up. Tonight she said the town is full of vultures, sitting in the eaves, waiting for her to make a misstep. Waiting to rip into what's left of her. And Tonie is a vulture for taking Joe Bob who was never anything anyhow but a piece of rotten meat. And then she started in calling Tonie names."

"She sounds like she's having a breakdown. You should get her to see a psychiatrist."

"But when you see her on the street—and when I call her back later in the evening—she's perfectly normal. She never mentions the calls."

"And you don't either?"

"Of course not! I've known her a long time, and she's always had a streak of strangeness. You know about her family—"

"That doesn't mean she isn't crazy. She used to do some pretty awful things in school. There was this one fat girl with freckles who cried easily. Frankie Gallo or one of the real dummies could miss every question, but if this girl got one measly homework question wrong, Miss Pickett would shake her finger under her nose and scream at her. And the girl would start sobbing her heart out. I mean this happened days on end."

"Poor Roe!"

"Poor Roe—what about us, the ones that were her students?"

"You seem to have managed pretty well."

"I don't know about that," said Lee, and she really didn't, sitting here in Mary Katherine's kitchen, feeling sorry for herself because Mary Katherine hadn't invited her to live with her, unable to bear the thought of going back to the house on High Street where she didn't even know if her mother and father were working something out or not by their silent sitting in different rooms.

Well, she thought, I've already chosen.

Chapter 9
Mary Katherine

Mary Katherine had been one of the first to know, long before John or Vera, at least she thought before Vera, you couldn't always tell when Vera was wrapped up in one of her plays. The late night phone calls from Roe had begun shortly after Tonie came back from college. The first time she had not recognized the voice.

"Who is this?" said Mary Katherine, suspecting pranksters.

"You don't know me," said the voice. "You only know your own blood relations."

She didn't tell Earl or John, and beneath the surface she must have recognized the voice, or at least that she knew it, because it troubled her and she kept trying to figure it out.

It called again, bitter and self-pitying: "She had everything and I had nothing but him, nothing and nothing and nothing. I thought no one would ever want such trash. I know what it's all about, I can read, you know. You always   seek out your own father. Well then that's what I want, the worst drunken trash that ever crept on the face of the earth and that's all I've ever had, but why would she want to take him away?"

"Is that you Roe?" said Mary Katherine, because no one else in Galatia would go down to craziness boasting about what they had read.

The voice said, "She's bunny fluff. These young girls have nothing inside them but little bunny tails. If they get a disease, they go for a shot of penicillin; if they get a baby, they get rid of it."

Mary Katherine had just had a whining call from John to complain that Vera had given Tonie bus fare to New York without telling him. She had seen Tonie with Joe Bob a few times too, sitting out on the wall in front of his house, just the two of them talking and smoking. It didn't look right to her, but she never would have said anything. Tonie was doing it to shock people, Tonie wanted to look bad. This is exactly what happens, she thought. This is what you let yourself in for. She said, "I don't know what you think you're doing, Roe, making anonymous phone calls, but I do know that Tonie went to New York to visit Lee and that's all."

"Oh no," it was such an evil voice. "The fluff twat went to get rid of his baby."

Vulgar language acted on her like a cold shower. "You sound like the Picketts, Roe."

The voice snickered. "Fluff twat. Fluff twat with its legs open. Easy come, easy go."

"I won't talk to you if you're going to use language like that. You wouldn't want me to hear it."

"Fluff twat!" it shrieked, "open legs!" and Mary Katherine hung up and was almost knocked over by the force of a headache that struck through her forehead like a sling of bricks. She just managed to put her casserole in the oven and slip upstairs to bed. Even lying down she had to cover her eyes with her apron against the ugliness she kept seeing on the wall, shadows from the tree outside. She kept seeing Roe who believed that whatever happened to her, she was still like her parents on the inside. Those people who used to beg on the streets of Galatia and then beat one another and their children.

Mary Katherine once saw Roe's mother pull up her skirt over her behind, no underpants, and squat over Thelma Shinn's decorative border of pinks. It's all in the home training, they used to say, who used to say that? The sins of the fathers are visited. And if so, what did it say about John and Vera, if it were true about Tonie? And if about John, then Mary Katherine was implicated herself. She hated secrets rearing their heads out of the quiet mud. She had no desire to lie, but there was mud in all the past, and she wanted to concentrate on what was good. Even with Roe and Joe Bob Farley, they had been a couple before Joe Bob got drunk every day.

She first saw Roe's craziness when they were fourteen, the summer John got her the job at Rogers's Rexall. It was his old job and she had never been so happy. It was her first separation from the Preacher, and she was learning every day. She loved that drugstore from the first time she polished the ice cream freezer and the soda fountain spigots. She cleaned the mixing blades of the milk shaker with minute care. She wiped down the gold-speckled mirror behind the counter and taped up cutouts of banana splits and identical strawberry ice cream cones in three different sizes. She never stopped working and of course Doc Rogers the pharmacist and Gladys Shingleton who had worked there forever liked her work, but they liked her anyhow, they gave her gifts, brought her supper when she worked late, insisted that she tell them if she needed time off. She was a little timid of Doc Rogers, but comfortable with Gladys and listened to every word she said as wisdom. She used to say in her mind, Gladys, you know, I never had a mother, and she imagined that if she could say just that much, Gladys would fix it for her. Make sure she had a mother. Gladys taught her about using Mum under your arms and gave her lipstick which she had to wipe off before she went home to the Preacher.

During the summer Doc Rogers and Gladys gave her more and more responsibility. They went off for whole afternoons and left her in charge. The drugstore was quiet, nothing moving faster than butterscotch syrup, everything of that slow yellow brightness, yellow lights on the ceiling, the street through the cellophane shades dropped against the sun. She polished everything twice, made a list of paper products that needed reordering, swept the whole tiled floor. There was only one customer, and that was Roe Pickett on her afternoon break from selling movie tickets. Roe and Mary Katherine had made friends at school where they ate lunch together. They were both careful students, although Roe was far more successful. She took quizzes to win and planned her studying like a general. She came into the drugstore almost every afternoon and stayed until after football practice when Bill Rogers, Doc's son, and Joe Bob Farley and Earl Wright came in. At first Mary Katherine didn't know which one Roe was waiting for—she knew it wasn't Earl because Roe knew about her and Earl, so she thought it was probably Bill Rogers. Joe Bob didn't seem like the right one. He was polite, but he dressed too well, sharkskin summer slacks when the rest of them wore khaki and poplin. There were rumors about parties up at his uncle's mansion, but mostly he was just too sleek and citified to Mary Katherine's taste.

She and Roe talked awhile about jobs, Roe was already looking for something better than the movie theater. "What I want is to get a room," said Roe. "Just like your brother did."

"But John got a room because he couldn't get along with the Preacher."

Roe said, "You think I get along with my family?" Mary Katherine was ashamed for bringing them up, but just the same it always seemed to her that Roe looked for an excuse to drag them in. "You can't imagine what it's like. I have to hide my schoolbooks or they'll use the pages to start the stove in the morning. Or worse." There was a little silence while they drank Coke and watched the door for the boys. Roe said, "John would have found some excuse to get out on his own anyhow. You can't do anything with a family hanging around your neck. I just want to get rid of mine, I don't even feel ashamed anymore. I'd never feel ashamed again unless I thought shame could kill them, but otherwise I'm just going to go on my way.

The boys came in, and Roe went speechless, turning her face down to her drink. It was funny that Mary Katherine could talk to them more naturally than Roe could when Roe was so sure of what she had to say most of the time. Maybe, Mary Katherine thought, it was because she had an older brother.

They were damp and clean from the showers after football practice, cracking jokes and filling space, seeming bigger than usual, and they didn't speak at once to Roe or Mary Katherine, being very involved in discussing whether a particular small but quick sophomore was going to make first string. They three, of course, were sure of their places, the Galatia front line. Earl and Bill built thick and tall, Joe Bob even taller, but light.

Bill sat down first and slammed his hands on the counter. "Set 'em up, Mary Kay. Large cokes, plenty of ice. Where's my dad?"

Earl grinned at Mary Katherine, and Joe Bob took the stool next to Roe, who stared resolutely ahead. He leaned close and whispered under her fringe of pin curls. He never would have done that if Gladys or Doc had been here, nor would Bill have been so loud. Mary Katherine frowned at Earl. "Doc Rogers is out."

"On second thought," said Bill, "make mine a cherry coke. Joe Bob, Earl, what'll you have?"

Joe Bob was still whispering into Roe's ear as if he were a movie lover, and Roe wasn't saying a word, wasn't stopping him. Without looking up, Joe Bob said, "Lemon coke."

Mary Katherine didn't think things were as they should be. She would have given a lot for Gladys to come back or the dentist to drop over or anyone who would make Bill and Joe Bob get in line. John should come in, she thought. John would ask them how the team was shaping up, and everything would smooth out and become pleasant. She said to Bill, "You know you have to pay for the cokes."

"Sure," said Bill. "A lemon coke, a cherry coke, and a plain coke. Large with lots of ice."

"You better show me your money."

Bill's long soft cheeks blotched. "You'll get paid."

She didn't say anything.

"Come on, Mary Kay."

Joe Bob mimicked Bill. "Come on, Mary Kay." Even Earl gave a little snicker.

"Earl Wright," she said, "sometimes I think you're just the tail those two wag."

"Even if I didn't pay," said Bill, "it's none of your business Mary Kay. It isn't your drugstore, it's mine."

"It's Doc Rogers's drugstore, and it's Doc Rogers's rule that nobody gives anything away except him."

"And Gladys," said Joe Bob.

"It's my store," said Bill. "If it's my dad's, it's mine."

Mary Katherine felt a surge of power because she knew she wouldn't yield. They could beat her and torture her but Doc Rogers had made his rule and she would keep it. "I can give you free ice and carbonated water and that's all."

Joe Bob said, "See, Bill, she's saving the profits for you. That's your college education in that fountain, and Mary Katherine isn't going to give it away."

Bill said, "I'll come around and serve myself."

"We'll see about that." She leaned her weight on the hinged section of the counter. Don't let that boy push you around, Doc Rogers had said. Bill will walk all over you.

Earl said, "Aw, Billy, leave her alone."

And Joe Bob said, "I've got some change. I'll pay for the stuff."

Bill stared Mary Katherine in the face. "It's my daddy's store."

"Hey!" said Joe Bob. "I'm buying! Set 'em up, Mary Katherine! Bill is just being stubborn because he's used to Gladys giving him stuff for free. Hey, Bill, we could wait till Gladys gets back. Gladys always gives stuff to Bill, he's her favorite; she wishes he was her boy."

"Shut up about Gladys."

"But even if Gladys was here, I'd pay, Bill, because your dad needs every penny he can get, to send you to college, what with two families to support—"

Bill gave Joe Bob a little shove in the shoulder. "Shut up about Gladys."

"Say, Mary Katherine, where is Gladys? Did she and Doc go off together again? I hear they go out every afternoon, just about—"

An explosion seemed to throw chunks of bodies all over the floor and Mary Katherine had an impression of fan blades falling from the ceiling, stools overturned, and merchandise swept from the shelves. "Stop it!" she screamed, running from behind the counter, leaping over Bill's legs just in time to rescue the magazine rack.

Bill was on top of Joe Bob shrieking, "Shut up!" and pounding Joe Bob's back and shoulders, but Joe Bob wouldn't fight back, he just laughed and protected his head.

"Earl! Make them stop!"

Earl shrugged. "Joe Bob's been asking for it all day. They'll get tired soon. They're friends."

"They're going to break something!" Mostly she was in terror of someone coming in and seeing that she had let things get out of hand. Where's Johnny? she thought. Where's Johnny, he always comes in about now.

But it did seem that Bill was slowing down, that he was getting tired of pounding on Joe Bob's back, but that was when the other thing happened, the thing that no one was expecting. Roe Pickett had been like a statue, looking straight ahead as Joe Bob whispered to her, ignoring the teasing between the boys, the tension. Roe had been perfectly still in her cotton blouse and cotton skirt, her anklets and powdery home-polished white sandals. She didn't scream or threaten now, but suddenly leaned over the counter and pounced on the ice cream scoop and came careening off her stool at Bill. She struck him hard in the temple and then brought the scoop down hard again on the top of his head. He grabbed his ears and rolled off Joe Bob and Mary Katherine screamed at Roe and Earl grabbed her. Roe's face was completely twisted, completely baring her ugly teeth. She twisted her head and tried to bite Earl with them. "Roe!" screamed Mary Katherine, "Roe!" But Roe didn't stop twisting and fighting until Joe Bob got up and took the scoop away from her. He took her by the shoulders and pushed her toward the door. She backed out and finally made a noise. "Son of a bitch! Son of a bitch, you sons of bitches!"

"What is going on?" said Mary Katherine. "What's the matter with her?"

Joe Bob and Earl knelt down beside Bill, who seemed to be gasping for air or else sobbing and had his knees tucked up under his chin. There was an ugly strawberry mark on the side of his face. He moaned. "I think I blacked out. Have I been here long?"

"Not long," said Joe Bob.

Mary Katherine got a paper container of Coke and gave it to Earl to give to Bill. In silence they helped him sit up and drink. Mary Katherine refilled it, and when he had drunk again, he rubbed his hands on his face and they helped him up.

"Maybe he needs a doctor," she said. "It was his head."

"Nah," said Earl. "You should see what happens in football practice."

She could hardly wait for John, she trusted that John would explain it all to her. She said, "I couldn't believe it, Johnny, she cursed all of us, Joe Bob too. She just got as ugly as anything and cursed a blue streak."

John nodded. "She's to be pitied, Mary Katherine."

"But how will I ever be able to be friends with her after that? It changes the way you look at a person after something like that."

"Well, it's in all of us. There's something in all of us."

"I don't even know what Joe Bob was teasing Bill about."

Looking back, Mary Katherine could still feel sorry for herself at that moment. It wasn't a matter of right or wrong, but she felt so sorry for herself because she had thought Roe was a friend of hers, a person like herself. She had thought Gladys Shingleton was the one person she could finally trust to look up to.

"Why," said John, "he was teasing Bill about Gladys and Doc Rogers, of course. I thought you knew. Doc and Gladys live together like man and wife—not in the same house, but they live together like man and wife."

Mary Katherine wanted to throw up. It was a can of worms, a pit of vipers in the daylight. Everything illuminated, Doc and Gladys making certain private jokes, things said between Gladys and Bill, How's your mother, Billy? Oh fine, she's fine. Never when Doc was around. Any number of things that had been mere little ordinary events began to choke her.

John said, "Doc and Mrs. Rogers haven't got along for years, long before Gladys came into the picture. She won't give him a divorce, though."

"Why didn't you tell me?"

"I don't like gossip. Besides, I thought you'd know. This is Galatia, everyone knows everything."

"I don't know anything unless you tell me."

"To be perfectly frank," he said, "I was afraid you'd do something dumb like refuse to take the job."

"You knew all about it and still convinced me to work here?"

"Convinced you? Are you saying I tricked you?" John turned completely white. It was the beginning of their first fight.

"What about right from wrong?" she said, "How is a person supposed to know right from wrong if they start liking wrong people before they know they're wrong?"

Then he called her a stiff-necked little ignorant Pharisee and demanded to know if she thought he had corrupted her by getting her a job in here and she said that wasn't what she meant, but it wasn't enough to stop him from saying he wasn't going to stand around and be told he corrupted his sister, and he stormed out and she was left alone without even the comfort of thinking John would be coming soon to make everything okay.

In terror of the landslide of dirt, she began cleaning again, polishing things she had already polished, the counter, the pie case. She found a little crust of dirt around the brand name bolted to the milk shake mixer and scratched that out with a toothpick. Doc and Gladys came in together, arguing in their genial back and forth way about which summer it was that there was a rabid dog up on Robinson Run. They were so homey and familiar that she almost cried out Stop it! Stop teasing me! They had brought her a glassine bag of oatmeal cookies from Saint Anthony's Altar Society bazaar, and after Doc went back in the pharmacy Gladys said Mary Katherine looked peaked and wanted to know if it was her time of the month and said she should take it easy the rest of the day.

Every minute Mary Katherine passed without standing up and pointing her finger and quoting Bible, without taking off her apron and walking out, the less disgusted she became and the less chance she had of keeping herself from liking them again. She made some prayers in her head that they would see the light before it was too late, that Roe would get control of her temper and not go too far with Joe Bob Farley, but the older Mary Katherine got, the more convinced she became that those things that disgusted and pained her in other people were really none of her business. She forgave Gladys and Doc before the day was out, and she and Roe went on pretty much as before, because two days later Roe just walked in and sat down and started drinking Coke and talking, without a word about what happened.

But with John she always took a long time getting over it. She couldn't ever say for sure that she really got over anything with him. Years would go by and something would happen, and it would be as if her new anger were starting on top of the old.

It was three weeks since he had announced he was walking out on Galatia, and she could not get over it. Lee had gone, Johnny and Jimmy came home and went off again to their summer jobs; Tonie's boyfriend drifted away. Emzie had her testimonial dinner and now was lying around the house prostrate with fatigue, moaning that the headache powder had passed its expiration date and would Mary Katherine please go to town to get her a fresh packet. Mary Katherine, through all this, was still angry. Gladys used to say, Don't let the sun go down on your anger, and she and Doc Rogers never did. And with Earl and the boys Mary Katherine didn't either. But with John, with the old Preacher, when she thought of how many suns had set on those angers, it was like an empty overturned ruin of a town behind and around her. As far as she could see, the only improvement she had made over the old Preacher was that she could separate her anger from the wrath of God. That blasted disastrous village was the one where she had lived with the Preacher. Compared to it, the real town of Galatia was a vision of grace.

This is the day, she decided, I'm going to town for Emzie's medicine, and the sun won't go down before I talk to John. She was going to say, Johnny, forgive me. I've been blaming you for a dozen things, for hurting Vera, for hurting the girls. For walking out on me. I haven't given you a chance to explain, and I don't think I want an

149

explanation now. I just want there to be peace. Maybe after you retire, you'll come back here and we'll all be together again.

Feeling much better she walked along Pike Street. She was wearing a green leaf print skirt and blouse set and stockings. She always wore stockings to town, even if she was only coming for a quart of milk. It meant something in Galatia to have once been a scraggly little girl who didn't even wear socks in the summer and now to be a woman with a sense of what was proper. Pike Street was utilitarian, not beautiful, a street of three-story brick buildings from the turn of the century. The best buildings, the churches and the big, porched frame houses, were all set on the side streets. No boastfulness in the appearance of Galatia. A town where you did your commerce without needing ornamentation. Except for the geraniums around the street lamps. If you wanted beauty, all you had to do was lift your eyes, and there in any direction were the hills rising, and no matter how high up someone had stuck a farmhouse or a water tank, there was always some dense tree-nubby hill above.

She went in the drugstore, completely remodeled by Bill after Doc's death. She missed the way it had been; Bill had gone into debt to buy the store next door and tear down a wall. He put in air conditioning before anyone else in town, fluorescent lights instead of the old hanging fans. People gossiped about how much he put into the place, but they gossiped about everything Bill did. He seemed to attract it. People thought he was a playboy and still remembered how many times he had dropped out of college before he finally got his B.S. and then how long before he got into pharmacy school. They remembered the parties he and Joe Bob used to throw at the Farley mansion. There were still stories that he came back from a druggists' convention with gonorrhea and treated it himself. That he was the father of his counter girl's baby, but that one was hard to ignore because the girl told it herself. Now there was this sad business with his daughter Ruthie who had run off with the older man and had the car accident. John said she was sitting around that brand new fieldstone house wallowing. John said they all were. But Mary Katherine had always respected Bill for the way he treated Gladys after Doc died. How he kept her on and paid up all the back quarters on her Social Security that Doc never bothered with.

He was sitting at one of the little tables in the back, wearing his professional smock with his large fair-haired arms crossed over his chest. Mary Katherine waved. He said, "Hey, Mary Kay! Gladys was in here again this morning. She asked about you."

The counter girl was leaning on her elbows smoking. "Big as life. I said, 'Gladys, what the hell are you doing in here when the doctor says you couldn't hardly get out of bed?' and she said she needed the exercise. Can you beat that? Bill drove her home after she sat awhile. She was worn out, just as white."

Mary Katherine sat down too. "I don't get over to see her as often as I should."

The girl said, "Well, how could you? A person has their own life to live."

Mary Katherine never knew whether to ignore the girl or not. She said, "Gladys is the closest thing I ever had to a mother. You'd think I'd find a better way to pay her back than dropping by her house once a week. I keep thinking I could take her to live with me. I've got plenty of bedrooms."

Bill rolled his eyes. "How about Earl's mama?"

"We'd manage. Emzie keeps talking about getting her own place one of these days. "

A customer came in for the girl, and Mary Katherine followed Bill back to the pharmacy gate and stood halfway inside while he put pills from a big bottle into a little one.

She said, "No mortar and pestle these days."

"We don't do anything these days but rake up the money."

"That wasn't what I meant, Bill Rogers. I just get nostalgic for the drugstore the way it was when I worked here."

Out of his long morose face he flashed her a grin. "You know what, Mary Katherine, you and I should have got married. I never did have sense to know what was good for me. I shouldn't have let Earl get a step on me."

Mary Katherine definitely ignored that. "I'll probably never get Gladys to come and live with me. I'm already going to have Tonie Scarlin after John and Vera leave."

"She says she's staying with you, does she?"

"She is staying with me."

"Well, it's none of my business. I've had my wild times, but I always tried to keep it out of sight."

Mary Katherine closed her ears to him. She did not choose to inquire further. If there was something new, if Tonie had done something else. But I've really had enough, she thought. I'm going to go get Gladys and take her to the Barbeque for lunch. Or take one in to her if she's tired. Let Emzie open her own can of chicken noodle soup. Then I'll go find John. But as though she were not to be allowed to forget, as soon as she walked out on the street, she saw Roe Pickett. Roe always dressed to come down the street too. She used to say, there's no room for error for a person like me. People would as soon say I was getting sloppy as not, people would as soon say I was starting to drink if I ever so much as let my slip hang. Her hair had just been done and her white pocketbook matched her shoes. She didn't smile when she saw Mary Katherine, but made a gesture to wait,

"Well," she said, "I'm going to Europe. I went over my checking account and my savings account, and I decided to go anyhow. I've been to Canada and the Caribbean, but this time I'm going to Europe. I'll be in debt for the rest of my life."

"Oh, Roe! I'm glad you're going!" She thought, Why didn't John go traveling instead? Why does he have to go so far away?

Roe said, "Don't think I'm fooling myself. I don't expect anything is going to change."

"But you'll have a good time, Roe, that changes things."

"At the price I'm paying I'd better have a good time."

Delicately, dangerously, Mary Katherine said, "Things do change, Roe, over time. Little by little." She meant the calls; Roe hadn't called since that night Lee was over.

"I'll trot all over Europe and come back here and they'll still talk about me like I was dirt. Well, at least the trip counts the same as a postgraduate course on the county salary rate."

"That's not why you're going!"

Roe peeled back her lips, and Mary Katherine almost exclaimed because her teeth had been repaired. It must have happened very recently.

"I'm going to get away from him, it's no secret. Ask anyone. And the funny thing is, I have that niece of yours to thank."

Again the crawling on Mary Katherine's neck. "Well, I hope Tonie is out of that too—"

"She's not. Don't you know she's staying up there with him? Everyone knows. The mailman sees her, the grocery boy. She's living with him."

"No," said Mary Katherine.

"You can say no. But she is. And I say thanks to her. I might have sat around waiting another twenty years. I'll be away till school starts, then that will occupy my mind."

The question was, did John and Vera know. No, the question was whether or not Roe was making this up, and it didn't sound like it. No, she thought, the real question is whether or not to interfere. "Why is she making it hard for herself?" said Mary Katherine. "I don't understand what she's doing."

Roe said, "She's just like me at that age except she'll try to get by on her looks."

Mary Katherine could have gone to the church, but she drove up to High Street instead, telling herself she might catch both of them that way, but hardly even lying to herself. John would be at church. Their house had always seemed to be on the edge of a cliff to her, with the roofs of the other houses piled down below and the hillside rising so steeply behind it. The blinds were drawn in the front room, the way they had been for the first year they lived up there, when Vera said she was in hiding. Vera had said, That front room has nothing in it but boxes, and I don't want some neighbor up on the porch peeking in and telling the world I'm not unpacked yet. They had eventually bought a living room suite, but now the room was full of boxes again. Boxes and boxes. There had been panic in Vera's voice when they spoke last on the phone. She walked through, calling Vera's name as she went, and found her on the patio in the back, sitting in a canvas sling chair wearing blue jeans and drinking iced tea.

"You caught me," said Vera, who looked extraordinarily good. Her weight was down, her hair all tied back, barefoot. For some reason you always thought of Vera at her best barefoot. "At least I have my clothes on. I think it's a sign I'm getting the packing under control. I went the first two weeks in my nightgown. The same nightgown. I finally threw it in the trash. Let me get you some tea—"

"No, stay there. I have to tell you some things."

"Oh dear," said Vera.

Mary Katherine sat on the wall that held the hillside back. it was tipping in further and further these days, but that suited her because she could stretch out her legs, lean forward and see Vera, sunk back in the lounge chair. "I had some errands in town today," she started, "but the main thing I had in mind was to find John and apologize, set things straight. We've been very cool to each other for the past few weeks."

"John is cool towards everyone these days except the people in Montana when he talks to them on the phone. Or the moving people. Anybody who has anything to do with Montana. He overflows with brotherly love. He's expecting a lot out of this move."

It chilled Mary Katherine and she thought, Supposing she didn't get to make her apology, if it was an apology. She and Earl were already planning a camping trip west next summer, and they'd visit with John and Vera of course. After all that time passing everything would have worked itself out, surely.

She said, "Not to beat around the bush, I heard today—this may be gossip and it may be true—but I heard that Tonie is living with Joe Bob Farley."

Vera started to sit upright, then dropped back again. "I don't think so, Mary Kay. She's been sleeping here. I don't think—I mean—there's a limit to what she'd do, I think. She pretends that it doesn't mean anything to her that this is Galatia, but it's like I used to pretend the old harpies checking up on my housekeeping didn't mean anything to me either

"Then she is back with Joe Bob."

"I don't know. I'm packing."

"Vera!"

"I really don't know. I'm a bad mother in the best of times, but when I'm packing I'm completely hopeless. Don't think I'm not worried—I think about her all the time, Mary Kay, but I don't know what to do. I walk in the bathroom and see her toothbrush which she makes a point of leaving in a puddle of water on top of her travel case as if she didn't have a slot in the toothbrush holder. She leaves her depressing little messages all over the place, and I feel like crying, but I don't know what I can do because it's so late in the day and because John has decided we're moving to Montana. What am I supposed to do, beat myself for being a bad mother?"

"For one thing, get her moved into my house before you leave."

"But what are you going to do if she doesn't come in? Sometimes I think the best thing would be if she did move in with Joe Bob."

"Vera!"

"And get married. How about if they get married? I can't think of anything to do for her. Lee offered for her to come up there— you've offered, and she sits up in her room waiting for something to happen. What am I supposed to do, stay here with her instead of going with John?"

For an instant Mary Katherine almost said, Yes, I hadn't thought of that, but it's the best idea yet. Stay here until you're sure of her and then go. Let John wait. She was shocked at herself for not choosing John. Would I rather have Vera than my own brother?

She got up to go. "I told you what I know. What I heard."

Vera smiled. "You always do your duty, Mary Katherine. I've always envied you your duty."

But her duty had been her satisfaction and even her pleasure, at least since the Preacher died. Until maybe this moment, because she didn't think she was going to be able to make her peace with John after all. She said, "Where is he anyhow?"

Vera waved her hands. "Everyone is looking for him, and no one can find him."

Mary Katherine decided to take Gladys out for lunch.

Chapter 10
Vera

She is walking on some railroad tracks across a trestle, far above the valley floor. Dragonflies hover; sometimes a bird passes; you can see the thick tufty green of the treetops through the spaces between the ties.

She hears the train whistle as it approaches town, and she hurries, although there is more than enough time to get across safely. She tries not to take steps that are too big for the little girl with her, but the little girl stumbles, and her foot slips between two of the closely spaced ties. Quickly she stoops to reassure the little girl and free the foot; it seems they could get it out easily if they took the shoe off, but the little girl's ankle blows up fat and salmon pink, and in spite of sawing the foot back and forth, they can't get it free.

The train whistles at the junction, less than a mile away. She hears it, but it still sounds far off, as do the little girl's wails, several in quick succession, the same pattern as the train. Only ten yards behind her is a platform with a water barrel. She hears the chugging of the train now and has a glimpse of black through the trees. In a few seconds they will see the teeth of the cowcatcher head on, and the engineer will try to stop, but he will be going much too fast. It is already too late. Like the ankle, the little girl's face is swollen and ugly with screaming. She begins to back away to save herself. The little girl spreads her arms to beg. She knows that the right thing would be to keep the little girl company. The locomotive is on the trestle now, bristling with smoke and metal, whistling and screeching as it tries to stop. The clamor is distasteful; the little girl is distasteful. She is furious with the unfairness of the right thing to do.

Reluctantly she starts back. Below the air seems thick as water, and some birds swim by without a sound, dipping and swooping. The green tufted bedspread would like to enfold and mother her softly. She makes a perfect three-step approach and dives off the trestle, somersaulting slowly over and over in the green air, feeling the sun.

The sin they accused her of over and over as she was growing up was selfishness. When she lived with her aunt, her aunt accused her; when she lived with her mother, her mother accused her. Only her grandmother never accused her. Her aunt and her mother's lips became little white rosettes: Vera, you are the most selfish child that ever lived, you never think for one minute not one second about anyone but yourself.

My Self, thought Vera. My, how selfish, my center of myself. It swelled inside her, growing faster than she did, and clamoring. She took a sort of pride in its monstrosity, and when her own daughters hunkered on the floor sullenly refusing to pick up their toys, she never wanted to discipline them, but to give in, at once, unconditionally: to feed them and make them grow strong enough to contain the ravenous self. But that would be a Bad Mother. A selfish mother looking for an easy way out.

Sometimes people praised Vera for her church pageants or her choir singing. They praised her for taking on the senior class play at the high school, and she dodged their praise as if it would scald. She didn't want anyone to notice how she treasured these selfish successes. Perhaps even above her family. With the pageants she had always had the excuse at least that they were for the church or for Lee or Tonie. But the high school class play was only for herself; it was like getting lost in a good book, a complete indulgence. She had been so completely centered in herself that there had been no room to see Tonie slouching from room to room balancing an ashtray on top of her coffee cup, wandering and smoking. Or rather, she had seen it but stored it in her mind to look at later. She had gray curtains in her head with which she could divide off her space and conceal things for a while. And even when she knew unmistakably that Tonie was full of rage and confusion, and sleeping with Joe Bob Farley, she had said to herself, It's almost time for the play, I'll pay attention to her just as soon as the play's over. She let Lee take the responsibility, take care of Tonie. And when they came back from New York and Vera saw that Tonie was still alive—she wanted them to leave her alone again. She wanted to say to them, Look, when I was Tonie's age I was already married, and by the time I was Lee's age I had both of you. She wanted to say to Tonie, Stop lying on the floor with that boyfriend draped over your thighs. And I don't want to hear Lee tell me what a bad mother I am. I know it, I know it, I already know it.

She thought her badness and her selfishness were as visible as a glorious bloody sunset. She could not understand why others hadn't given up on her when it was so obvious. The time she chased off the people from Parkersburg had been nothing compared to this desertion of Tonie.

"Sometimes," she said to Lee, "I wonder how I could have brought children into the world in the first place."

"Thanks a lot," said Lee with her new city wit, "but don't despair, maybe we'll die young."

It wasn't what she had meant, of course, and why was Lee the one who always misinterpreted her. "Why don't you grow up and have some compassion?"

"Did you have compassion for us when we were growing up? You never taught us the things we really needed to know."

"I didn't know enough myself. I was ignorant."

So she avoided discussions in order to be left alone. Sometimes she thought about the boy in the play. She was infatuated with the boy. He was a friend of Tonie's, and sometimes she made up little stories pairing them. She made Tonie smile and the boy smile and made them hold hands and kiss and tell her they were getting married and coming to live happily forever in her house with her. They would have a baby like Tonie's baby should have been. Like her own babies. I always thought my little baby girls would always love me and smile the way they did then. When I put my face close to their faces, it was like touching a flame to a candle: light, light, aglow! When I took my face away, they dimmed.

The boy Eddie Salerno was not an actor until Vera lit the magic candle. According to the teachers, he had leadership qualities; the principal directed Vera to him as the customary spokesman of his class. He was tall, a varsity athlete like all the Salerno boys. With the deep voice and even temper that impressed adults. He had the role of the ghost in the play because no one could imagine a class activity without him, and he shambled through his part with responsible gravity. At the second rehearsal Vera said, "Wait a minute, stop everything," and mounted the stage. "Look, Eddie, I know it's supposed to be a comedy, but at the same time, those girls are really scared when they see the ghost." He nodded, good boy. "Eddie," she said, "we need some tension. Do you play basketball this relaxed? Can't you make your body tight? Do it without glasses. You can hardly see these people—you don't believe in them any more than they believe in ghosts." She took the glasses off his face, and the others tittered.

Eddie said, "What would a ghost be thinking about?"

A flush of pleasure, her first genuine request for guidance. "I think the ghost would just be doing what it had no choice but to do. Ghosts are very bound up in their fate."

Without the glasses Eddie was even more handsome and more distant. He came across the stage while the girls chattered without seeing him. He was supposed to bump a table, they would hear it, turn and scream. Eddie paused in the middle of the stage as if he were just then noticing the girls. He moved slowly, as if puzzled, and the girls ran out of lines, but their silence was charged with expectation and Eddie's sleepwalker advance. His face was still, but his hands took on consequence, he carried them poised outward; they might have been feeling the way, or they might have been threatening. He bumped nothing, he was far too graceful to knock things over, but the girls finally turned anyway, unable to bear the tension of waiting, and they leaped up spontaneously, and his fingers spread as if to encompass them, and they screamed and ran. Eddie stood with his hands out toward the audience, as if inquiring into the meaning of the scream.

Vera wanted them all to cheer, but instead, they gathered around him on the stage, especially the boys, and punched his arms: Are you still with us, Eddie? He nudged the air a little with his nearsighted face, over the heads of his friends, and Vera passed him his glasses. She was just beginning to congratulate him when his eyes came into focus and found hers. He was for half a second tuned entirely to her approval "That's what we wanted," she said, and at that instant knew how to rewrite the play, knew what she wanted for the actors, for the audience. Eddie gave her the ending for the play. At the end of each scene Eddie's face would rotate toward hers: Yes? Yes, Eddie, yes.

In the rehearsals of her play, she had been everything, and they were all extensions of her, but the performances belonged to them. She could not shout anymore, Stop everything I just had an idea! Her most important function was wearing a chain of safety pins on her dress front. Just before the final act, Eddie's shirt button was torn off. While she worked at his shirt, he dropped his forehead against hers briefly. But they all did something like that. They would come and stand near her or touch her to get her attention. She felt their bodies around her and pinned them all together. She made arrangements for cases of Coca-Cola and tubs of ice for the cast party. She kept her head full of dreamy mists and made herself a pool of calm in the midst of their play.

Afterwards of course there was praise for her. It was a hot night and most of the crowd left quickly. The janitor turned off half the auditorium lights, and she stood on the stage apron. Behind her there were the kids setting up their record player; the whole stale auditorium was sweet and damp with success. Congratulators came to her then, mostly men who stayed close to her the way the kids had, as if she had something they liked to be near. The principal hoped sincerely she would take on the play next year too; he thought there might even be some money to compensate her for her time. Eddie Salerno's father said he forgot it was his son Eddie up there. Bill Rogers stood beside her for a long time too, and when she asked what relative of his had a child in the play, he said he had come because of her.

After that it was harder to hold onto dreaminess. Her skull seemed very thin, and this warm bath of praise and touching was really a storm about to break. And inside the curtain was rising: her guilt for being here while Tonie was there.

She had called New York three times before the performance. The first time Lee reassured her; it was a clean wonderful clinic, full of doctors and nurses. She didn't believe Lee's confidence, strained her ears for what was hidden in it. It's legal in New York now, said Lee. Very professional. How do you know they're doctors? How did you choose that one? Later she talked to Tonie herself and Tonie said she was fine, they had just got back to Lee's apartment and she was going to take a nap. You sound groggy, said Vera. They had given her Valium; she giggled through the whole operation, she said. She called up a third time later and Tonie said she'd been up for hours, she had only slept forty-five minutes and she and Lee were making spaghetti.

Vera didn't believe a word of it; she went home and sat by the phone, waiting for that call, waiting to hear that Tonie was bleeding, that something ugly and brutal had happened at the last minute. Vera had an instinct that if she could sweat enough and suffer enough, and above all not sleep or think about the success and praise, then the phone call wouldn't come.

She promised herself that when the play was over she would concentrate on the house. She planned to organize the drawers and throw out the half-empty jars in the refrigerator. For the girls' homecoming she would prepare several days' meals in advance and really get the house organized. It was easier somehow to keep the house when the girls were home. She had fewer doubts about what was important. It always used to be so obvious: Buy school shoes; make dentist appointments. Dinner every night. In those days her guilt had been greater when she got involved in one of her projects, but on the other hand, she knew how to make up for them afterwards. She straightened drawers now and tried to imagine what to do for Tonie. What would they tell John? Should she discuss rightness and wrongness? She was sorry to have lost the grandchild baby; but that was selfish, of course. If Tonie had died on the operating table, she would have been selfish enough to think that was to punish her, Vera. It had been easier to be a child. Then someone else took care of all the punishing. All that was expected of you was to be quiet, to play by yourself, run errands. Someone always told you what to do, what was bad. Easy to know when you were bad, that way.

The day Lee and Tonie came home, she baked a cake. Patiently she formed decorative waves in the icing with the flat of a knife blade. She pinched off a little icing here and there, worked the waves up again with her fingers. This caused a roughness in the troughs between waves which she tried to smooth by running her thumbnail along the edge of the plate where extra icing had flowed. Suddenly she allowed the thumb to slide up the side of the cake, pulling off icing all along the way. Slowly, fingerful by fingerful she denuded her cake until in the end she was forced to make a second batch of icing. She felt great satisfaction that no one would ever know how she had mutilated the cake, even with her upset stomach.

When she was very young, she had developed the skill of taking bits and slivers of a cut cake in such balanced quantities from one side and then the other that no one ever knew she had been foraging. She thought of eating cake in the dark as stealing, even when it was her mother she was living with rather than her aunt. For years she wrote letters to her mother calling her aunt a mean old maid and begging her mother to take her, but when her mother finally did remarry and set up housekeeping, Vera was already thirteen and in her heart so bitter that she secretly refused to call the succession of company houses in company towns her home. Shortly after she went back to her mother, her aunt moved to Alaska and Vera started writing letters to her, complaining about the stupid people in the stupid towns where they made her live. What a sneaky nasty person I've always been, she thought, remembering all the evenings after a filling meal when she would slip back into one kitchen or another and attack the leftover pie. Sneak up on it and work a finger between the crusts, feeling for a cherry, then patting the filling back into the hole she had made. When they were all eating pie again, she would think how her fingers had been all over it and inside it. Other times she went into her mother's bedroom and applied so much lipstick that her lips stuck together, and then she would slowly eat it off and finally smooth and round the lipstick so it looked as if it hadn't been used. When she was very little, she didn't suppose she had been so selfish and sneaky and hungry. When she was very little, her mother and her real father were still married. But then they started to fight and she was sent to live a couple of months with her grandparents, old-fashioned country people who lived up on the side of a mountain. He wore overalls and she wore long dresses and aprons. The very first evening they sat Vera between them on the swing, her grandfather on the yard side so he could spit his tobacco juice, and they asked her questions: Did she know her Bible stories? Did her mother take her to Sunday school, and did her father go to church? Did he by any chance keep liquor in the house? They took turns with their questions, and while she answered, she watched their hands: her grandmother's red ones plucking at the fabric of her apron, her grandfather's brown and still, with one black nail. After a while they ran out of questions and didn't speak for a while, but let the swing creak back and forth. Vera thought they were so old that they must be solid and unchangeable all the way through like wood. She was just about to fall asleep when they began to sing in high whining voices. They sang "Barbry Allen" a song Vera's mother sometimes sang, and Vera started to cry. The grandparents each put a hand on one of her knees and sang more and more verses. She thought the song was really about her mother and father: it was a sad song about the Merry month of May, and her mother's name was Mary and her father was Sweet William. She thought the song was about her parents dying. Mother mother, said the song, go make my bed, Father father go dig my grave. Every night that summer her grandparents sang for her on the porch, hymns and ballads, always ending with "Barbry Allen" so Vera could contentedly, safely, cry herself to sleep with her head in her grandmother's lap.

Vera thought sometimes that the best thing in life would be to be a grandmother herself, to be as solid and consistent as her country grandmother. She broke herself in two, a thick grandmother and a little girl. The grandmother had a dried corn ear, and she peeled back the husk for a skirt and popped off all the kernels except for eyes and a mouth. What's its name? asked the little girl with her hands out to touch it. You can name it, said the grandmother. Well, said the little girl, I name it Miss Jezebel from the Bible.

I would have made corn ear dolls for Tonie's baby, she thought. I would have taught that baby to sing its first words. She wished that somehow it could have been given to her to grow; she had never minded being pregnant. No question about what you should be doing; you were pregnant. You were a whole farm and a farmer. With her own babies she had been anxious about doing right, but a grandmother is always right. A grandmother just loves its little hands and loves its little heart. She knew it was true; she had heard her mother and aunt many times complain about her grandmother and how strict she was and mean, and old-fashioned and fundamentalist, but Vera only heard the deep country voice saying, Love its little heart, love it, love it, love it.

Tonie used to say, How come Jimmy has a grandmother and I don't? And she would feel a terrible stab of guilt. They didn't let me live long enough with my grandmother. She and my mother never agreed about anything, and I had to live with my aunt who had bad teeth and always frowned. They took me away and my grandmother died.

She said that to Tonie, but sometimes she didn't really believe they would have changed enough to die. Sometimes she thought they were still up in the mountains singing hymns and stirring up flour gravy. She did not believe that she herself would ever be old either. She would never get a grandchild to love, or get to rest in dignity or even finish the things she had to do like clean the dog's dish that was caked with dried food. Collars to iron, hems ripped out by high heels. She had crinkles in the corners of her eyes and tiny dry smile lines, but she, Vera, would spoil on the outside before she ever ripened on the inside. And all she wanted was to stop hurrying and talking and spend the rest of her life singing to a little grandchild. But Lee and Tonie were going to kill all their babies.

That's what a family is, she thought, something that never fulfills its promises and is never satisfied. Something that keeps leaving you but never leaves you alone. Lee moved away; Lee came home to criticize. Lee went away again. Vera had once thought that she found a family as families should be when she married the Scarlins. She loved John for beauty and Mary Katherine for moral excellence and the old Preacher for being perfectly himself. Everything had seemed to be there that she needed: one to love, one to take care of her, one to take care of. She loved Galatia. It was as if John and Mary Katherine were giving her a whole town to be at home in. She wore baby Lee like a jewel, and was herself set in John and Mary Katherine and they in Galatia and Galatia in the mountains. A moment at the beginning when she almost became an adult, when everything almost fell into place.

But Galatia grew as vast and uncertain as the whole world. The Preacher died, Mary Katherine moved out. She wrote a few times to her mother but didn't invite her to visit. Lee and Tonie became old enough to judge, and there were too many people in John's church to please. John's Montana job had a look about it of another new beginning that would simplify for her. There would be nothing there but John.

She thought she would go with him.

In the dark John touched her shoulder and said, I don't know myself why I didn't talk to you first. It was a terrible thing to do.

She said, You were wrong not to tell me.

He put his face between her breasts and murmured so that she could hardly make out what he said. You're coming with me, aren't you?

Of course, she answered, not even bothering to tease him. Where else would I go?

The movers carried away the large pieces of furniture, and Vera began to tear her house apart in earnest. She developed a passion for bare shelves, so she lined up pots and pans on the kitchen floor and threw out balls of shelving paper and collections of old mayonnaise jars. She used up her packing boxes for trash, even throwing away old china that someone else might have used; she loved to hear it smash. She laughed at how easy it was after all to extricate yourself from a house. Tonie came into the kitchen and then backed out. "What are you doing?"

"I'm getting rid of everything, and watch out, because your room is next."

"You had better not touch my room."

"Everything! I'm getting rid of everything."

She dumped a whole file cabinet of Bible school scrap craft. Also dried-up tempera paints, and stacks of magazines she had been saving for paper dolls and decoupage. Separating the wheat from the chaff, the sheep from the goats. To an unfinished needlepoint pillow: Go where there is howling and gnashing of teeth. She dragged her bags and boxes of trash out in front of the house.

John came in for lunch with the unfinished needlepoint pillow. "Did you mean to throw this out?"

"Get rid of it! I don't want to see it or anything like it."

"But you're using up all the boxes."

She massaged her scalp, fingers deep in her hair. "I'm a whirlwind," she said. "I'm cleaning out our lives."

He grimaced and made himself a lunch of peanut butter and crackers from the floor. She carried out an armload of dress-up clothes from Lee's room.

"Lee isn't going to like that."

"She isn't here. It's all going to be swept away."

She felt that John and Tonie both were discreetly avoiding her, and that was fine. People all seemed soft and vague; their faces didn't hold together for her. But she saw vividly the old crushed shoes, the extra serving platter, and boxes of broken crayons and pencil butts, loved these things even as she destroyed them. Neighbors had begun to slip up to her trash pile and take things without speaking to her. She noticed that her six tall ugly snake plants were gone, and the vase of dried bittersweet.

She stripped the bathroom last, and then showered, scrubbing and pumicing her body, scraping off dead skin and excess flesh. She used to take soaking baths, sometimes an hour long, lying in water deep enough that her breasts floated and her hands and feet swam in little circles. She used to do this to make her mind dormant. Tonie would pound on the door and yell "Mama! Mama! I gotta go!"

"Can't you hold it?" she would answer, and then, "Well go outside, Tonie, and do it in the woods."

Poor Tonie, to have been wounded by such a selfish mother. Even her poor little bladder. Vera was sorry, even angry at that other woman who sent her children outside to tinkle. She had dumped that self with the snake plants and broken crayons.

She had a new dress; it was Lee's, but Lee had talked her into trying it on, and then said Take it, it was made for you. It had a big floppy pale blue collar, dark blue and purple flowers in the print, and it fit her princess style like a glove, except it was shorter than anything she had ever worn. She felt breezes on her thighs. She went to Tonie's room to get a reaction to the shortness and to the curve of her abdomen that the dress didn't hide.

Tonie was listening to rock and roll music and reading letters. Her room hadn't been touched by the movers; in fact no one had touched Tonie's room since she was in grade school: the same magazine horse pictures were still taped all over the walls, the same collection of horse statues cluttering the window sills. There was a look in Tonie's eyes that she didn't like. "You haven't started packing yet, Tonie."

"Aunt Mary Katherine isn't ready for me yet."

"Yes she is, she told me so herself, and you have to do something with all these little horses—"

"You want me to throw them away."

"You know I'd never touch your things."

"I don't like moving and I don't intend to pack until the last minute."

Outside the tree and the fence posts cast long shadows into the field. There was an orangeness to the light falling on the brush that used to make Vera cry in her afternoon bath. But she had thrown away that person—she wished she had some way to make Tonie get untangled from the past too, wired to her stereo, hampered by minute tendrils from her horse collection. Did she dare ask her her plans? Is it true you're going back with that alcoholic, Tonie? Will you be going back to school?

Tonie sank her face into her neck, looking jowly and recalcitrant. Vera said, "I used to watch you sometimes when you were too little to go up on the hill by yourself. You'd stand by the fence and stick your hand through with an apple or some sugar or just grass if that's all you could find, and call and call for the horses. I can still hear your little voice. You were so earnest, and the horses never would come."

"They came sometimes. They're more dependable than people." She stared at Vera with a particularly mean accusation in her eyes.

What did I do today? thought Vera. She said, "Come to Montana,

Tonie. I'll buy you a horse."

Tonie said, "I got a letter."

"From Rick?"

"I got one from him too. Not that I care. I'll probably write back to him just because I like getting mail."

"He's a nice boy."

"You and Daddy would like to see me safely married, wouldn't you? You'd like to see me married to anybody."

"Not anybody. We'd like to think you were safe, but I don't know that marriage is so safe." The light on the hill was making her restless. She was closer and closer to asking her right out, Tonie, are you back with him again? Is it true what I hear? But what if the reply were a chin thrust out and a yes? "Who's the letter from?"

Tonie shook her head no.

Well, thought Vera, it's true, I was a wrongheaded mother. And I still don't know how to talk to her. She waited for a wave of suffering, but instead itched to get moving. An activity, an act to perform. She said, "I have to go down town before the drugstore closes. Will you be here?"

Tonie shrugged.

Vera said, "I'm going to say good-bye," she said. "That's really why I'm going."

She got to Pike Street very late, while everyone was home for supper. There were the boys in front of Nuzzi's, but no one she had to smile at, no one to get in the way of her trying to make an adventure of standing stock still and feeling the town all around her. The sun was going down, but she looked at the bricks of Galatia which had begun to glow in bay, salmon, and old gold. There were reflections in all the glass, the ordinary shop clutter hidden behind flashes like signals. Overhead were black clouds and the pink. Galatia was solid and short. Now, saying good-bye, she thought this was what Galatia was really like.

She thought then of the people she had for one reason or another failed to make friends with. Thelma Shinn, who was of an older generation, but Vera always enjoyed her funny complaints about her husband and her spike-heeled shoes. And there was the checkout woman at the A&P, an aunt of Eddie Salerno's, so beautiful, Vera had always thought, with dark hair knotted at the back of her neck, and a scattering of white at the temples. But Vera never saw her except at the grocery store for a few minutes. It's just a little town, she thought, it looks like I could have made friends with her sometime in the last twenty-three years even if she was a Catholic. Thelma was a Baptist and that didn't do me any good.

She stopped at the door of the drugstore and saw Bill Rogers inside at his counter all alone with a coffee cup and a ledger book. He rubbed the bald spot on top of his head from time to time. He was a big man, not overweight so much as shapeless, with thick wrists and long soft jowls. He always flirted with her. Once he volunteered to help Earl Wright build a cross and platform for the Easter pageant, but while Earl worked, he kept following Vera and trying to lay a hand on her shoulder. There were always so many titillating stories about Bill. If someone said there was a whorehouse on a farm on Black Run, then the certain businessman who frequented it always turned out to be Bill Rogers. There was his illegitimate child too, and of course his poor daughter and his wife, Ruth, and her short housecoats that John liked to talk about. She tapped on the plate glass.

He took his time raising his head from the ledger book, but then Vera had the pleasure of seeing his expression slide to anticipation and he hurried to the door and fumbled to open it. You'd think it was an assignation, she thought.

"You don't have to be in such a hurry, Bill. I shouldn't even have knocked when I saw you were closed."

"You're all dressed up," he said. "That dress—in that dress you look mighty good."

"Lee gave it to me. It's my experiment dress." Bill put a hand on her elbow and directed her to a seat at one of the little wrought iron tables in back. "I'm sorry to bother you so late—all I came for were allergy pills—I'm worried about the ragweed out West—"

"It's a dirty shame," said Bill, "after all these years for John to get run out. I hate to see that kind of thing happen."

"Oh no, Bill—he really isn't being chased. I think he was looking for an excuse. Anything would have set him off. We've both been needing an adventure for a long time."

Bill gave a curt little nod. "I'll get you the pills," he said. He talked from the back, his voice coming now from one part of the pharmacy, now muffled from another. "My mother is taking it hard for John to leave. She acts like her best beau jilted her."

"Older women have always been John's specialty."

"Ruth too. She doesn't know how she'll get along without him. No offense to John, but he's going to miss all the attention from the ladies. Hey Vera, come back here a minute, I want to show you something."

She didn't see him at first, then noticed a door between some shelves, a storeroom with a cot where Bill was sitting with a bottle of plum wine and two plastic cups. She immediately thought of the girl who worked for him, all the girls who'd worked late and had a glass of wine with him.

"Now don't refuse to have a drink with me, Vera. I don't mean anything but to wish you well. I'll give you a peppermint afterwards so John won't find out. There aren't many people in this town that I care whether they come or go, but I wish the best for you and John too."

She smiled but didn't sit, accepted the wine but didn't drink. Bill asked her if she wanted to sit down and be comfortable, but she preferred to lean against a stack of cartons. "So you keep a cot in the back, Bill."

"Things aren't always so inviting at my house. I sleep over here sometimes."

Vera said, "I always used to feel like Galatia wasn't my town. It was John's and Mary Katherine's or even Lee and Tonie's, but never mine."

Bill took his glasses off and swayed forward in an odd way, leaning closer and closer to her until his face was about on a level with her ribcage. He even had his eyes closed.

She said, "I used to think everyone belonged except me, or if I was feeling really good, I would decide the trick was they were all only pretending—"

He embraced her thighs and pressed his mouth against her ribs. He made little groaning noises, working his mouth around on her side. She kept talking and set her wine down on a box so it wouldn't spill. "I always felt like there were all these possibilities that were only for the real Galatians, things like, I don't know, starting friendships—"

Bill panted. "You could take this all day, couldn't you? You love it, don't you?"

She was slowly, regularly expanding to fill the closet. She was going to calmly, gravely, burst out of Bill's arms, out of the drugstore and fill the town. Engulf it and make it her own. She was being lifted now, his hands on her buttocks, his face in her belly. She could have done without his grunts and the dampness of his hot breath, and then he began to fumble for her bra hook and failing that, reached for her zipper.

"Oh, don't fool with my clothes," she said.

He pulled her back onto the cot with him, stuck a hand on her thigh under the dress.

"I don't want to take my clothes off, Bill."

"Clothes on then—that's fine—"

Grunting he tried to roll on top of her on the cot, burrowing into her belly again, but he was balanced badly and she got a grip on his forehead and pushed off, wriggled onto her feet.

"Come on, Vera, don't be a tease—"

She almost shrank away when he told her she was being bad, but the shrinking stopped when she was about the same size as Bill. "I'm being completely selfish today," she said. "I'm taking just exactly as much as I want, just so much and no more."

"Listen, Vera, you can trust me. It's just between us."

"You're missing the point."

"I've always wanted you, you have this body—You really want to do it, too, I can tell. I can feel how soft you are—" He looked young and soft himself. Pudgy-wristed, round-shouldered. He was curled on his side on the cot, and he held her hand. "I can wait," he said. "I can wait till you're ready."

"Go to sleep." She pressed him down on the cot; he grabbed her knee. She ran her thumbs over his eyelids to make them close. He didn't let go of her knee until she pried his fingers off gently one by one. "Go to sleep and dream, Bill."

"Tell me what to dream about."

He thought it was a game, thought that since she'd let him lay his hands on her, she would have to go all the way. "Dream about being a boy again."

He grinned with his eyes shut, and Vera grabbed her pocket-book and ran. Through the dim drugstore, bursting out onto the street which was darker but somehow more clear, and she kept running for half a block, then turned up an alley wondering if anyone had seen her headlong flight, the short dress climbing her thighs.

She never got the allergy pills.

The bricks had stopped glowing, and this alley she had chosen was especially dark, overhung with trees and heavy loads of black leaves. She began to walk up the hill slowly, a great bubble of honeysuckle air from one backyard, frying onions from a window. I almost had an affair, she thought. Well, I thought about it. Not all that close. She had let a man touch her who wasn't John, and that was pretty adventuresome all by itself. She hadn't been excited the way John made her excited. She recalled the sensation of growing and shrinking, and the sound of her own voice.

She kept walking, heading out North Avenue, with Mary Katherine's more or less for a destination, but when she came to the wall and Farley's driveway, her heart started to pound. Between the stone gate pillars she saw a light up at the house. A voice in her head said, Having sex is just sex, what is exciting is having no idea what will happen next. She felt a sort of light of grace; this was what she really wanted to do. She had a right to ask Joe Bob his intentions. It was so stupid when you thought of it, that no one spoke to him. I have nothing against you, she would say. Goodness knows there are plenty of ways to waste your days, and I don't suppose drinking is all that much worse than needlepoint. But what do you intend to do with Tonie?

She found the front porch, but no light, and she found a heavy brass knocker. When she first came to Galatia, there used to be parties up here. Mary Katherine and Earl stopped attending them, and John and Vera were never invited. After a while a figure with a flashlight came around the side of the house.

"Who is it?" he said.

"Vera Scarlin." Feeling foolish now, especially when he played the flashlight over Lee's slinky dress.

"That's not the door," he said. "That's nailed shut. We used to have vandals coming in. You have to come around the side."

She went toward the light and when she got to the edge of the porch, he switched it off and took her elbow to help her down. Very firmly. He had a solid grip. She said, "I've never been up here. Mary Katherine used to tell me about the parties."

"Look," said Joe Bob over his shoulder, leading the way. "I'm not going to make any excuses, or try to get rid of you. She's here."

"Oh. I didn't think she would be. I mean, I just saw her at home, so I didn't come to get her—I don't think 1 came to get her."

She didn't know what to make of him, except that she was pretty sure he wasn't drunk right now. She felt like something quicksilver and skittish compared to him, and thought that maybe if he stopped drinking, he would be good for Tonie.

She said, "I really came to talk to you—I thought I did. Maybe it was just to find out about her—"

"If you find out anything about her, tell me."

Tonie and old Mrs. Farley, Joe Bob's aunt, were in the kitchen drinking something in cups. It was an old-fashioned kitchen with little glass-paned windows in the cabinets and an actual icebox sitting beside the refrigerator. The old woman looked cold; she was wrapped in a tufted bathrobe with a shawl over her shoulders. Tonie shared a corner of the table with her.

"Look at those two," said Joe Bob, "thick as thieves. Do you want some Postum?"

"No, no thank you," said Vera. "How do you do, Mrs. Farley? I'm Vera Scarlin, Tonie's mother?"

The old woman was intensely bright-eyed, and her hand was light and cold. She said, tossing her chin at Tonie, "You come for her?"

Vera could feel a fit of chattering coming on. "No, no, I really didn't come to get her. Really, Tonie—I didn't expect to find you here—"

Joe Bob laughed. "Tonie spends a lot of time out here these days, but I'm not sure why. I think she comes to see Aunt Josephine, maybe to check up on me."

"You're all right, Joe Bob," said Tonie, and Vera had no idea whether her tone was sarcastic or sincere or both at once. Tonie was sitting in the same position she had been in when Vera walked into her bedroom two hours ago, slightly tipped back in the chair, chin lowered.

"I don't mind," said Joe Bob. "It's the best thing that happened to Aunt Josephine in years. She gets up out of bed now just to talk to Tonie. She's deaf as stones, but she always knows when Tonie comes. They play dominoes and I referee. I guess it's the best thing for me too, although Tonie makes no promises. I may be suffering for my own entertainment—"

Vera was thankful to Joe Bob for talking. He was not the same man as when she first met him, when he and Earl came back from Korea. He always used to have hair in his eyes, or was that only because she always saw him driving his convertible? She said, "You don't look well, Joe Bob."

"I told you I'm suffering. It's your daughter's fault."

Tonie finally had a change of expression, and she looked pretty. A little smug maybe, but pleasant. "He goes up to Morgantown to the Alcoholics Anonymous. He's doing very well. I sit with Aunt Josephine on his meeting nights."

"That's wonderful!"

Joe Bob waved his hands. "Oh yeah. Real wonderful!"

"You're doing this for yourself, not for me," said Tonie.

He looked hurt. Vera felt an enormous gaiety bubbling up. Everything was going to be fine. "I don't guess it will hurt now—I can go ahead and ask my questions. About the future —what your plans are—"

"Don't ask me, ask Tonie."

Tonie made a face. "Mom wants us to get married."

Joe Bob looked up. "That's the kiss of death. No offense, but your daughter is the most contrary person I know. If you mention marriage, she goes berserk."

Vera wasn't satisfied, but before she could ask anything else, the old woman shouted, pointing at her, "Who is that?"

"My mother!" shouted Tonie.

"Your sister. You got a sister?"

"It's my mother."

"Too young," said Mrs. Farley, and no one argued.

"Well," said Vera. "Maybe I'd better head on home. I can't think of anything else to ask you."

"I guess I'll go along," said Tonie.

Vera shook hands with Mrs. Farley again and thanked her for insisting she looked too young to be Tonie's mother, and then she shook hands with Joe Bob and wished him luck, and she really did. She hoped he would dry out at once and become young and handsome for Tonie.

It had been a good adventure, she thought, walking along North Avenue with Tonie. "I really am proud of you about Joe Bob, honey," she said.

Tonie said, "I've got a letter I want you to read."

"In the dark?"

"Here's a streetlight. I've had it a couple of days. I was looking at it when you were in my room. It's the answer to a letter I wrote to my grandmother. She wants me to come and visit her."

A piece of paper with a design of rambling roses across the top and down the side was extended, but Vera didn't touch it. For a few seconds she thought it was *her* grandmother, her country grandmother, that Tonie meant. "How," said Vera, "how did you—" She was going to say Find Out, but it seemed too dramatic. Ludicrous, now that Tonie had said the words My Grandmother so easily.

"She said she'd like to see you too. It isn't the first letter I've had from her either. I found a Christmas card from her to you and she asked how were your dear darling girls and signed it your mother and I wrote to her."

"I never told you she was a bad person. She just wasn't any good with children. She and my aunt both. I was the only child they had between them and they passed me back and forth like a hot potato."

"What did she do that made you run away?"

"I never ran away." She tried to draw a picture in the air with her hands so she wouldn't have to talk, but it was too dark and Tonie couldn't see. She was going to have to say something in so many words. "I always said I ran away, but actually it was more like they helped me find a place to stay so I could finish high school where I started. I was supposed to go live with them after I graduated, but I met John and got married instead." There were whole years and months of her life that she never thought about. She promised herself she was going to spend a week in the new house in Montana just getting her memories organized, watching them like old movies.

"You mean you lied," said Tonie. "You lied to me and Lee about our grandmother."

171

She wished Mary Katherine were here now. Mary Katherine would say, Now Tonie, don't be so hard on your mother. It hasn't been easy for her either. She said, "I was always hard on my mother. I didn't even tell her I was getting married until after I did it. She didn't tell me my stepfather was dead either until after the funeral."

"You should have gone to see her, especially now when she's old. She says she always invites you. She says she always wanted to see me and Lee."

"All my life I've been bad about going back, Tonie. I told you how I used to throw a fit every time they moved. Then after the move was over, I would always start to hate the place I'd been, and all the people there. I used to say to myself, 'I'll never go back there; they'd have to take me in a box.' I can't retrace my steps—"

Tonie did not stir with sympathy. She kept her distance and they started walking again. "I'm going to see her. You should have taken us, but I'm going to go anyhow. I have a right to see my grandmother."

"Did you tell Lee?"

"Not yet."

It occurred to her that Tonie was being greedy. She had finally found a grandmother, and she wasn't so eager to share her. "Listen, I have an idea. Pack a suitcase and come with us and we'll stop in Ohio and see her. All of us." Tonie couldn't see the whole vision, the singing in the car, the laughing. Maybe Lee would come too. "She'll put out cake for us. She has a three-tiered milk glass cake carrier she has always taken with her through two marriages and a dozen houses. She'll bring it out with a different cake on every tier. She'll love John, of course, she's the kind that always falls for him."

"He won't do it."

"Of course he will. It's a duty." Her power was coming back. She was seeing the clarity, the justice of it. She was annoyed at Lee for not being here to make it perfect. "And then you'll drive to Montana with us and help us get settled."

"Maybe I'll stay with her. She sounds lonely."

"You could do that too." Tonie thought it was a threat, but of course it wasn't really. It was the best thing. And if Tonie came to love her grandmother, then maybe someday she would give Vera a chance to be one. "We could call Lee and see if she would fly out and meet us."

"How come you're so willing to go all of a sudden?"

Vera waved her arms, attempted to lift off. It had to do with mists parting. It had to do with flying. "Some things change. It's like I can look in different directions now. It used to be something I could only do with a play. But now I see my whole life. I see the town of Galatia. I see it like an idea for a play."

"I don't know what you're talking about."

And you don't intend to try, do you? she thought. Tonie was going to sulk and punish her with furious looks for a long time to come. For years. Well, she had punished her own mother for twenty. Tonie didn't want to understand, but to demand an explanation. So the understanding was all for Vera.

The End

Afterword

In preparing this new edition of my first novel, *A Space Apart*, I have had the opportunity to correct a few small errors and to explore the world as I saw it in the nineteen-seventies. The most remarkable thing to me as I went over it was how little I then knew about West Virginia and the Appalachian region. I grew up there, and had a deep emotional connection– I could close my eyes and see it and smell it, but I did not know the history or the literature. For that reason, as I reread *A Space Apart* now I find an odd combination of literary sophistication and a surreal world that, when I was writing the book, I thought was completely realistic. In this edition, I didn't try to change that, but I did add a few markers to make the novel align better with what was happening in current events.

The first half of the novel is set just after World War II, and the second half is set in the spring of 1970. There are the years of my own childhood and early twenties. For all children, of course, there is no history: there is now and there is an ahistorical past, an Age of Giants inhabited by your parents and your ancestors. The West Virginia of *A Space Apart* is extremely concrete but mythic in tone.

When I wrote it, I had been living in New York City for a number of years. I had participated in political events of the late sixties and early seventies–demonstrations against war, community organizing with people abandoned to poverty, but my West Virginia was captured in a snow crystal. It was a place where the only important buildings were churches and schools. The largest social gap was between those who lived genteelly in town and those who lived without indoor plumbing in the outlying hollows.

In the 1970 part of the novel, I have given Lee an awareness that this is the spring of Kent State and Jackson State. She is more interested in her interior life, but she makes reference to what was happening in the news. The emphasis of the novel is still emotions and tensions largely outside of history, but I wanted to create a reminder that history was happening at the same time.

After the publication of *A Space Apart*, I was privileged to meet a whole new group of West Virginians–writers and librarians and scholars. These friends have been educating me ever since about West Virginia and Appalachia, and, I hope, influencing what I write.

Meredith Sue Willis
Spring, 2017

About the Author

Meredith Sue Willis grew up in West Virginia and attended Bucknell University for two years before spending a year as a Volunteer in Service to America. She then took degrees from Barnard College and Columbia University in New York City.

Her fiction has been published by Charles Scribner's Sons, HarperCollins, West Virginia University Press,  Mercury House, Ohio University Press and other presses. Her book of literary short stories, *In the Mountains of America*, was praised in the *New York Times Book Review* as an "important lesson on the nature and function of literature itself." Her latest books include two collections of short stories, *Out of the Mountains* from Ohio University Press and *Re-Visions* from Hamilton Stone Editions; a book about writing from Montemayor Press called *Ten Strategies to Write a Novel;* and a young adult novel, *Meli's Way*, also from Montemayor.

She now lives in New Jersey, a short train ride from New York City, where she is an Adjunct Assistant Professor of Creative Writing at New York University's School of Continuing and Professional Studies. She is an occasional visiting writer-in-the-schools in New York and New Jersey, keeps a four season organic garden, and is active in local racial integration politics.

To learn more about her and her books, see her web page at www.meredithsuewillis.com.